Board Stiff

Board Stiff

A DEAD-END JOB MYSTERY

Elaine Viets

AN OBSIDIAN MYSTERY

OBSIDIAN
Published by the Penguin Group
Penguin Group (USA) Inc., 375 Hudson Street,
New York, New York 10014, USA

USA | Canada | UK | Ireland | Australia | New Zealand | India | South Africa | China

Penguin Books Ltd., Registered Offices: 80 Strand, London WC2R 0RL, England
For more information about the Penguin Group visit penguin.com.

First published by Obsidian, an imprint of New American Library,
a division of Penguin Group (USA) Inc.

First Printing, May 2013

LIBRARY OF CONGRESS CATALOGING–IN–PUBLICATION DATA:

Viets, Elaine, 1950–
Board stiff: a dead-end job mystery/Elaine Viets.
pages cm.
ISBN 978-0-451-23985-3 (hardback)
1. Hawthorne, Helen (Fictitious character)—Fiction.
2. Women detectives—Fiction.   3. Local government—
Corrupt practices—Florida—Fiction.   4. Florida—Fiction.
I. Title.
PS3572.I325B63   2013
813'.54—dc23   2013001051

Printed in the United States of America
10 9 8 7 6 5 4 3 2 1

Set in Bembo
Designed by Elke Sigal

PUBLISHER'S NOTE
This is a work of fiction. Names, characters, places, and incidents either are the product of the author's
imagination or are used fictitiously, and any resemblance to actual persons, living or dead, business establish-
ments, events, or locales is entirely coincidental.
    The publisher does not have any control over and does not assume any responsibility for author or third-
party Web sites or their content.

For the real Valerie Cannata,
who has fast friends

ACKNOWLEDGMENTS

Riggs Beach is a mythical Florida town, but the cutthroat competition for tourist dollars is real.

Florida lifeguards are exceptional professionals. Ocean-rescue guards are trained paramedics and amazing athletes. Thank you, Lieutenant Jim McCrady, Fort Lauderdale Ocean Rescue, as well as Ben Hutchinson and Christine Jackson for your help with the rescue scenes. Any mistakes are mine.

Thank you, Nora E. Saunders, Saunders & Taylor Insurance, Inc., Fort Lauderdale, and Dr. Robin Waldron. Dina Willner and mystery writer Marcia Talley supplied technical advice.

Novel writing is a team effort, and I have help from the best: senior editor Sandra Harding and the ever-helpful Elizabeth Bistrow at New American Library; my agent, David Hendin; and my reporter husband, Don Crinklaw, who valiantly rattles cages in Fort Lauderdale in between reading my novels. Thanks to Dick Richmond, my friend and former newspaper editor.

Some friends let me borrow their names. Valerie Cannata was transformed into an investigative TV reporter. Nancie Hays let me turn her into a lawyer. Nan Siemer and her bichon, Benji, are all grown-up now, and Nan has her own consulting company, Breakers, in Alexandria, Virginia. The real Margery Flax is much younger but just as crafty as the fictional Margery. Both love purple, but the real Margery wishes she could smoke. Joan Right is not a Riggs Beach server, but a generous woman who made a donation at a charity auction to have her name in this novel.

Karen Grace and I spent many hours discussing who really blackmailed Helen and her sister. I didn't have a clue when I first wrote that scene until Karen explained it to me.

Thank you, Alan Portman, Molly Zuckerman Portman, Doris Ann Norris, Kay Gordy, Jack Klobnak, Robert Levine, Janet Smith, Jinny Gender and Mary Alice Gorman.

Private investigator William Simon gave invaluable information. So did Detective R. C. White, Fort Lauderdale Police Department (retired), and Rick McMahan, ATF special agent.

Thank you to the sources who can't be named.

Anne Watts, assistant director of the Boynton Beach City Library, lent me her six-toed cat, Thumbs, for this series. Once again, I am grateful to all the librarians who helped with this book, especially the staff of the St. Louis Public Library, the St. Louis County Library, and the Broward County Library. Librarians are the original search engines.

I can't forget super-saleswoman Carole Wantz, who could sell a Chevy to a Ford dealer.

I'm grateful to the booksellers who recommend my novels to their customers.

Helen still works those dead-end jobs, but now that she and Phil have their own private eye agency, she takes them to solve cases. *Board Stiff* required my own in-depth research. I took stand-up paddleboard lessons and landed in about nine feet of water. Mario St. Cyr of Paddlesandboards.com said I fell very gracefully.

Thank you to the Femmes Fatales & Freres. I rely on your

encouragement and advice, and appreciate the help of my blog sister, mystery writer Hank Phillippi Ryan, who knows all about being a star TV reporter. Read our blog at http://www.femmesfatales.typepad .com/.

Questions or comments? E-mail me at eviets@aol.com.

Board Stiff

CHAPTER 1

"They're trying to kill me," Sunny Jim Sundusky said. "They nearly succeeded in March, but I'm one tough buzzard. I survived. They almost got me in April, but I escaped again."

Helen Hawthorne and her husband, Phil Sagemont, sat across from Sunny Jim in their black-and-chrome chairs in the Coronado Investigations office. Sunny Jim sat in the yellow client chair, looking anything but sunny. Sun-dried was more like it, Helen thought as she studied him.

His face was red leather. His blond hair was dyed and flash-fried in a crinkly permanent. But he did look tough.

"They're gonna keep coming after me until they stop me for good," he said. "That's why I wanna hire you two. I hear you're the best private eyes in South Florida."

"We were lucky to get good publicity," Helen said.

"That wasn't luck," Phil said. "That was good detecting."

"That's what I need," Sunny Jim said. "Detecting. I want you to stop them before they stop me—permanently." He stabbed his chest with a brown callused hand, right in the smiling sun on his yellow

SUNNY JIM'S STAND-UP PADDLEBOARD RENTAL T-shirt. His arms and legs were roped with muscle and his chest was a solid slab.

Helen had seen enough steroid hardbodies to know that Jim had built that beef the old-fashioned way. She thought he was attractive in a dated disco style, except he was too young to have caught the seventies disco fever. She guessed his age on the shady side of thirty-five.

"So you gonna save my business or not?" Jim's eyes were hidden behind expensive shades—Floridians rarely had naked eyes—but his chin jutted in a challenge.

Helen tried to pick up a cue from Phil, but he stayed poker-faced. "Tell us a little about your business," he said.

"Like I said, I own a stand-up paddleboard rental company," Jim said. "I got two locations in Riggs Beach."

"The beach town just south of Fort Lauderdale," Helen said.

"Right," Jim said, and smiled for the first time. "There's Lauderdale, then Dania, Hollywood, Hallandale and Riggs Beach. You ever been to Riggs Beach?" He shifted in his chair and Helen tried not to stare at the little golden hairs on his long, tanned legs.

"I walk along that beach sometimes," she said. "Nice fishing pier."

"That's where I rent my boards," Sunny Jim said. "Near the base of the pier. Riggs Pier is owned by the city."

"Good fishing off that pier," Phil said.

"Primo," Sunny Jim said. "There's a reef just past the pier. Saw a loggerhead turtle there when I was diving."

"You were telling us about your business," Phil said.

"There's a little restaurant and bait shop on the beach end of the pier, run by Cyrus Reed Horton. The restaurant is called Cy's on the Pier. Locals joke that Cy fries up whatever bait he doesn't sell, but the food's not half-bad.

"Cy owns some real estate along Riggs Beach, including a T-shirt shop and a fancy boutique. He's got the parking lot by the pier, too. That place is a gold mine. Tourists are begging to park there.

"I keep a trailer—like a lawn service trailer—at the foot of the pier and rent my paddleboards, but you gotta be good to go out on the ocean. I also give lessons at Riggs Lake about two blocks away: one hour of personal instruction and a half hour of practice for a hundred bucks. The water is quieter and calmer on the lake. It's a good place to learn. You ever do stand-up paddleboarding?"

"No," Helen said. "I've seen guys paddling along on those big surfboard-like things on the Intracoastal Waterway. I gather those are paddleboards."

"They are. Stand-up paddleboarding is the hot new sport. Everybody wants a piece of the action, and I've got the best spot in the city. That's why they're after me."

"Who is?" Phil asked.

"The two people who want the lease on my spot," Jim said, as if it were obvious.

"And they are?" Phil asked.

"Bill's Boards. I've caught him poaching on my territory. He was giving lessons right next to my space on Riggs Lake. Even set up a sign like he belonged there. His lessons are cheaper, but he doesn't have to pay the city to rent the land or buy the license or carry liability insurance like I do. He can afford to undercut me."

"How come Bill doesn't have to follow the rules?" Helen asked.

"I'm getting to that," Jim said. "Bill's Boards parked its trailer next to mine here on the beach and started renting their boards. He was just an employee, not the owner, and I chased him off the first time. But Bill stands there and defies me. He refuses to leave. I called the cops and they shrugged and said it wasn't their problem.

"Now if I don't open up early and drag my boards out on the beach so Bill's Boards can't park there, he tries to set up his business again. I'm out there at six a.m., though most of my customers don't show up until after nine in the morning."

"Sounds stressful," Helen said.

"Stress! Hell, it's cutthroat. He'll do anything to put me out of business. Even stole Randy, my best employee."

"How'd he do that?" Phil asked.

"Offered Randy more money," Sunny Jim said. "I can't afford to pay him eleven dollars an hour. Not when I'm stuck with all the costs of being a legitimate businessman."

"Did you complain to Riggs Beach?" Helen asked.

"Hah! Rigged Beach is more like it," Jim said. "I've made more than two hundred complaints to the police, the beach patrol and Riggs Lake park rangers. The city commission won't do a blessed thing.

"I finally went to a meeting and complained. Put on a suit in Florida. One commissioner said it would cost too much to enforce the rules. Cost too much! What about the fees the city is missing? What about following the rules?

"The commissioners said they wanted proof that my competitors are poaching. I even stood behind a palm tree and took photos, but the commission said that still wasn't proof unless I caught 'em when the money was changing hands. I was never cynical about government, but after that meeting, I saw that same commissioner say hi to his good buddy Bill. Slapped him on the back and they left together. In public. No wonder the police won't arrest him when he poaches on my territory. That was February.

"Once I turned up the heat, the sabotage started. In March, two of my paddleboards were stolen and twelve paddles were trashed. Someone broke into my trailer at the height of spring break, the busiest time of the year, so I didn't have enough boards or paddles for rentals. By the time my insurance claim was settled, spring break was over and so was the demand.

"That cost me thousands in equipment and even more in lost business. But they weren't counting on me having insurance. See, that's where the extra cost comes in, but it saved my bacon.

"I had video cameras on my beach trailer, and the cameras caught two men on tape. One man is the same size and height as Randy Henshall, my old employee, but he and his accomplice are wearing dive suits and masks, so you can't see their faces."

"And even though Randy was a good employee," Helen asked, "you think he'd break into your trailer to ruin your business?"

"Yes, I do," Jim said and stuck out his chin defiantly. "He left me for money. I think he'd break into my trailer for money, too. But I can't prove that. He knew about the cameras, didn't he? And he disguised himself."

"Not sure that means anything," Phil said. "Many businesses use security cameras. What did the police say?"

"They took a report and that's about it." Jim's face showed his disgust. "Riggs Beach police aren't interested in tracking down the thieves. They called it a spring break prank and said the stolen boards were probably strapped to a car roof and heading up north."

"The break-in was in March," Phil said. "What happened next?"

"I started getting tons of calls for reservations and lessons. I was fully booked every day of the week. Thought I was in fat city. Except half of the callers never showed for their lessons or board rentals. After four days of twiddling my thumbs, I changed my policy. Now if you want a lesson or you want to rent a board, you gotta give me a credit card. And I run the card while you're on the phone. Nipped that in the bud."

"Who made the false reservations?" Helen asked. "Men? Women?"

"Both," Jim said. "They all sounded young, but then most of my business is people under thirty."

"Anybody else you can think of who'd want to cause you trouble?" Phil asked.

"Well, like I said, there's Cy," Jim said. "He wants my beach spot, too, so he can expand his parking lot. He's like this with the city commissioners." He held up two fingers, stuck together.

"But I give Cy some credit. He told me up front. That other bird went behind my back. Only my lease with the city is keeping me on Riggs Beach, and the renewal is coming up for a vote in June."

"So what do you want Coronado Investigations to do?" Phil said.

"Catch 'em!" he said. "Catch them when they're sabotaging me.

I'm still looking for a new employee since I lost Randy. I can't find a good one. I'll pay you seven seventy-five an hour, Phil, to work the pier location. That's in addition to your regular fee. You can keep the money."

"Thanks," Phil said. Jim missed the slight note of sarcasm, but Helen didn't.

"Minimum wage in Florida is seven dollars and sixty-five cents, so I'm overpaying you.

"And I want your lady to work for me, too."

"You want two people to suddenly start working at your ocean paddleboard location?" Helen asked. "Won't that look suspicious?"

"You're a smart girl," Sunny Jim said. "But I got a better job for you. I want you to sit on the beach with a video camera. Like a tourist. You can document my competitors stealing my business. Make sure you get them exchanging the money. Nobody will think anything of it. Tourists video everything—even palm trees doing nothing but standing there. I want Helen to get to know some of the staff at Cy's restaurant and his two shops. Cy's a tightwad and he has enemies. Some of his employees are angry enough that they'll talk about Cy or whatever else they see here in Riggs Beach."

"My cover can be that I'm a Fort Lauderdale salesclerk on a staycation," Helen said. "I've got some days off and I'm too broke to go anywhere for a real vacation."

"So are you going to be Phil's wife while he's working for me?" Sunny Jim asked.

"It's better if we don't even know each other for this job," Helen said. "I'll have to take off my wedding ring."

"And put on a bikini," Jim said. "A fine-looking lady like you belongs in a bikini, you know what I mean?"

Helen didn't like his smirk.

"You know that Ms. Hawthorne is my partner—and my wife," Phil said.

"I meant no disrespect," Jim said. "It's hard not to admire a woman like Ms. Hawthorne. Tell you what. I'll even throw in free paddleboard lessons for you both after work. As my personal apology.

"How about if you start tomorrow at six with me, Phil? Ms. Hawthorne, you don't have to go to work until nine. What do you say, huh?"

"You can call me Helen," she said. "Apology accepted."

I'm getting paid to sleep late and sit on the beach, she thought. Finally, a dead-end job I can enjoy. Phil gave her a slight nod, his signal that he wanted this client.

"It's a deal," she said.

CHAPTER 2

Helen slathered coconut sunscreen on her arms and breathed in the soft, salty ocean air. A light breeze pulled at her big-brimmed straw hat.

Her short, gauzy caftan covered her black-and-white two-piece suit but showed off her long, tanned legs. She kicked off her black sandals and wiggled her toes in the warm, damp sand.

Riggs Beach was starting to come to life that morning. Weedy teens rode their boogie boards into the waves while coltish girls squealed and flirted with them. One scrawny boy boldly backstroked past the NO SWIMMING markers. A dark-skinned lifeguard blew her whistle and shouted at him to return.

Helen heard cheers from the nearby beach volleyball court. A muscular woman in a purple bikini was playing against a goateed dude in red shorts. The beer-chugging spectators were cheering for Ms. Purple—or her skimpy suit, which shifted with every lunge.

Red Dude has a definite disadvantage, Helen thought. He's watching her chest bounce instead of the volleyball. No wonder he's losing. The breakfast beers didn't bother her. This was Florida.

On Riggs Pier, a cluster of anglers tried their luck at the far end near the reef, coolers waiting to hold their catch.

Helen set her rented lounge at an angle so she could see the ocean and Sunny Jim's trailer. The yellow windowless trailer was wide open. Inside was a homemade plywood fold-down desk for an iPad and a laptop. The sand in front was shaded by a yellow canopy that said SUNNY JIM'S STAND-UP PADDLEBOARDING—RENTALS & LESSONS.

Parked next to the trailer was a metal rack with eight yellow paddleboards, black paddles stacked on top.

Helen saw Phil lounging under the canopy in a lawn chair, a cold bottle of water in the cup holder. The bottle was sweating. Phil was not. He was watching the volleyball game.

Helen settled back into her padded lime green lounge. Green should be the official color of Riggs Beach, she decided. She was glad she could write off the ten-dollar chair—and the equally steep pier parking lot fee—as expenses.

Now, this is how to live, she thought. The whoosh of the waves was soothing and Helen felt her eyes closing.

Whoa! she reminded herself. You're supposed to be working. She pulled the camcorder out of her beach bag, checked the time and date stamp, and started videoing the beach.

Helen zoomed in on a young man playing a mournful version of "Guantanamera" on a guitar to two beach bunnies under a palm tree. His long brown hair and pink lips gave him a romantic prettiness, like an old-time cavalier. But his red thong didn't have enough material for a cavalier's cuff. Mr. Romantic finished his guitar solo and the two young women applauded. He stood up, bent to take a bow, and Helen saw his hairy bottom.

She winced. Mooned in daylight. Helen wanted to run over with a tube of hair remover and say, "Use this! Keep Florida beautiful."

Helen abruptly swung the camera away, toward the sound of an argument. A fleshy topless woman was screaming in French at the curvy brown lifeguard in a modest red suit. The lifeguard handed the topless woman a towel and pointed toward the street. The sturdy woman flipped the lifeguard the bird, a gesture understood in any language. She left without covering herself, her bare breasts swinging defiantly.

Helen turned her camera to a family playing by the shore. A brown-haired mother watched her toddler squeal and chase the waves. The chubby-cheeked baby had a duck's fluff of blond hair.

Helen was so charmed by the Madonna with her water baby, she forgot she was supposed to be watching Sunny Jim's. She aimed her camcorder toward the trailer and found her husband talking and laughing with the brown-skinned lifeguard. Her muscular body, carved out of mahogany, gleamed with sunscreen, a slippery surface for any man. Phil didn't wear his ring for this assignment, either, and he sure wasn't acting married.

Movement at the edge of the viewfinder caught Helen's eye, and she shifted her camcorder toward two twentysomething men near the open trailer.

The curly-headed one in loud Hawaiian shorts seemed to be watching Phil. The other, with hair gelled into spikes and black board shorts, edged toward the laptop and iPad on the trailer desk.

Helen stood up, camcorder still at her eye, and strolled over as if she was fascinated by Riggs Pier from that angle. Mr. Hawaiian tapped Mr. Spike lightly on the arm and they casually wandered away.

Too casually, Helen thought. She kept the camcorder trained on them until they were splashing in the waves near the squealing teens.

Then she turned her camcorder back to Sunny Jim's. The shapely lifeguard was sashaying back to her tower, long brown hair blowing in the ocean breeze, while Phil stared at her and waved good-bye. Helen wanted to wipe that silly grin off his face.

There's no reason to be jealous, she thought. Not after last night. Phil's yellow Sunny Jim T-shirt covered the nail marks she'd left on his muscled shoulders. They'd started celebrating their new contract with a bottle of wine on the couch and ended up in bed. They'd been married less than a year, and Phil's touch still set off delicious responses. The soft, sensuous Florida nights seemed made for long sessions of lovemaking.

Helen's viewfinder examined Phil's lean face with its aristocratic, slightly crooked nose. She thought his startling silver hair made him look younger than forty-five. This morning, he wore it in a ponytail.

He's not like Rob, she told herself. The thought of her dead ex-husband gave her a guilty shiver on this warm morning. She wished she could bury her guilt as well as she'd buried Rob. The secret of his death weighed on her conscience, heavy as the concrete that covered his unmarked grave.

Her uneasy thoughts were interrupted when a yellow pickup truck parked behind the trailer.

Phil waved at Sunny Jim. "Hey, you're back already," he said. The wind carried their conversation straight to Helen.

"'Already'? It's been two hours," Jim said. His french-fried hair was hidden under a yellow baseball cap. He dug a tanned, muscular arm into a foam cooler in the trailer, pulled out a cold bottle, and leaned against the paddleboard rack, chugging his water.

"How did the lesson go with your St. Louis tourists?" Phil asked.

"Better than I expected," Jim said. "The husband, Daniel, was an experienced paddleboarder, so he rented a board and explored Riggs Lake on his own.

"His wife, Ceci, was scared at first, but Riggs Lake is a good place for beginners. Once her husband was out of sight, she was way more confident. She only fell once. After she got her balance and felt comfortable standing up on the board, she enjoyed it. Went paddling around near the shore, watching the birds—until some meathead roared by in a speedboat. Set off a hell of a wake—big waves, one right after the other. Ceci kept her balance on the board. She knew how to handle the paddle to keep from tipping."

"That's good," Phil said.

"I guess," Jim said. "Except now Ceci says she's ready to try ocean stand-up paddleboarding. Her husband reserved two boards on the beach for tomorrow morning."

"What's wrong with that?" Phil said.

"Look at those waves," Jim said. "They'll be coming at her steady, and the ocean is way worse than any boat wake. I asked her if she was ready for the ocean. I explained the water's not as smooth as the lake.

"But Ceci insisted. I said, Why not go out in the early morning, when the ocean can be smooth as glass? But Ceci said she wasn't going to get up early on her vacation. She only has one more day left and she wants to get out on the ocean before she loses her nerve."

"Makes sense," Phil said. "The East Coast doesn't get big waves like Malibu."

Jim finished his water and dropped the bottle in the beach recycling can. "Are you and your lady coming for your lessons on the lake after work today?"

"You bet," Phil said. "Helen and I can't wait."

"Help me clean off their paddleboards, will you?" Jim asked. He opened the truck and pulled out one board by its handle in the center. Phil took the other.

"Watch the fins on the bottom," Jim said. They leaned the boards against the side of the trailer and Jim hosed them off.

"Do we have to wax them?" Phil asked.

"No," Jim said, and laughed. "These aren't surfboards. Usually rinsing them off with freshwater is sufficient for removing salt water and dirt. Ceci left hers facedown on the lakeshore and got it sandy."

"Are you really worried about her going out on the ocean tomorrow?" Phil asked.

"Not worried, exactly," Jim said. "But Ceci's only had one lesson. Her husband made a ten o'clock reservation for two boards. And look at this."

Jim pulled a Riggs Pier tide table from his pocket and pointed to a line of dark type. "Tomorrow's a full moon," he said. "High tide is at ten twenty-six a.m. and there's always a nasty rip current next to that pier. Ceci doesn't know what she's getting into. She gets dragged into that current and she could drown."

"But her husband will be paddling with her, won't he?" Phil asked. "And we'll be here."

"Yeah, you're right," Jim said. "Hell, I'm just borrowing trouble. We'll all watch her. She'll be okay."

CHAPTER 3

● ● ● ● ● ● ● ● ● ● ● ●

"That's it! That's the proof I need!" Sunny Jim said. His shout echoed across the serene surface of Riggs Lake, sending a startled flock of white birds skyward. "You caught them on your camcorder, Helen."

Jim, Helen and Phil were sitting on lawn chairs outside Jim's lakeside paddleboard trailer. His lake trailer was just like the one on the beach, except for the brown-speckled banana on the plywood desk.

Jim stabbed the camcorder's playback screen with a callused finger. "I told you they were out to get me," he said. "See that dude with the spiky hair and black shorts? That's Randy, my old employee. The one I told you about. He works for Bill's Boards now. In March, he and some other douche bag stole two paddleboards and broke a dozen paddles. They ruined my spring break business."

"You think," Phil said.

"I know," Jim said. He thrust out his chin and his dry-fried hair flopped forward. "If the cops were doing their job, they'd know, too, and arrest him."

"Randy looks like a lot of guys on the beach," Helen said.

"No, he doesn't," Jim said. "See that barbed wire tattoo on his biceps? That's Randy. The dude with him is the same one in my surveillance video. I caught them stealing red-handed and you did, too."

"Any distinguishing marks on the other man?" Phil asked.

"Yeah. He hangs around with Randy," Jim said. "Buncha thieves. This time, they were going to steal my laptop and iPad in broad daylight. Except you caught them."

"They wandered away when I went toward them," Helen said. "But they didn't enter your trailer. This video doesn't prove anything."

"Yes, it does," Jim said. "It proves that they mean to ruin my business. I keep my waivers and appointments in those computers. I've got a set for the lake location and the beach. I lose them, and I'm out of luck—and out of business."

"Don't you have backup?" Phil asked.

"I've been meaning to get it . . . ," Jim said, his words trailing off. "Been busy. I was short an employee for a while. Which gets us back to Randy. He knew how important that equipment was. He nearly wiped me out, until you stopped him."

"I'm glad you're happy, Jim," Helen said, "but I'm not sure I did anything."

Phil flashed her a warning glare and said, "We're always happy when a client is satisfied. We'll get you the hard evidence. I agree Helen did an amazing job. It's been a long, hot day on the beach and I'd like to get out on that lake before it gets dark. How about those paddleboard lessons?"

Riggs Lake was a polished silver disc under a tender pink sky. Tree branches dipped gracefully into the silvery water. Helen could hear the rustling of pelicans settling in for the night.

"Sure thing," Jim said. "Just sign this waiver of liability on my iPad, and you're ready for your free lesson."

Phil stepped up to the trailer desk and scrawled his name on the electronic signature pad.

Helen hesitated. "Why do I need a waiver?" she asked. "Is paddleboarding dangerous?"

"Never lost a client yet," Jim said.

Helen didn't like the way his eyes shifted away.

"Just sign, Helen," Phil said. "The lake's only nine feet deep in the center and it's smooth as a mirror. I want to get out on the water and start paddling."

Helen signed, then followed Phil to the white sand crescent at the foot of the trailer—a castaway's beach, complete with broken shells and a coconut. Three yellow boards floated in the shallow water near the shore, each with an orange life vest on its nose.

Jim took two black plastic paddles off the rack and stood them up next to Helen and Phil. Phil got the longer one. "The paddle should be about eight inches taller than you."

Jim picked up another paddle and waded to the closest board. Helen and Phil followed him into the lake. The sun-warmed water felt good on Helen's bare legs and the white sandy lake bottom was toe-friendly.

"See this handle in the middle of the board?" Jim asked. "That's the center. You get on there with your paddle, in a kneeling position."

He gracefully kneeled on his board. It rocked slightly, like a well-filled waterbed.

"Then you stand up, holding your paddle. You need to keep your feet eight inches apart. It's a misconception that if you have a nice, wide stance you'll be stable."

He rose up gracefully as a sea god, paddle in both hands, then made wide, smooth strokes, moving slightly away from the shore. "Come on," he said. "Try it. The secret is don't look down. Look forward or you'll lose your balance."

Helen climbed awkwardly onto her board. The long, wide board had shrunk to a skinny, unstable strip. It shifted under her weight, but she was kneeling on it. Helen felt so relieved, she wanted to sit down.

She was glad she'd changed into a long red T-shirt. She felt exposed on the unsteady board and knew if she tumbled into the lake, she'd be a flailing bundle of limbs.

She glanced over at Phil. He hopped on the paddleboard as if he'd been born in the water, stood up in one smooth motion and slowly paddled out toward Jim with long, even strokes.

"Good, Phil!" Jim said. "You're a natural. Keep your paddle close to your board. That drives it in a straight line. Your turn, Helen."

Helen stood up gingerly and the board shifted like a seesaw. But she was standing and still holding her paddle.

"Great!" he said. "You did it. Now relax your hips, knees and ankles." Jim did a little dance on his shifting board. "You should be so loose you can do the merengue," he said.

Why is it when people say "relax," my body goes as rigid as this board? Helen wondered. She stuck her paddle awkwardly into the water and took a few tentative strokes.

"Wider, Helen," Jim said. "Flex your knees. Reach forward and pull your board through the water, not your paddle. Use your core to move forward. Keep your arms straight, like this."

He looked like a praying mantis with a paddle as he skimmed across the surface. "You want to cover eleven or twelve feet per stroke."

Phil, the star pupil, paddled over toward the pelican roost near the shore.

Helen took a few longer strokes with her paddle and moved away from the beach toward Jim.

"Excellent. Excellent," he said.

She relaxed a bit and felt her body shift. The panic must have showed in her face. Jim's voice became soothing. "Don't look down. Paddle away from that pipe sticking into the water. It's covered with rocks and barnacles."

And green mold, she thought, eying the pipe uneasily. She rowed away from the corrugated metal drainage pipe studded with sharp and slimy disaster.

"Good. Row!" Jim cried. "Now, switch! Other side. Straighten your arms and you'll get more pull."

The tense muscles in Helen's arms ached. She eased up on her paddling, and the board tipped toward the right side.

"Whoa," she said, but kept her balance.

"Feet wider apart," Jim said.

"Do you take your paddleboard out on the ocean?" she asked.

"All the time," he said. "I love wild water. I've been paddleboarding in Hawaii, where there's real surf. I love riding the big waves."

Helen found it easier to paddleboard while she talked to Jim. "Do you surf, too?" she asked.

"Oh, yeah. My dream is to compete in the Molokai 2 Oahu World Championships in Hawaii and paddle thirty-two miles. Hawaii has serious paddleboarding and surfing. Some surfers use paddleboards to build upper-body strength and endurance."

"So surfing and paddleboarding are kind of alike?" Helen asked.

"Not really," Jim said. "Stand-up paddleboarding is the opposite of surfing. When you surf, you want speed. You're in a hurry to catch the wave. Paddleboarding is slow and steady—unless you're racing. I have a racing paddleboard, too. It's got a little different shape, but I can really go on it. I beat a kayaker when I raced him on my stand-up paddleboard."

"Amazing," Helen said.

"I had a lot at stake," Jim said, and grinned. "The loser bought the beer."

"You must have a natural sense of balance," Helen said.

Jim shrugged. "You'd be amazed what you can do on a paddleboard. Fishing. Yoga."

"People do yoga on these boards?" Helen asked.

"Sure," he said. "Fall off and it's an instant cooldown. Beats sweating in hot yoga. I like leading paddleboard tours on the river."

Helen and Jim were paddling along the tree-lined shore. A long-necked brown bird that looked like a weathered tree branch watched

Helen with beady eyes until her paddleboard floated too close. It moved reluctantly.

"Sorry," Helen said to the bird. "It's your house."

Helen and Jim paddled quietly past nesting birds, long, low homes with hurricane shutters on the windows, and a pink condo with a pool jutting over the water. They could see the white glare of televisions in some living rooms.

Helen noticed Phil paddling on the far side of the lake. The setting sun bronzed his body. Muscles rippled in his arms and back as he paddled.

I am married to one good-looking man, she thought, admiring the view until Phil disappeared around a curve.

"Well, what do you think of stand-up paddleboarding?" Jim asked.

"I like it," Helen said. "I'm feeling more comfortable on the board. I like how I paddled right up to that bird. Paddleboarding really lets you get close to nature."

"Certainly does," said Jim, studying a bikinied redhead by the condo pool.

"I'd like to go out again," Helen said. "Do you think I'm ready for the ocean?"

"Maybe," Jim said. "I haven't seen how you do in a boat wake yet."

On cue, Helen heard a distant burring, and a speeding blue Jet Ski whipped into view, spewing rooster tails of water. The roaring Jet Ski left a wide wake. Four thick waves rocked their paddleboards. Helen braced herself successfully.

"Nice," Jim said. "You stayed with the board. Ocean paddleboarding feels like a perpetual wake. The only fairly smooth time is early morning."

"Could I try it tomorrow?" Helen asked.

"Sure. How about seven o'clock?"

"I'll be there," Helen said. They heard the sound of a gigantic mosquito. The annoying Jet Ski was back, ripping through the tranquil water and leaving bigger, stronger waves in its wake. One. Two. Three. Helen toppled into the water when the fourth wave slapped her board. She felt a shock when her head went underwater. She thrashed around and surfaced sputtering. Helen bobbed in the water, pulled her long wet brown hair out of her eyes and swam toward her paddle. Her yellow board floated just beyond it.

"You fell very gracefully," Jim said.

"I'd rather stay standing up," Helen said. She swam over to her board and sat on the edge, her legs dangling in the warm water.

"Works better if you've got both legs on the board," Jim said.

Helen kneeled on the board and rose shakily, then started paddling. She distracted herself by asking more questions. "Ever rescue anyone?"

"I only had one real rescue," Jim said. "A kid—a teenager—with his own paddleboard was out near Riggs Pier. I saw him fall off by the pilings and he didn't get back on. I paddled over. He wasn't swimming. He was barely staying afloat in that strong rip current.

"I dragged him back to the beach. He was coughing and spitting up water. Kid said he couldn't swim. He was scared, and I made sure he stayed that way. I said, 'Don't let me see you out here again until you know how to swim.' I haven't seen him since."

"Is that why you're worried about Ceci the tourist going out on her board tomorrow?" Helen asked.

"No, I'm worried because she's too confident," Jim said. "She had one lesson and one good experience and now she thinks nothing bad can happen to her. Ceci doesn't know enough to respect the ocean or its power."

Helen's legs felt wobbly and both arms ached. She slowed her paddling.

"Tired?" Jim asked.

Helen nodded, sending drops of water over her board.

"You've been paddling for over an hour," he said.

"I'm ready to call it a day," she said.

"You done good," Jim said. "Your paddling is fine, but you need to work on your balance. Try practicing at home getting up from a kneeling position."

Helen and Jim carried their paddleboards up by the trailer. Jim hosed them down and stowed the equipment on the long rack.

Helen saw Phil paddling toward them and met him on the tiny beach.

"How was your first stand-up paddleboard lesson?" he asked.

"More like a falling-off paddleboard lesson," Helen said.

"Not true," Jim shouted. "She did good for a first timer. So good she's going out on the ocean tomorrow."

CHAPTER 4

At seven a.m., the sea was silver silk under a pearl gray sky. Helen was so entranced, she stood up on her board and started paddling without thinking about it. She breathed in the water's warm, salty scent and watched the seabirds wheel overhead.

A pelican dove headfirst into the water, startling Helen. The lumbering brown bird became a sleek killing machine when it was hunting. Her board rocked, but Helen kept her balance and paddled farther away from the beach.

Phil doesn't know what he's missing, she thought with the fervor of a newly converted early riser. Yesterday she'd slept late without any qualms. Today she wondered how she'd managed to miss such early morning beauty.

Helen could almost believe she was the only person out here. Sunny Jim was quietly working around his beach trailer. She could see Riggs Pier off to the right, bristling with fishing rods, red warning buoys and danger signs. She paddled hard to keep away from the pier's treacherous rip current.

Her arms and thighs still ached from yesterday's paddleboard session, but she ignored that discomfort. The sun was now rising in a golden haze, surrounded by whipped cream clouds. A breeze softly brushed her hair away from her face.

After some fifty minutes, the spell was broken by the chunk and roar of the beach cleaner. The tractor-pulled machine raked the wet sand to remove cans, cigarette butts and other trash left by yesterday's beachgoers.

Now Helen's legs felt slightly wobbly and the sun started burning her skin. Time to turn back.

"You've been out on the water for a full hour," Sunny Jim said when she dropped off her board. "You're turning into a pro. Proud of you."

Helen was proud of herself. She popped on her cover-up, then stopped for breakfast at Cy's on the Pier restaurant. The long, low wood building was painted a cool sea green.

Every table was packed, but a young couple stood up just as she arrived and Helen scored a choice outside booth on the pier. A honey blond server in a green polo shirt filled her coffee cup. Her name tag read JOAN. The fortyish server had a tired beauty. Even at eight in the morning, Joan looked like she needed a night's sleep. Her white shorts and sneakers set off her slender tanned legs.

Sunny Jim wanted Helen to get to know Cy's staff, but Joan was so busy, Helen didn't try to talk to her. Joan quickly delivered her scrambled eggs and toast and kept refilling Helen's coffee cup.

Helen decided the food was okay, but the view was sensational. She watched the deadly waves swirl around the pilings. Successful anglers dragged carriers filled with their morning catch past Helen's booth. Hopeful fish hunters loaded with equipment and coolers paid their five-dollar fee at the pier gate. Helen felt slightly queasy when she saw them buying bait from the back of the restaurant. At eight forty-seven, Helen got her check, left a twenty-dollar bill, and received a grateful smile from Joan the server for her generous tip.

Back on the beach Helen rented another green lounge, smoothed on more sunscreen, then checked the time and date stamp on her camcorder and started videoing. This morning, she saw no sign of Jim's competitor or the possible pilferers, Randy and his friend.

Phil arrived for work at nine. Helen wanted to tell him about her extraordinary morning on the water, but they were working undercover. She couldn't acknowledge him again until they left Riggs Beach.

She swung her camcorder toward a thirtysomething father with an elaborate tribal tattoo on his back. A blond boy of about four clutched one hand and held a blue plastic pail and shovel in the other. Father and son settled near the water's edge and started a sand castle.

They were deep into their project when a tanned, wrinkled, gray-haired woman came dancing along the hard-packed sand. She waved to the father and son and shouted, "Isn't it great to be alive?"

Her enthusiasm made Helen smile.

The smile vanished when she swung her camera farther down the beach and saw Phil chatting with the stunning dark-skinned lifeguard. The guard laughed and tossed her mane of dark hair. Phil grinned at her like he'd been hit on the head with a coconut.

He's not your ex, Helen told herself. He's never given you any reason to doubt him. Just because you married a hound once doesn't mean you've picked another.

A shrill squeal made Helen shift her camcorder toward a teen girl being dunked by a boy. The giggling girl launched herself at the boy and they fell into the ocean together, laughing and splashing.

The father-son castle builders had made progress. Their castle was now three feet tall with two bucket-sized crenulated towers. The boy was earnestly digging a moat.

Helen heard a whistle blast, and the mahogany lifeguard shouted into a bullhorn at a swimming man, "You've gone too far! Come back! Now!"

The swimmer returned. So did Phil. He strolled back toward Sunny Jim's rental stand.

"Hey, there, Daniel and Ceci," Jim said, waving at a couple in swimsuits. "Glad you made it. I have your boards ready."

Helen's viewfinder gave her a close-up of the St. Louisans. Plump, pretty Ceci's bouncy brown curls were wilting in the Florida humidity. Helen guessed her age at thirty, but the fat padding her arms and stomach aged her. Ceci's matronly one-piece red suit clashed with her painful pink sunburn.

Her husband had a chiseled chin and lean, hard muscles. Helen couldn't imagine Ceci cuddling that rock-hard chest, even when it wasn't slippery with sunscreen. He wasn't sunburned like Ceci. Daniel was as bronzed as an oven-roasted turkey.

"Phil, this is Daniel and Ceci from St. Louis," Jim said.

"I've been there," Phil said. "Great city. What part?"

"We live in Kirkwood," Daniel said. "It's a suburb."

"I was in Webster Groves," Phil said. "That's next door, right? Lots of beautiful big houses."

"With big ugly utility bills," Daniel said.

"At least you can console yourself with good beer," Phil said.

"Plenty of beer, but no beaches," Ceci said. "I can't wait to get out on that ocean. This is our last full day here in Florida and it couldn't be more perfect. Can I leave my beach bag in your trailer?"

"Sure, we'll watch it," Phil said.

"I need you both to sign these waivers," Sunny Jim said. He took the bag, while Phil pulled a paddleboard and paddle off the trailer. He started to remove another, longer board, but Daniel said, "Not me. I'm not going out."

"You've already paid for it," Jim said. "I can't refund your money."

"That's okay," he said. "I want to relax. I'm tired and hungover."

Hungover? Helen thought. The man looked like he binged on bottled water.

"You go have fun, honeybunch," he said. "Don't let me spoil your good time." His voice was slick with insincerity.

"You promised," Ceci said, and gave a little-girl pout.

"I know I did," he said, "but I'm not up to it today. You can use the exercise, Chubbette." He swatted her on the bottom.

Helen would have flattened Phil if he had said that, but Ceci looked at her husband like a whipped dog. "I did put on a couple of pounds," she said.

Show some spine, woman, Helen wanted to say.

"A couple? More like forty," Daniel said.

"I've been trying to lose it," she said, "but it won't come off."

"Not the way you ate last night," Daniel said.

Jeez, Helen thought. Let the woman enjoy her vacation.

"That's why I want to go stand-up paddleboarding this morning. It will get rid of the spare tire around my middle."

"Not unless you paddle to Cuba," Daniel said.

Helen was relieved when Sunny Jim interrupted the insult fest. "I'm not sure you should go out this morning, Ceci," he said. "It's high tide and there's a west wind blowing against you. I don't think you're experienced enough to handle a paddleboard in those conditions."

"It's an *ocean* breeze," Ceci said. "And the water's not that deep. Look at those people out there at the no-swimming markers. The water's only up to their armpits. It's not that deep."

"You can drown in a bathtub," Jim said.

"And I could get hit by a car in the parking lot," Ceci said. "If you won't rent me a board, I'll call your competition—what's his name?"

"Bill's Boards," Daniel said.

"Bill will deliver a board to me right here," she said. "Are you going to rent me a board or not?"

At the mention of his hated rival, Jim caved. He pointed to the pier and said, "You can't go within five hundred feet of the pilings. See where those mint green shower stands are?"

"Where the two boys are washing sand off their feet?" Ceci asked.

"That's it," Jim said. "The no-swimming signs are posted beside them, and you can see the red warning buoys. Don't go past them or you'll get in a wicked rip current. Stay away from it, or you could get pulled under."

Ceci nodded.

"There's another reason you should avoid that pier," Jim said. "Folks are fishing off it. You could get a hook stuck in you. And don't go out past the orange no-swimming markers. Are you a good swimmer?"

"Yes," Ceci said.

"She'll be fine. Fat floats better than muscle." Daniel insulted his wife with a smile.

Ceci's face clouded briefly. Phil was frowning, too. Or was that the sun?

"Can you remember all that?" Jim asked.

"Yes," Ceci said. She squared her shoulders and said, "I'm ready."

"Here's a life vest," Jim said.

Ceci buckled it on and her husband gave a jackass bray. "You look like a freakin' pumpkin in that orange vest," he said.

"She looks nice and safe," Phil said.

Ceci unbuckled the vest and handed it to Jim. "Thanks, but it will throw off my balance. You didn't make me wear one yesterday."

"You don't have to wear one in a swimming area, but you do have to keep it on your board," Jim said. "That's a Coast Guard rule. If you go outside that swimming area I showed you, you have to wear the jacket." Phil grabbed Ceci's board by the handle and carried it toward the water. Jim followed with the paddle and the life jacket.

"Bye, honey," Ceci said. "Enjoy your rest on the beach."

"So long. All that talk about St. Louis beer made me thirsty," Daniel said. "Think I'll get me a burger with extra onions and an ice-cold beer. Best cure for a hangover."

Helen wondered if Daniel knew—or cared—how cruel he was to his dieting wife. She shifted her camcorder back toward Sunny

Jim's, watching the trailer. No one approached. Ten minutes later, Phil and Jim were back.

"Ceci fell off the board twice, but she seems fine now that she's up," Phil told Jim.

"She has more confidence when her husband isn't around," Jim said.

"Who wouldn't?" Phil said. "Where is he?"

Daniel was draped on a green lounge, chomping a cheeseburger. A cold beer sweated by his side.

I hope that food turns into lard that sticks on you forever, Helen thought. It will go well with your fat head.

She could see Ceci's paddleboard moving steadily out on the water. Ceci was getting as far away from her husband as she could.

Helen shifted her camcorder back to the castle builders. Father and son were carefully picking shells from the bucket and embedding them along the castle's walls and towers.

Sunny Jim had a sudden rush of customers. Two giggling women in bikinis wanted boards. "We're taking a mental health day," the tall brunette in the skimpy yellow suit said.

"Because we're crazy!" her friend in pink said.

Behind them were two young men with charming Aussie accents. They were carrying their boards to the ocean when someone cried from the pier, "A dolphin! A dolphin!"

Helen saw a pair of dolphins playing near the far end of the pier. Anglers tossed the dolphins bait and fresh-caught fish.

"Here, Flipper!" someone said. The restaurant customers and servers ran out to see the dolphins. Helen saw a red-suited figure paddle toward the pier.

"No, Ceci!" Jim yelled.

Was she trying to get a better look at the dolphins? Was she strong enough to paddle against the wind?

The lifeguard blew her whistle, then called on her bullhorn, "Turn away from the pier, ma'am. Turn away from the pier."

"Turn back! Ceci, don't go there," Jim screamed and waved, but she didn't seem to hear. Her yellow paddleboard was heading straight toward the pier.

Now even her husband had abandoned his food. "Honeybunch, no!" Daniel shouted. "Go back."

The wind blew sand in Helen's eyes and a sandwich wrapper skimmed along the sand. The west wind had picked up. This was no soft ocean breeze. Helen wasn't sure if Ceci tried to turn back or simply lost her balance. But she definitely saw Ceci lurch, then tumble off the paddleboard.

She did not get back on.

CHAPTER 5

"Rescue Tower Three! Rescue Tower Three!" the female lifeguard shouted into her radio, then jumped on her ATV and headed toward the pier.

The lifeguard in the tower south of hers took up the call on his radio: "Rescue Tower Four. One victim near the pier." The second guard had short, dark hair and a slender, wiry strength.

Now both guards were roaring toward the pier. Ceci's yellow paddleboard bumped against the pier pilings, but Helen saw no sign of her—not even a glimpse of her red suit in the swirling water.

"Watch the shop, Phil," Sunny Jim said. "I'm going to save her." He hauled a paddleboard off the rack and sprinted for the water. Ceci's husband, Daniel, grabbed another board and paddle and ran after him. "Where's my wife?" he screamed at Jim. "I don't see her."

"We'll paddle out together and look for her," Jim said, hopping on his board with a practiced move. Daniel tried the same maneuver and fell into the water.

"Hey! Can I get some help here?" A beefy man slammed his fist down on the trailer's plywood desk, and the iPad and laptop jumped.

"I said I want to rent a board. I'm trying to give you some business."
He waved his credit card.

"Not now," Phil said. "There's a rescue going on. A woman is in
danger. You'll be in the way."

"Not going nowhere near there," Mr. Beefy said. "Take my card
and let me rent a board."

Helen saw Phil block the entrance to the paddleboard trailer.
"I'm sorry, sir," he said. "You'll have to come back later."

"I don't have to do nothing," Mr. Beefy said, with what sounded
like a Western drawl. "I'm leaving and I'm not coming back."

"Good," Phil said.

Helen stashed her camcorder in her beach bag and ran over to
Sunny Jim's trailer. "Glad to see that guy go," she said. "What a twit.
I can't see Ceci. Can the lifeguards get to her in time?"

"Kim's fast," Phil said. "Look. She's at the pier already—less than
a minute after she spotted Ceci in trouble. The Tower Four guard,
Garcia, is already helping her."

"You know their names?" Helen asked.

"It's my job," Phil said.

"I saw you talking to Kim," Helen said, then wished she hadn't. It
sounded like an accusation.

Phil flushed. "She kind of brushed me off," he said. "Said she had
to work."

Kim jumped off her ATV and ran toward the water with long,
strong strides, carrying an orange tube. Garcia hauled what looked
like an orange surfboard with straps and cutouts off his ATV.

"What's Kim got?" Helen asked.

"A rescue tube," Phil said. "Garcia has a rescue board."

Daniel was still trying to get on his paddleboard to reach his wife.
Jim floated nearby, angling his paddle like a kickstand. He had better
balance than Ceci or Daniel and stayed on his board despite the wind.

"Those two should leave Ceci's rescue to the lifeguards," Helen
said.

That must have been what Kim thought. "Please go back, sir," the lifeguard said.

"I have to save Ceci," Daniel said. He seemed to be crying. "I have to help." He reached for Kim's arm.

She pushed past him and waded into the water. "Please move away so we can save her," she said. "We're paramedics."

"She's my wife," Daniel said. "Let me do something, please! I'll call 911."

"Already did that. Go back on the beach, sir. Please."

"Let's see if we can help Jim get Daniel out of the way," Phil said. "He's losing it."

Helen tossed her beach bag into the paddleboard trailer and Phil slammed the door shut. She'd abandoned the pretense that she and Phil were undercover. She figured no one would notice in the confusion.

The frantic activity had attracted a crowd. Swimmers and sunbathers swarmed past the pier restaurant servers and ran out on the deck, shoving each other away from the rails for a better look. Others clustered at the water's edge. Everyone seemed to be taking photos.

Helen and Phil elbowed their way through the crowd. Jim and Daniel were both out of the water, their boards abandoned on the sand. They paced back and forth at the water's edge. Jim's hair stuck out like an electrified Brillo pad, and his face was white under his tan. Daniel was wringing his hands and making excuses. "I should have listened to you," he said. "She wasn't ready to go out. I should have gone out with her. She should have never been alone on the water."

Now Helen could see the two lifeguards about a third of the way down the pier, trying to pull Ceci's body out of the roiling water. The water was nearly up to their chests, maybe three and a half feet deep. Both lifeguards were younger and fitter than Jim and Daniel, but they still struggled to keep from being carried away in the swirling current. It looked like they were trying to stand up in a washing machine.

They'd lifted Ceci's body off the bottom, but she was still face-down, her brown hair spread out like seaweed on the water.

Helen shivered in the hot sun. "Oh, no," she said. "No, no, no."

"What?" Phil asked.

"I think Ceci's dead," Helen said.

"It's too early to give up hope," Phil said. "You'd be surprised what lifeguards can do."

"Ceci!" Daniel screamed when he saw his wife. He started out toward her, splashing water everywhere. Jim and Phil held him back by the arms.

"Stay here, dude," Jim said. "The guards know what they're doing."

On the pier, people shouted confusing suggestions: "You both should get on her right side," one screamed. "Take her head by the hair," another shouted. "Flip her over and drag her out by her feet," a third said. Others snapped cameras and cell phones like demented paparazzi.

Helen saw Kim snap the rescue tube onto Garcia's rescue board, while Daniel struggled to break free of Phil and Jim's grasp.

"She's my wife," he said. "Let me do something, please!"

Now Kim waded to Ceci's right side, pushed the closest arm under the water and reached for the other. Garcia, the second life-guard, helped her turn Ceci. At last she was faceup, her head cradled in Kim's brown arm, her body floating in a straight line.

"Her face is out of the water," Daniel cried. "Brilliant!"

The crowd cheered.

Helen didn't see anything to cheer about. Ceci's head lolled against the lifeguard's shoulder. Her mouth hung open. She didn't gasp or sputter. Her arms and legs were lifeless. Her lips were nearly blue and she had a jagged gash on her forehead, but it wasn't bleeding.

"This is bad," Helen whispered.

"It doesn't look good," Phil said, "but the lifeguards will work on Ceci when they get her on the beach."

Garcia slid the rescue board under Ceci's body, while Kim held her face out of the water. Kim took the front of the board, Garcia took the back, and they hauled it toward the shore.

The water was shallow now, only about two feet deep. Spectators crowded closer, watching with avid eyes, as if Ceci's drowning had been staged for their entertainment.

"Please move," Kim said to them, with a polite tone Helen didn't think the ghouls deserved.

In less than three minutes, they were back on the beach. The rescue board had skids and moved easily across the sand. Ceci was still rubbery and slack jawed. One pink-nailed hand flopped over the side. Helen watched closely but didn't see Ceci's chest move.

Garcia ran to the red ATV and came back with a thermal blanket and a small plastic suitcase.

"Back off so we can resuscitate this woman. Move, please," Kim said to the crowd. Sand Castle Daddy gathered up his son's bucket and toys and carried the boy away. Others were not as courteous.

"Please back off," Kim said, her voice harder. "Clear the beach. Now."

The sharp command got through. The gaggle of men and women shuffled back, never stopping their obscene staring.

Kim opened a pouch around her waist and snapped on blue protective latex gloves. Garcia wrapped the blanket around Ceci. Kim placed two hands in the center of her chest and pushed down hard, twice.

"Ow," said a scrawny tattooed guy with a cigarette butt dangling from his mouth. "Right on the boobs. That's gotta hurt."

Daniel turned on Mr. Tattoo, his voice soft with menace. "That's my wife, asshole," he said. "Get out. Get out or I'll kick your ass up between your shoulder blades. This isn't a show, losers. My wife is in danger. Beat it."

A large woman in a World's Best Grandma T-shirt looked ashamed and left. The rest of the crowd slunk farther back. Mr. Tattoo tossed his cigarette butt in the sand but stayed. The crowd had a scruffy, feral look, like a coyote pack.

Kim continued the chest compressions, but Helen didn't see any sign of life.

Garcia had opened the small suitcase and snapped on his gloves. "The AED is ready," he said.

"What's an AED and why is Garcia attaching those wires to Ceci's chest?" Helen asked.

"That's an automated external defibrillator," Phil said. "It's supposed to help restart her heart."

"But Kim is still pressing on Ceci's chest while Garcia uses the AED," Helen said.

"They're doing the right thing," Phil said. "She's still out cold. Combining an AED with chest compressions and rescue breaths is the best treatment for someone who isn't breathing."

"She's still not breathing," Helen said.

"Come on, Ceci," Phil said quietly. "Breathe, dammit."

But Ceci didn't move. Her skin was gray under the pink sunburn. Her wet brown hair was a flat cap.

Helen heard a siren now, then another howl as Daniel wailed, "Honeybunch, wake up. Please."

Ceci could have been a wax doll.

An EMS ambulance slammed to a stop in front of Sunny Jim's trailer. Four muscular paramedics bounded out, spoke briefly to the lifeguards, then rushed Ceci onto a wheeled stretcher without removing the blanket or the rescue board. The paramedics worked briefly on Ceci. Helen thought they were attaching an oxygen mask, but it was hard to tell.

Seconds later, they hustled her into the ambulance, still trying to revive her.

"Ceci!" Daniel cried. "That's my wife. Where are you taking her?"

"Riggs Beach General," a ponytailed woman paramedic shouted as she slammed the ambulance door.

"Where's that?" Daniel said.

"I'll drive you," Sunny Jim said. "Phil, get the boards and lock up. Then meet me at the hospital." He tossed Phil a set of keys.

"Will do," Phil said, running toward the trailer.

The ambulance rolled off in a blur of flashing lights and sirens. The feral crowd melted away and left Helen alone on the trampled sand.

A huge wave washed up and wiped out the sand castle, caving in the crenulated towers and taking back its seashells.

CHAPTER 6

Helen couldn't stop shivering. Phil ran to Sunny Jim's trailer, threw open the door, yanked out a beach towel and wrapped Helen in it.

The sun-warmed towel felt good, but Helen was still shaking. It was too much: Ceci's awful husband, the botched rescue, the lifeguards bringing her possibly dead body back from the strong current. Phil held her in his arms. Helen leaned her head against his chest and he rocked her gently.

"That poor woman," she said. "Do you think Ceci will make it?"

"I don't know," he said. "She still wasn't breathing when the ambulance took off. Even if she survives, there might be brain damage if she didn't get enough oxygen."

"I hope her husband feels good and guilty," Helen said. "He told her she looked like an orange pumpkin in that life jacket."

"Those kind never feel guilty," Phil said.

"Sir?" It was a third lifeguard, a woman clutching a red plastic clipboard. "I'm Zone Lieutenant Samantha Jenecek." Lieutenant Jenecek was about five foot six and had a red pixie cut. But those weren't Tinker Bell muscles. She had an athlete's fit frame. "Do you know the victim's name? Could I get a witness statement from you and your friend?"

Helen said quickly, "I'm Helen Hawthorne," in case Phil introduced her as his wife and blew their flimsy cover.

The lifeguard nodded.

"Did Ceci ever start breathing?" Helen asked.

"She's going to a good hospital," the zone lieutenant said, evading the question. "Riggs Beach General handles all the beach and boating accidents. Do you know the victim's last name?"

Before Phil could answer, a second siren shrieked and a Riggs Beach police car swung to a stop in front of Sunny Jim's, spraying sand. The officer sauntered over to them like a gunslinger in an old cowboy movie. Helen had a hard time taking the officer's John Wayne strut seriously when she saw the Riggs Beach logo on the police car: a blazing yellow sun wearing a smile and shades.

He was scrawny, with no-color hair and a pale complexion pebbled with pimples. "Officer James, Riggs Beach Police," he said. "Did you witness the drowning?"

"Has the woman been pronounced dead?" Lieutenant Jenecek asked.

"Don't know if she's dead or alive. She's at the hospital," the pimpled officer said. "We already had an officer at the ER. He said the victim had arrived but didn't report her status. What did you see?"

"Two of our lifeguards pulled her out of the water about twenty minutes ago," Lieutenant Jenecek said. "The woman's husband and Jim Sundusky, the paddleboard concession operator, followed her to the hospital. The lifeguards returned to their towers, as per Riggs Beach Ocean Rescue procedure. We can't leave the beach unguarded. These two civilians were with Sundusky. They stayed behind."

"Stick around, you two," Officer James said. "I need to talk to other witnesses."

What other witnesses? Helen wondered. The beach was nearly

deserted. The ghoulish gawkers had melted away, leaving a residue of trash-strewn sand. The camera clickers were gone, too. A few swimmers were splashing near the lifeguard tower, as if Ceci's emergency had never happened.

"What's the victim's name?" Officer James asked, giving Lieutenant Jenecek a lazy smile. He wasn't immune to her good looks.

The lieutenant was all business. "Her husband called her Ceci. He took off before I could get more information."

"I have it in our company computer," Phil said. "Ceci and Daniel rented paddleboards from Sunny Jim. Okay if I look it up?"

Officer James nodded yes. Helen stayed to eavesdrop.

"What caused the victim to fall into the water?" Officer James asked.

"I didn't see that," Lieutenant Jenecek said. "Kim, the Tower Three lifeguard, witnessed it. I took her statement. She reported that the victim was on a stand-up paddleboard. The victim strayed into the no-swimming area near the pier. The lifeguard blew her whistle and shouted at the woman to turn back. She thought the woman was trying to turn around when she toppled off her board. There was a strong west wind and she couldn't handle the board. When the victim didn't get back on, the lifeguard radioed emergency response and I alerted 911. I came on the scene when the lifeguards were carrying her out of the water."

"Did the lifeguards see anything that looked like she'd been pushed or deliberately harmed?" Officer James asked.

"I asked the Tower Three guard," Lieutenant Jenecek said. "She said no. But visibility isn't good in that area. The waters are murky from the rip current."

"Did she see anyone in the water who was close but not making an effort to render aid?" the officer asked.

"Like I said, the victim was in a no-swimming area," Lieutenant Jenecek said. "No one else was in the water there. As soon as the lifeguard blew her whistle, Jim Sundusky and the woman's husband tried to run out to rescue her, but they didn't know what they were doing. Our lifeguards arrived first: Kim, the Tower Three guard, and Garcia, in Tower Four."

"Did the husband impede the rescue?" Officer James asked.

"He didn't aid or impede it," Lieutenant Jenecek said. "He obeyed their orders and let them proceed. The lifeguards got the victim faceup and on a rescue board. She had a cut on her forehead. They thought maybe she hit a piling when she fell and was knocked unconscious."

"How would you describe the current?" he asked.

"Strong," Lieutenant Jenecek said. "The lifeguards carried the rescue board with the victim to the beach, where they tried to revive her until the paramedics showed up. The paramedics were still working on her when she was loaded into the ambulance."

"Did the paddleboard rental operator follow proper safety procedures?" Officer James asked.

"Like what?" Lieutenant Jenecek looked puzzled.

"Was the victim wearing a life jacket?"

"No, but stand-up paddleboarders aren't required to wear jackets in a swimming area. When she strayed into the restricted area, the lifeguard signaled her to turn around, but it was too late."

Phil returned and read from the iPad screen. "The couple's name is Odell, Daniel Marcus and Cecilia Ryan Odell," he said. "They live at 225 Clafin Drive, Kirkwood, Missouri. That's part of St. Louis, I think."

"A very nice part," Helen said.

"What did you see, Miss, uh . . . ?" Officer James asked.

"Hawthorne," Helen said. She gave him her name and address but didn't mention that she and Phil were working undercover. Florida state law wouldn't let private eyes divulge much about their work without their clients' okay.

"It happened so quick," she said. "One second Ceci was paddling on the board and the next she was underwater."

"Did you hear the lifeguard blow her whistle? Did she warn the victim to move to a safer area?" Officer James asked.

"Oh, yes," Helen said. "It looked like Ceci was trying to do that when she fell off the board."

"Where was Mrs. Odell when the lifeguards reached her?" Officer James asked.

"About a third of the way out on that pier," Helen said, pointing toward the area. "Where that couple is standing. Except she was in the water. Under it, actually."

"Was the victim wearing a life jacket?" he asked.

"No," Helen said. "She put one on, but her husband made fun of her and she refused to wear it."

"Did you take any photos or videos of the incident?"

"Lots of people did, but I locked up my camcorder in the trailer when I ran out to help," Helen said.

The officer asked Phil similar questions. Phil said he first noticed Ceci was in trouble when the Tower Three lifeguard blew her whistle. Sunny Jim wanted to paddle out to help her. Her husband, Daniel, took a paddleboard to rescue his wife, but he couldn't get on his board. The lifeguards asked them to stay away and they followed their orders.

"Did the victim have any paddleboard training?" Officer James asked.

"One lesson from Sunny Jim on Riggs Lake," Phil said. "Ceci did well and wanted to go out on the ocean today. She and Daniel made reservations, but this morning he said he didn't want to go out even though he'd paid for a board."

"And Mrs. Odell didn't wear a life jacket?"

"Not after her husband said it made her look fat," Phil said.

"Did Sunny Jim insist she wear the life jacket?" the officer asked.

"No, he couldn't force her to," Phil said. "He did insist that she keep the jacket on her paddleboard. I carried her board out to the water and Jim brought the paddle and the life jacket."

"Was Mrs. Odell a good swimmer?" Officer James asked.

"She said she was," Phil said.

The officer turned back to Lieutenant Jenecek. "Did the tower guards see a life jacket on the paddleboard?"

"You'll have to ask them," she said. "If you have any further questions, you can interview them. They're off duty at five o'clock."

"What about you, Miss Hawthorne?" the officer asked.

"I saw Jim carry a life jacket and a paddle when Phil took her board to the ocean. Jim didn't come back with either one."

"But you didn't actually see him put it on the board?"

"No," Helen said.

"Did you notice a life jacket in the water when the lifeguards went out to help Mrs. Odell?" he asked.

"No," Helen said, "but it could have been swept away in the rip current."

"Are you an expert on ocean currents?" Officer James asked.

"No," Helen said. Why was the officer cross-examining her?

"Officer, if we're finished here," Phil said, "my customers are waiting to return their paddleboards. Can I help them?"

"I have your contact information," he said. "You can go. You, too, Miss Hawthorne." He pulled out two business cards, wrote a number on them and said, "If you remember anything, contact me. That's the case number."

"What was that about?" Helen said, as she and Phil loped across the trampled sand. "That police officer sounded like a frustrated trial lawyer."

"I didn't like it, either," Phil said. "Seemed like he had it in for Sunny Jim."

The two Aussie tourists stood by the trailer with their boards, flirting with a pair of bikini-clad office workers. Their damp hair hung in ringlets and their noses were sunburned.

"Have a good time?" Phil asked the muscular blond Aussie in the blue board shorts.

"Bloody right, mate, until we saw the amby and then the blue heelers," he said.

"The what?" Phil asked.

"The ambulance and the cops—the police. Something happen?"

"A woman fell off her board and was taken to the hospital," Phil said.

After an awkward silence, the blond Aussie said, "Hey, it's beer o'clock. We should get out of the bloody hot sun and into a cold beer."

"We like beer," said the tall office worker in the yellow bikini.

"Is the woman going to be okay?" Ms. Pink Bikini asked.

"We hope so," Phil said. "How was your mental health day?"

"We're still crazy," Ms. Yellow Bikini said, "but now we're thirsty. We're going to decide whether the USA or Australia makes better beer."

"An important step toward better international relations," said the blond Aussie solemnly. The group left together, laughing.

"We can go when we find the last three boards," Phil told Helen.

Daniel and Sunny Jim's boards were still on the beach, next to their paddles. Helen and Phil carried them back. Ceci's board wasn't floating near the pier.

They walked along the beach. The board and paddle had washed up a quarter mile south, sandy but undamaged. There was no sign of the missing life jacket.

Phil brushed the sand off the board. "I'll get it," Helen said.

"Let me," he said. "You carry the paddle."

Helen found it hard to trudge through the trash-littered sand on this part of the beach.

"I'm dreading the hospital," she said.

"Me, too," Phil said. "I don't think we're going to get good news."

At last they reached Sunny Jim's. Helen helped Phil lean the sandy boards and paddles against the trailer. "I'll hose these down and lock up," he said. "We'll take Ceci's stuff to Daniel at the hospital."

"Let me turn in my beach lounge," Helen said. "I should take Daniel's back, too."

Helen dropped both lounges at the rental kiosk. Then she gathered Daniel's book, sunscreen and rolled-up towel. When she grabbed the towel, a white card slipped out. She picked it up off the sand.

"Riggs Pier Bait Shop," the card read. "On beautiful Riggs Pier. No fishing license required on the pier."

The card had tide tables for May 2013, with high-tide dates and times and strong-tide warnings. One warning was for ten twenty-six a.m. today. The time was circled.

That was when Ceci went paddleboarding. Alone.

CHAPTER 7

"Ceci's dead," Helen said to Phil.

Sunny Jim didn't have to tell them. Helen knew by looking at him.

He sat alone in the ER waiting room at Riggs Beach General, isolated by an almost visible cloud of shock and sorrow. The room's fluorescent lights gave his tanned skin a greenish tinge—unless the news of Ceci's death had caused that color. The TV blared overhead, but Jim stared at nothing. He clutched his chair's wooden arms as if he needed to cling to them to save himself.

Helen and Phil sat on either side of him.

"Jim," Phil said. "Are you okay?"

"No." Jim's voice was as flat and colorless as the tile floor. "Ceci's dead. The doctors couldn't revive her. The ER doctor said it was a blessing because she would have been brain damaged. A blessing? She's dead! Why do people say stuff like that?"

"I guess they assume she'd want a full life," Helen said.

Jim slammed one callused fist on the chair. "She's dead and it's all my fault."

"Quiet," Phil said. "Ceci's death isn't your fault. If you have to blame someone, it's Ceci. She insisted on going into the ocean after one lesson. You told her the wind was dangerous and she dismissed your warning. She went paddling in a forbidden area—where you told her not to go."

"Her husband should share that responsibility," Helen said. "He said the life jacket made her look fat and she took it off. Where is Daniel, by the way?"

Jim nodded at the oak double doors marked EMERGENCY ROOM— NO ADMITTANCE.

"Inside there," Jim said. "He asked to be alone with his wife after she was pronounced dead. Becky, one of the ER nurses, is a friend. She's been keeping tabs on him. Becky checked on me about ten minutes ago. She says the staff is disgusted by his behavior."

"What did he do?" Helen asked.

"He didn't cry or even act sorry," Jim said.

"Maybe he's in shock," Phil said.

"Becky says a lot of men don't cry, and shock makes some people numb or confused. Daniel just looked at his wife, then asked for a place to make calls. Becky took him to the family lounge and offered him juice and graham crackers. When she came back with his apple juice and crackers, he was on his cell phone talking to a lawyer. That was his first call! She heard him say, 'So do I have grounds for a wrongful death suit?' Becky came straight out to tell me. She says she's seen people more upset when their dog died."

"Do you have liability insurance?" Phil asked.

"Five million dollars," Jim said.

"That much?" Phil raised his eyebrows in surprise.

"I have to," Jim said. "It's what a responsible company does. I have a lot of exposure renting paddleboards to the public. My business does well and I have some family money. My dad died in a car accident and his insurance paid out a million dollars. When I was in the ER after Dad got hit, I wasn't calling any lawyer. I felt like I was moving underwater."

"When are they going to release the body?" Helen asked.

"After the autopsy," Jim said.

"An autopsy! Why? She drowned," Helen said. "It was an accident."

"They have to find out why she died," Phil said. "Ceci's death looks like a drowning accident, but it could have been caused by a medical problem, a stroke or an aneurysm."

"She's too young to have a stroke," Jim said.

"They happen at any age," Phil said.

"Her death is just wrong," Jim said. "Ceci was a nice lady. She was supposed to go home tomorrow after a vacation. Now she's going back in a box with that greedy bastard."

"It is sad," Helen said, patting his hand. "But you can't blame yourself. I liked Ceci. Can't say the same about her husband—she might still be alive if she was wearing that life jacket. You look pale, Jim. Have you had any lunch? Can we get you coffee? A sandwich?"

"Not hungry. Too jittery for coffee," Jim said. "I've had four cups since I got here. I'm gonna use the men's room. I'll be back."

He headed down the hall, his walk oddly jangly, as if he couldn't get his legs in sync.

"Phil, do we tell him about Officer James's odd questions?" Helen asked when Jim was out of earshot.

"Not yet," Phil said. "We'll face those problems if and when they happen. I just hope the husband doesn't decide to sue."

"Can he do that?" Helen asked. "Daniel laughed his wife right out of her lifesaving life jacket."

"You'd be surprised how a good lawyer can twist this situation," Phil said.

"I wish I'd called that police officer when I found the tide table in Daniel's towel," Helen said.

"So what if Daniel had one?" Phil said.

"He circled the tide time when Ceci went out on her board."

"Still doesn't prove anything," Phil said. "They give them away on the pier."

"But he sent his wife out at the worst time," Helen said.

"She went herself," Phil said. "He was on the beach when she drowned. He even tried to rescue her."

"Looked to me like he was trying to hinder the rescue," Helen said. "Screaming and thrashing around in the water."

"He panicked when he didn't see his wife," Phil said. "Not everybody has a cool head in a crisis. Why are you shivering?"

"Because all I'm wearing is a swimsuit and a thin cover-up," Helen said.

Phil dropped some coins in the coffee machine and handed her a cup of black coffee. She wrapped her hands around its warmth gratefully, then sipped the bitter brew.

"Thanks," she said. "I feel much better. I still don't like Daniel."

"Me, neither," Phil said. "Sh! Jim's coming back."

Helen pretended to watch the TV on the waiting room wall. Then a red banner crawling along the bottom of the screen caught her eyes. "Missouri Tourist Killed at Riggs Beach," it said. "Details on Channel 54 at 4."

"Phil!" she said. "Look!"

"I saw it," he said. He glanced up at the ER clock. "It's three fifty-five."

Jim saw the bad news, too. He sat down heavily in his chair and put his head in his hands. "Oh, no," he said. "Riggs Beach will use this to get me."

"You don't know that," Phil said. "We know Valerie Cannata at Channel Seventy-seven. She's won a slew of Emmys, and she did some good stories about us. That's probably how you learned about Coronado Investigations in the first place."

"You wait and see," Jim said.

The trio spent a tense twelve minutes. The top news stories seemed endless and pointless. Helen thought there were stories about a high-speed car chase and a robbery at a strip mall store. Then an anchor with a blond bubble of hair assumed a professionally sad expression and said, "A thirty-year-old tourist from Kirkwood, Missouri, was killed while stand-up paddleboarding on Riggs Beach."

A photo of Ceci smiling adoringly at her husband, Daniel, flashed on the screen. It must have been taken a while ago. She wore a white ruffled top and was forty pounds slimmer than the woman Helen had seen. Ceci and Daniel looked deeply in love.

"Where the hell did they get that photo?" Sunny Jim said. "She's only been dead an hour."

"Her husband could have e-mailed it to them," Phil said. "That means he's going to sue. He'll try the case in the court of public opinion first."

Jim groaned. None of them could tear their eyes away from the news story.

Now a police spokesman was talking on-screen. "The victim was identified as Cecilia Odell," he said. The spokesman looked like he was facing a firing squad instead of a camera. "Mrs. Odell was with her husband, Daniel Odell, on Riggs Beach this morning. Mr. Odell was sunbathing on the beach while his wife was stand-up paddleboarding. Mrs. Odell fell off her board and was found unconscious in the water. She was transported to Riggs Beach General Hospital and died at the hospital without regaining consciousness."

The blond anchor said, "The company that rented Mrs. Odell her paddleboard was Sunny Jim's Stand-Up Paddleboard Rental, based in Riggs Beach and owned by Mr. James Sundusky. Mr. Sundusky did not return our phone calls."

"What?" Jim said. "They didn't call."

"Is your phone on?" Helen asked.

Jim fished it out of his pocket and checked the display. "The station called five times," he said. "I should call them back now."

"No," Phil said. "Let's see where this story is going."

A blurred, shaky video clip was rolling. Helen could see the two lifeguards carrying Ceci out of the water on the rescue board. "A Channel Fifty-four viewer took this exclusive video of the rescue," the blond bubblehead intoned. "Remember, if you see news and can safely do so, send your photos and videos to your Fifty-four news station. If we use your video, we'll give you fifty-four dollars."

Professional video replaced the snippet of amateur work. It showed a hefty man with a comb-over and a dingy white short-sleeved shirt.

"Oh, no," Jim said. "That's Commissioner Charlie 'Want More' Wyman. He's always got his hand out for a bribe."

Charlie earnestly folded his chubby hands over his paunch while the blond anchor said, "Police say the incident is under investigation. But here's what Riggs Beach city commissioner Charles Harrison Wyman told us."

Commissioner Wyman had a reedy voice for a big man. "I have repeatedly called for more regulation for water sports companies," he said. "South Florida has had tragic deaths from parasailing providers, Jet Ski rentals, and now in Riggs Beach, stand-up paddleboarding rentals. These companies and their equipment should be inspected on a regular basis. And right now, that's not occurring. My rules would change that. We need to protect our citizens and the good name of Riggs Beach as a family vacation spot.

"If companies like Sunny Jim's Stand-Up Paddleboard Rental can't follow safety procedures, they don't deserve to be on our beach."

"See? I told you," Jim said. "The Riggs Beach City Commission is going to vote to take my license and my spot near the pier. They'll do anything to ruin my business."

"Even kill an innocent woman?" Phil asked.

"What better way to get rid of me?" Jim asked. "That poor lady was unlucky enough to be in the wrong place at the wrong time."

Phil flashed Helen a look over the top of Jim's head that told her he thought their client was astoundingly self-centered.

Helen heard an engine pulling up to the emergency room entrance, then a short, sharp horn honk. A yellow cab was waiting outside the door.

The emergency room's inner doors swung open and Daniel burst into the waiting room. Sunny Jim stood up and approached Daniel carefully, as if an energetic movement could cause the newly bereaved husband more pain.

"Daniel, I'm sorry for your loss," he said, his voice a mournful whisper.

"Get away!" Daniel shouted. "You killed my wife." He pushed Jim in the chest. "Get out of my way. That's my cab."

"No, that's not true," Jim said, but he backed away. "I didn't kill Ceci. Her death was an accident."

"An accident?" Daniel gave a harsh, ugly laugh. "You endangered my wife's life with your reckless policies. You failed to provide her with proper training and safety equipment."

What? Helen thought. Daniel had mocked his wife when she put on a life jacket. He sure didn't sound like a grief-stricken husband. He was using legal language.

"I'd give anything for your wife to be alive," Jim said. "I'd rather it was me who died than Ceci."

"Yeah, right," Daniel said. His thin lip curled like a cankered leaf. "By the time my lawyer finishes with you, you're going to wish you did die."

CHAPTER 8

Helen and Phil straggled through the gate at the Coronado Tropic Apartments a little after six that night. Phil's paddleboard T-shirt was stained and wrinkled. Helen's hair hung in limp strings, and she felt ridiculous in her swimsuit and cover-up. At least she was thawing out after the hospital's chill air.

Margery Flax, their landlady, was stretched out on a chaise by the pool, white wine in one hand and a Marlboro in the other. She looked like a giant lavender butterfly in her caftan. She was seventy-six and wrinkled as a linen summer suit, but Margery's wrinkles seemed like awards for distinguished living.

"You two look like particular hell," she said. "You need a drink. Let me get you a beer, Phil. Helen, pour yourself a white wine. The box is on the umbrella table."

"You are a goddess," Phil said. "Don't get up. I can run to my apartment and get my own beer."

"You are a humanitarian," Helen said, filling a plastic wineglass from the box of wine. She took a long sip. "Hey, this is actually good wine." Usually, Margery's box wine tasted like Kool-Aid with top notes of tile cleaner.

"Got it on sale," Margery said. "The label says it has strawberry notes and a dry, slightly floral finish."

Helen took another sip and said, "My sensitive taste buds can detect that it's cold, wet and has alcohol. Tastes good, too."

Phil was back with a cold Heineken and a big bowl of popcorn.

"What a man," Margery said. "Good-looking and you cook." She helped herself to a generous handful of popcorn. Helen grabbed some for herself.

Before they settled into serious munching, Margery said, "Who died?"

"How did you know?" Helen said. Her hand shook and she spilled popcorn on her cover-up.

"I didn't," Margery said. "But I know something is off. You're prancing around in a swimsuit cover-up and Phil's wearing a T-shirt that looks like it's been in a food fight."

"We're working undercover in Riggs Beach," Helen said. "We saw a woman drown today. It was awful."

"Was she a client?" Margery asked, her voice softer and more sympathetic.

"She rented a paddleboard from our client," Helen said, and told Margery about Ceci's death. Margery did some subcontracting work for Coronado Investigations. She also was a good listener and a source for local information.

"You never mentioned who you're working for," Margery said.

"It's on my shirt," Phil said, and pointed to his chest. "Sunny Jim's Stand-Up Paddleboard Rentals."

"Not Jimmy Sundusky?" Margery said.

"You know him?" Helen said.

"Him and his daddy, Johnny. Johnny Sundusky was a beach bum, but the ladies loved him. Jim has his father's charm and better business sense. He opened up that paddleboard rental company and seems to be doing well for himself."

"Maybe too well," Phil said. "He thinks Riggs Beach is out to get him."

"Paranoia. He got that from his father," Margery said. "Johnny owned Sundusky's Sun Spot, a bar on Riggs Beach. Johnny claimed the city put him out of business."

"That's what Sunny Jim says the city is doing to him," Phil said. "Was it true? Did Riggs Beach have it in for his old man?" He took a long drink of beer.

"Johnny was his own worst enemy," Margery said. "He loved a good time and treated his customers like friends. He was always giving away drinks on the house. When he felt like celebrating, it was free booze all around. When he felt down, he gave away liquor to liven up the place. Johnny ran that bar like a perpetual party, and every mooch in town hung out there. When Johnny died in a car crash five years ago, he left his son barely enough to bury him and settle his debts. The only smart business decision Johnny made was taking out a hefty life insurance policy. That allowed Jimmy to start his business."

"That's what he said," Phil said. "Are our client's claims that Riggs Beach is crooked and his enemies are out to ruin his business true?" Helen noticed that Phil's nose was sunburned and his tan was darker. This job made him even better looking.

"Not exactly," Margery said. "The town is crooked. Riggs Beach has been called Rigged Beach since Prohibition days. Lowest-paid police force in South Florida, but they've always had big homes and expensive cars. When liquor was legalized, the smugglers switched to drugs. But Jim inherited his father's paranoid streak, along with his debts. Don't believe everything he tells you."

"Great," Phil said. "An impossible job just got worse. Sunny Jim is convinced Ceci was murdered."

"Was she?" Margery asked.

"We watched that poor lady die," Phil said. "Ceci paddled out against a strong west wind. She had no experience in ocean paddle-boarding. Jim warned her about the wind and the rip current near the pier, but she went there anyway. She fell off her board and was knocked unconscious. Daniel, the husband, is threatening to sue Sunny Jim. But Jim says she was murdered, maybe by someone in the Riggs Beach government. We didn't see a soul near Ceci when she went under. We've got nothing."

"Except Jim is paying you," Margery said. She took a puff on her cigarette. The tip gleamed in the evening light like an angry firefly.

"Definitely," Helen said. "Until Ceci died, we had the perfect job. Phil did the heavy lifting, working at the rental stand, and I got paid to sit on the beach."

"So what's your plan now?" Margery asked.

"Keep investigating. Daniel is passing himself off as the heartbro-ken husband," Helen said. "An ER nurse said he sure didn't act like a grieving husband. The first thing he did when Ceci died was call his lawyer.

"The TV station ran a story at four today about the accident. We think Daniel e-mailed Channel Fifty-four the photo of him and Ceci looking like newlyweds. Phil thinks it's a sure sign he's suing."

"So here's a man supposed to be devastated by his wife's death, yet he manages to call a lawyer and e-mail a photo of her to a TV station in time for a breaking news story," Margery said. The exhaled smoke formed a swirling cloud around her gray hair.

"In the photo, he looks like the perfect husband," Helen said. "But Phil and I know better. He was cruel to Ceci. I would have walked out on Phil for the things he said to her—and Daniel didn't care he was insulting Ceci in front of us."

"But she took it?" Margery asked. More smoke and another sip of wine.

"Meek as a lamb," Helen said. "Acted like she'd committed some terrible crime and deserved punishment. I hated watching a woman abase herself like that."

"We think Daniel, the husband, sent the photo to the station to show he and his wife had an ideal marriage," Phil said. "He's setting up our client for a major wrongful death suit."

"If we can't prove he murdered his wife, we have to at least ruin that lovebird image," Helen said. "It will make Daniel less sympathetic if he sues Jim. He's staying at Sybil's Full Moon Hotel here in Lauderdale."

"That's where you worked as a hotel maid," Margery said.

"Right," Helen said. "I've stayed in touch. Some of the maids have moved on, but Sybil, the owner, still runs the hotel. She's indestructible. I'll talk to her tomorrow and see if I can find out anything about Daniel and Ceci."

"Like what?" Margery waved her cigarette in the air. "They dropped their towels on the floor?"

"Couples on vacation reveal a lot about themselves," Helen said. "Hotel maids know who's cheap, who drinks, maybe even if Daniel and Ceci were really as much in love as they looked in the photo."

"I don't think Daniel was," Phil said. "That's a younger, thinner Ceci in that photograph. I think Ceci's terrible crime is she got heavier."

"Any man who rejects his wife because she gained a few pounds is a rat," Helen said. "We want to make sure Daniel doesn't look like a model husband to an insurance company or a jury." She reached for a third handful of popcorn and then changed her mind. Wearing a bathing suit all day had made her body conscious.

"He may look like a rat to other women," Margery said, "but you'd be surprised how many men think it's a wife's job to stay young and thin forever. What are you doing, Phil?"

"Besides helping Jim?" he said. "And trying to keep him from making crazy accusations? That's full-time work."

"Just in case there's some truth in what Sunny Jim's saying—that someone is out to get him—I'd look into his ex-wife," Margery said. "Bet he never mentioned her."

"My boss? He was married?" Phil said. "I had no idea he was divorced. Who did he marry?"

"Wilma Jane Wyman," Margery said.

"Wyman," Helen said. "Where have I heard that name?" She took another sip of wine and inspiration struck. "Not the Riggs Beach city commissioner?"

"Yep, only daughter of Charlie 'Want More' Wyman," Margery said, "and the apple of her father's eye. Lucky for Wilma Jane, she looks like her mother."

Helen winced. "I saw Charlie on TV," she said. "He's definitely not one of Florida's beauty spots."

"Commissioner Wyman was on that TV report of Ceci's death," Phil said, "demanding a full investigation of Sunny Jim."

"He'll get it, too," Margery said. "He'll keep that commission riled up until they take away Jim's city lease."

"Sure glad we talked to you," Helen said. "You've really cheered us up."

"At least you know what you're facing," Margery said.

"Or not," Helen said. She tried to stifle a yawn and failed.

"Come on, Helen," Phil said. "You're exhausted. You need rest. We have a lot of work tomorrow."

"Your place or mine?" Helen asked.

"Mine," Phil said.

After their wedding, Helen and Phil had kept their two small apartments side by side at the Coronado. Their office was in 2C, a third apartment conveniently across the courtyard and up the stairs. Separate apartments helped the newlyweds ease into marriage. Helen's cat, Thumbs, moved easily between the two places.

"Okay, but you have to feed the cat in the morning," Helen said.

"Thumbs loves me," Phil said.

"Because you overfeed him," Helen said.

"You're so cynical," Phil said.

"Are you two ever going to live together?" Margery asked.

"We already do," Phil said. "It's just more fun this way."

"It's the perfect arrangement," Helen said. "We're together when we want to be, but I can go to my apartment when I need to be alone. Phil can shut his door and blast his Clapton collection."

"But tonight we're going quietly to bed," Phil said. Helen kissed him on the nose and got up.

"Don't forget to refill your wineglass, Helen," Margery said. "I'll finish the popcorn and leave the bowl outside your door."

Helen and Phil walked hand in hand to his apartment. They could afford a house, but they loved this old L-shaped art moderne complex tucked away in downtown Fort Lauderdale.

"This is my favorite hour of the day," Helen said as the lengthening shadows softened the bright white Coronado to pale blue. Purple bougainvillea blossoms floated on the turquoise pool and rustling palms provided soothing background music.

"You don't see those slatted-glass jalousie windows anymore," Phil said. "It's like living in a noir movie."

"I even like the rattling window air conditioners," Helen said. "Reminds me of summer vacations when I was a kid."

"This is Old Florida," Phil said. "We'll enjoy it while we can."

They were almost to Phil's door when Helen yawned again and said, "Think we can save our client's business?"

"We're going to try," Phil said. "But the deck is stacked against Sunny Jim. He's sitting on valuable beach property. Daniel Odell may sue him. His competition may want to ruin him. And if he's got the city commissioners against him, even a lifeguard can't save Jim."

CHAPTER 9

"Which one is the death board?" A scrawny teen with a shaved head washed up at Sunny Jim's rental stand the next morning, just as Helen arrived.

"The what?" Jim's voice was as ominous as an approaching thundercloud.

The kid was clueless. He pointed to the rack of eight yellow paddleboards. "You know, the board that tourist lady rode when she died. I want the one with the blood."

At the word "blood," Phil strolled from behind the trailer and stood next to Helen. Only the ghoulish glamour of blood would get this scraggly character out of bed and on the beach at nine o'clock, Helen decided. She'd never seen a less appetizing specimen. Acne raged across his flour-white face. His baggy T-shirt had a double arrow pointing up to THE MAN and down to THE LEGEND.

Only in your mind, Helen thought.

Sunny Jim towered over the twerp. "There was no blood," he said, his voice quiet.

"Maybe not now, dude, after you washed it away," the Legend said. "But you could, like, spray the board with Luminol and turn out the lights. Blood glows in the dark. It's blue. Blue blood. Get it? Saw that on *CSI*. Blood lasts, like, forever."

His board shorts slid down his narrow hips, disastrously near the Legend. He yanked them up and pulled a wad of bills out of his pocket. "I'll pay extra," he said. "Riding the death board would be awesome."

Something snapped in Jim. His fists clenched as if he wanted to pound the stripling into the sand. "It wasn't awesome," he said. "It was sad. But not as sad as you. Get out of here before I drown your skinny ass."

He took a step forward and the Legend backed away. "Okay, okay. I was just trying to give you some business."

The Legend slunk up the beach past Kim's lifeguard tower and disappeared.

"Third creep this morning," Jim said. "They all want the death board. That's what they call it, like it's an amusement park ride. Here comes another weirdo. Why's he all dressed up?"

The large man was overdressed for the beach. A navy polo shirt, khaki shorts and loafers were formal dress in South Florida. He walked straight up to Jim and said, "Are you James Sundusky?"

"Yes," Jim said.

The man slapped a sheaf of papers into Jim's hand, said, "You've been served," and waddled off to the parking lot.

Jim paled under his tan and sat down heavily in his yellow folding chair. He read the first page and said, "Daniel Odell is suing me for the wrongful death of his wife." His voice was doormat flat. "The suit says I didn't give Ceci the appropriate basic training and failed to offer reasonable advice on currents, tides, rocks and other hidden and/or obvious threats."

"But you did," Helen said. "We both heard you warn her to stay away from the pier. I even videoed you when you pointed out the areas where she couldn't paddle."

"I know it's a shock to see it in print," Phil said, "but you were expecting the husband to sue."

"But not for this much," Jim said. "He wants ten million dollars. I carry five million in insurance. Most companies my size only carry a million. I thought I was covered for emergencies."

"Your insurance company will examine his claim and see you weren't negligent," Phil said. "Plus, Ceci signed a waiver. They'll deny the claim."

"Daniel Odell can still sue me," Jim said. "See this lawyer's name?" He pointed at the paper. "The guy's ads are on every bus bench in the county. He's already started his publicity campaign. That's why Daniel e-mailed the photo of him and Ceci to Channel Fifty-four."

"You don't know that," Phil said.

"I know juries act on emotion," Jim said. "I'll be the careless guy who killed Daniel's sweet wife."

"You weren't careless," Helen said. "We've got video that says otherwise."

"It won't make any difference," Jim said. "This lawyer is a pit bull. Defending that lawsuit will bleed me dry. That photo of Daniel and his wife says it all."

A hopeless silence descended. From far away, Helen heard children laughing and saw a couple walking in the surf. That broke the spell.

"Daniel didn't love his wife," Helen said. "We heard how mean he was. I bet there are other witnesses. He's staying at a tourist hotel called Sybil's Full Moon. I used to work there. Maybe it's time I pay Sybil a visit."

Jim managed a weak smile. "You really think I have a chance?"

"I know it," Helen said. "I'm glad I wore shorts today instead of a swimsuit. I can be at the hotel in twenty minutes."

The trip took half an hour in the tourist traffic. She shuddered as she drove past the Dumpster behind the hotel. She'd seen a young woman's body tossed in there like trash. The memory haunted Helen's nightmares, along with the suicidal shooting in the lobby. Two people had died violently at the hotel when she'd worked there.

Helen parked her car far away from the Dumpster, then made a wide circle around it and stepped into the hotel's sun-splashed lobby. A dozen tourists with painfully new sunburns and bulging flowered suitcases were waiting to go home.

Helen always returned to the Full Moon with mixed feelings. Her bond with the hotel staff had been forged with sweat as well as blood. When she worked there, Helen had cleaned twenty-one bathrooms, made thirty-eight beds and emptied sixty wastebaskets a day.

The Full Moon had survived the twin tragedies because it was clean, quirky and affordable. The biggest quirk was Sybil herself. She and her husband had built the hotel in 1953 and added the homey touches in the lobby. They'd even picked up the display of creamy pink and white seashells on Lauderdale Beach.

Sybil's husband had checked out permanently years ago, but she inhabited a smoky cave behind the front desk. Helen didn't recognize the desk clerk on duty this morning. The bronze-skinned young woman had dark hair pulled into a tight knot. Like all Sybil's employees, she was polite. The clerk promptly showed Helen back to Sybil's lair.

Helen braced herself for the nicotine stink. The dirty, bitter odor of cigarettes in the manager's rooms never seemed to seep out into the hotel. Sybil's desk was a landfill buried under layers of ash. A wiry, yellowed woman, Sybil was a year younger than Margery, but she looked infinitely older. A lit cigarette burned in a butt-studded ashtray, like an offering to an ancient god.

"Helen," Sybil said, and a nicotine-stained smile split her thin face. "I heard you and your hunky new husband opened up a PI business."

"We did. I'm a partner in Coronado Investigations," Helen said. "I wanted to ask you about one of your guests, Daniel Odell."

"That one," Sybil said, twisting her face into a thunderous frown. "If he never comes back here, it will be too soon. You know what that rat bastard did? Yesterday—the day his poor wife died—he came in here and had the nerve to ask me for a room discount."

"Why?" Helen asked.

"His reason was a real beauty: 'Only one person will be sleeping in the room now,' he says. 'I'll use half as many towels.' "

She took a long drag on her cigarette and puffed out smoke like a small gray-haired demon. "Real broken up, he was, the cheap son of a gun."

"I gather you didn't give him a discount," Helen said.

"Hell, no," Sybil said. "Not a nickel off. I hoped he'd get mad and leave, but he didn't. Mr. Odell won't find another place this good for what he wants to pay."

"Did he tell you how his wife died?" Helen asked.

"I saw the story on TV," she said, "with that lovey-dovey photo. I don't know where the station got that picture, but it sure wasn't taken here. He made that poor woman's life a misery. Hateful man." Sybil crushed out her cigarette as if she was grinding it into Daniel Odell's face.

"Did they argue?" Helen asked.

"Nonstop," Sybil said. "And he started them all. Poor woman couldn't do anything to please him. He bitched that she didn't wear her makeup right. She didn't do her hair nice. But mostly, he complained about her being fat. He supervised her breakfast like a prison guard. He'd bring her food to their table in my breakfast room. It was always the same: black coffee, one slice of dry wheat toast and half a banana.

"I put out a good free buffet, but he wouldn't let her eat anything else—no eggs, bacon or warm cinnamon buns. Not even a bowl of cereal.

"I don't know what they did for lunch or dinner, but I'm sure it was more of the same. That poor thing was starving. After he fell asleep, Ceci would sneak down here and stuff herself with candy bars from the machine. Drank Coke, too. She'd also leave a tip for the maids with the front desk. Her husband didn't bother.

"The last night, the night before she died, she snuck down, left two dollars for the maid at the front desk same as usual, then started to use the machine. Kelly, the night clerk, said, 'Why don't you order a pizza, Ceci? I'll make the call.' She got Ceci a large sausage-and-pepperoni pizza. Ceci was so grateful, she tipped Kelly five dollars for making a phone call. When the pizza arrived, Ceci took it into the hotel breakfast room and wolfed it down like she hadn't had a solid meal in months. Probably hadn't.

"She was finishing the last slice when the elevator doors flew open and Daniel Odell stomped out and demanded, 'Where's my wife?'

" 'I have no idea,' Kelly told him.

"But he saw Ceci cowering behind the table. 'Liar!' he screamed at Kelly and stormed into the breakfast room. He couldn't have been madder if he'd caught Ceci with another man.

"He grabbed her by the arm and shouted, *'What are you doing? You're hog fat and now you're sneaking downstairs and shoveling more food in your face. I told you, I won't have a fat wife.'*

"He yelled so loud, I heard him back here with the door closed. I went out and told him to keep it down or I'd call the cops.

" 'I'm doing this for her own good,' he said, and gave me that phony smile.

"I'd had enough of him. I said, 'You will not verbally abuse your wife in my hotel. You'll treat Ceci with respect or you'll leave.'

" 'How can I respect her if she won't respect herself?' he said. 'She's gained forty pounds. It's a health hazard. I'm a businessman and she makes me look bad.'

"I said, 'Handsome is as handsome does, and that makes you the ugliest bugger I've ever seen. You can shut up and stay, or you can pack your bags and get out now. Ceci, if you want to sleep in another room, you can. I won't charge you.'

"Ceci said, 'No, no, I'll go upstairs with Danny. This is all my fault.' They got into the elevator and up they went. She had tears running down her face, but at least he wasn't yelling at her."

"I don't understand why Ceci was such a doormat," Helen said.

"Some women get like that," Sybil said. "They're so used to men treating them bad, they don't think they deserve better. I saw them leave for the beach about nine thirty the next morning. That's the last time I saw that poor girl alive. I hope she's in heaven now, because her husband made her life hell on earth."

"Daniel said he didn't want to go stand-up paddleboarding that morning because he was drinking the night before," Helen said. "Was that true?"

"Oh, he was liquored up, all right," Sybil said. "Bourbon, by the smell of it. But he didn't need booze to be mean. It came natural."

"Did he make any calls from his room?" Helen asked.

"Used his cell phone," Sybil said. "He's not going to pay hotel rates for calls. This morning he asked me if I knew the name of a crematorium."

"He's going to cremate Ceci?" Helen asked. "So soon?"

"As soon as the medical examiner signs off on it," Sybil said. "Daniel said he should get the autopsy results by noon today. He's out making the arrangements now. He told me he's leaving Florida the minute the autopsy report is in and he can cremate that poor girl and bring her home."

"But her death was sudden," Helen said. "Her family won't get to say good-bye. Did she want to be cremated?"

"She's only thirty. Probably too young to think about it," Sybil said. "He's the husband, so he can do what he wants. That son of a bugger will have her cremated for two hundred dollars and carry her ashes on the plane. Save himself the expense of embalming, a casket, flying her body home and a St. Louis funeral."

She mashed out another cigarette, then lit a new one. As the flame flared up, Sybil said, "I'd like to see him burn. In hell."

CHAPTER 10

Helen breathed in the heavenly scent of the hotel's lemon polish. It was a relief to escape Sybil's smoky cave. Helen's hair reeked of cigarettes.

She was eager to hurry back to Riggs Beach in her cool white Igloo. The PT Cruiser had earned its nickname for its rounded shape and blasting cold air-conditioning. Even this early in May, Helen could feel the heat building. By June, South Florida would feel like warm soup.

Ceci Odell's autopsy report was due any moment, according to Sybil. Once the medical examiner declared her death an accidental drowning and Daniel took his wife home, Helen hoped Coronado Investigations could investigate Ceci's nasty husband. She'd love to destroy the hearts-and-flowers image of that photo flashed on TV. She didn't want Daniel getting rich from Ceci's death.

Maybe Sunny Jim will want us to go to St. Louis, Helen thought. It would be nice to have a free trip home to see my sister, Kathy, and her family.

No, it wouldn't be nice. Not anymore. Not since Kathy and I buried Rob.

Helen skidded away from the subject of her ex like a car sliding across a slippery road, and flipped on a classic rock station. Debbie Harry was singing "Eat to the Beat." She upped the volume, but even a blast of Blondie couldn't clear her conscience.

Rob was buried under tons of concrete. But he might as well be sitting in her car. He never left her.

She glanced in her rearview mirror and thought, I can almost see him. When I first met Rob, he had a kind of sexy teddy-bear cuteness. Women saw it and men didn't. I saw it, all right. I was blinded by love. So blind I didn't see that Rob cheated on me, starting with my own maid of honor.

Helen steered the Igloo onto I-95 toward Riggs Beach. She didn't notice the green Toyota behind her in her blind spot and got a well-deserved horn blast.

Now she was safely on the highway and quickly traveling back into the past.

I had a six-figure job in human resources and all the fast-track prizes, she thought. A closet full of pricy, sexless suits, a Lexus and a suburban McMansion I rarely saw. I worked from sunup to sundown.

I had it all. As long as I didn't look too closely.

The Igloo was barreling down the fast lane, but not fast enough for the pickup behind it. The truck impatiently roared around Helen.

I kept my eyes shut when Rob lost his job, she thought. I wanted to believe he couldn't find work worthy of his talents. For seven years I listened to his excuses while he lived off me.

A black Mercedes flashed its headlights at her. Helen realized she was going the speed limit—too slow for a South Florida fast lane. She switched to the middle lane.

The wife is the last to know, she thought. That sure was true for me. I was the only one who didn't know Rob was sneaking around. I didn't realize it until I caught him with his pants off.

I got my rude awakening when I was a restless forty. I bought a silly women's magazine for its ten tips to add romance to my married life. One was: surprise your man in the middle of the day. You'll find him ready to make love.

Rob was ready, she thought. Just not for me.

For the first time ever in my career, I left work early, hoping for hot honeymoon sex at three in the afternoon. Rob said he'd be working on our back deck. That's where I found him—nailing our neighbor, Sandy. I picked up a crowbar and started swinging.

Buck-naked Rob abandoned Sandy. He ran to his Land Cruiser, jumped in and locked the doors, while Sandy screeched behind the deck furniture.

And I slammed that crowbar into his true love—the Land Cruiser.

I couldn't stop myself. While I wrecked the Land Cruiser, Sandy called the police. I didn't see the cops enter our yard. One had to shout, "Drop the weapon, ma'am." I did. Rob, naked and pale as a boiled egg, crawled out of the ruined SUV, while the cops tried to hide their smiles.

Rob and Sandy refused to press charges for assault. She didn't want her husband to find out. He did, anyway, and she lost her meal ticket.

I filed for divorce. The judge, dumber than the crowbar but not as useful, awarded Rob half of our house. I expected that. But the judge also said Rob was entitled to one-half of my future income.

My lawyer, that blockhead, sat there like a stuffed vulture.

Good thing there wasn't a crowbar in the courtroom, or I'd have attacked all three men and gone to prison for triple homicide.

Instead, I swore on the Bible that Rob would never see another nickel of mine. Actually, I swore my oath on the Missouri Revised Statutes. But it was still binding.

I tossed my wedding ring in the Mississippi and left everything behind, driving in crazy crisscrosses around the country. Only Kathy knew how to reach me. My own mother thought I should forgive Rob and go back to him. Somewhere in Kansas, I traded in my

Lexus for a clunker. It died in Fort Lauderdale. That's how the Coronado became my home and Margery the mother I should have had.

Rob searched for me relentlessly. He wanted his money. If he'd
worked as hard to find a job, he would have been a millionaire. My
ex finally trapped me when I went back to St. Louis for Mom's funeral.

Funny, wasn't it? Mom brought us together again. They were
buried the same day.

Helen looked up and realized the Igloo was behind a flatbed
truck loaded with concrete burial vaults.

My mother's casket is in a vault like those, she thought. Rob is
sealed under the concrete of the church hall basement. Both of them
were buried in the church.

A horn blast brought Helen back to the present. She saw the
Riggs Beach exit, swung across two lanes and soon found herself at
the pier parking lot.

Once again, Helen couldn't bury her terrible memories. The air
in the Igloo felt dirty and bitter, but she knew Sybil's cigarette smoke
wasn't to blame. She would never rid herself of her ugly role in
Rob's burial.

Helen stepped out and breathed in the soft ocean air. She saw
Phil at Sunny Jim's, pulling a yellow paddleboard off the rack for a
dreadlocked beach bunny. As she got closer, Helen saw the young
woman had roses tattooed on her pale back and a green lizard on
her foot. The lizard's tail wrapped around her ankle.

Helen found the reptile oddly appealing. The woman's pale skin
was a good canvas for the needle artist's work. The roses-and-lizard
woman insisted on carrying her own board to the water, so Phil
loped alongside with her paddle and made sure she had the life
jacket on her board.

Sunny Jim was leaning against his trailer, pulling frantically at his
frizzy hair and talking on his cell phone. As she got closer, Helen
heard him say, "Are you sure?"

Then he punched his fist in the air and said, "Yes! I knew it. Thanks for telling me."

Phil rejoined Jim and Helen. Jim clicked off and smiled for the first time since Ceci died. "That was Becky, the nurse at Riggs Beach hospital," he said. "She told me Ceci Odell was murdered."

"What? She couldn't have been," Helen said. She felt like she'd been walloped with a wet towel.

"She was. The ME said so," Jim said. "Becky read me the autopsy report. It said she was stabbed twice in the back by a knife with a serrated edge, like a dive knife."

"Stabbed in the back?" Helen said. "Are you sure? I saw a cut on her forehead."

"That was there, too," Jim said. "The stab wounds went through two right ribs, lacerated the right lung and slashed some large vessels. They bled into her chest cavity and gave her a hema-something."

"Hemathorax?" Phil guessed.

"That's it," Jim said.

"Did Ceci drown, or did the stab wounds kill her?" Phil asked.

"She had salt water in her lungs," Jim said. "She might have been breathing for a little bit, but the stab wounds were enough to kill her. I don't know if she was conscious."

Now Helen felt sick. The sun seemed unbearably hot. "That poor woman," she said. Those three useless words were all she could manage.

"You gotta find out who murdered Ceci," Jim said.

"How? You saw her die," Phil said. "We were all there when it happened. There was nobody in the water near her. Her husband is the main suspect, and he was sitting on the beach in front of us."

"Somebody killed her," Sunny Jim said. "Maybe Daniel Odell hired the killer. Or one of my competitors did."

He must have seen the doubt on their faces. "I know what people say about me. They think I'm paranoid and my enemies are all in my head."

Helen felt a guilty stab. That was exactly what Margery had told them.

"But this killer is real," Jim said. "I want to pay you to find him. We couldn't save Ceci Odell, but it's not too late to save me."

"Tell me something," Phil said casually. "How did you get that information? That Ceci's death is murder. The police don't release autopsies in an open murder investigation."

"I told you: Becky is a friend," Jim said. "She's an ER nurse at Riggs Beach General Hospital. She has a friend who works at the Riggs County Medical Examiner's Office. That's how we do things here in Riggs Beach. There are no secrets in this city."

Except who killed Ceci Odell, Helen thought.

"Wait! I forgot something else," Sunny Jim said. "Becky told me there's going to be a story about the medical examiner's findings on the noon news. Channel Fifty-four again."

"We don't have a TV," Phil said.

"But I have an app for Channel Fifty-four on my iPad," Jim said. "They have streaming video. We can watch it here."

They ran for the trailer. "Maybe now I'll catch a break," he said. "Last time, Commissioner 'Want More' Wyman said my business wasn't safe. It's time for Fifty-four to tell the other side."

Good luck with that, Helen thought. You could trust Fifty-four to put the most sensational spin on any news.

Jim called up the station on his iPad, and they crowded around his plywood desk to watch it.

"The story is on now," Jim said, turning up the sound.

The same blond bubblehead was now reporting. She held a microphone up to a lean, lantern-jawed man identified on-screen as Riggs Beach crimes against persons detective Emmet Ebmeier.

"We have investigated the victim's husband," he said. "Mr. Odell was on the beach in front of witnesses when the murder occurred. His recent cell phone records show no calls to anyone but friends and family members. We do not believe he harmed his wife. The medical examiner has released Mrs. Odell's body to her husband."

"What about life insurance?" Helen asked the TV.

The blond reporter never asked that key question. "We also interviewed Commissioner Charles Wyman at his office," she said, "about this new development in the death of Mrs. Odell."

If the commissioner was lining his pockets with bribes, he sure wasn't spending the money on his office decor, Helen thought. The walls were covered with cheap plywood paneling and plastered with framed certificates, plaques and photos. Wyman was sitting behind a dented black metal desk. His comb-over emphasized his balding scalp.

"It is my duty to continue calling for more regulation for the water sports industry," the commissioner said, his voice as thin and high as if he'd sucked helium. "The Riggs Beach tourism industry needs to meet the highest standards of safety."

"Will you be voting to renew the city lease for Sunny Jim's Stand-Up Paddleboard Rental on Riggs Beach in June?" the blonde asked.

"At this point in time," he said, "I don't believe renewing Jim's lease is in the best interests of Riggs Beach. A tragedy occurred on his watch. Maybe it's not his fault, but his beach business will be a constant reminder of that death. We can't afford that on our beach."

"Then you'll vote to give the space to a competitor?" the news anchor said.

"That's one option," Commissioner Wyman said. "Another would be to use the area for more parking. I am carefully considering which would be best for the future prosperity of Riggs Beach."

"Hah!" Sunny Jim said. "He means the future prosperity of 'Want More' Wyman."

CHAPTER 11

"Now what?" Helen asked Phil.

The two partners of Coronado Investigations held a hasty meeting on a bench near Riggs Pier. Three feet away, a young mother washed salt and sand off her little girl. In front of them, two boys horsed around on boogie boards in the surf. Behind them was a beery game of beach volleyball.

No one paid them any attention.

"Jim wants us to solve a murder and we don't have a clue," Helen said.

"Clue?" Phil said. "We saw the woman die and had no idea she was being murdered."

"We can't even call this a locked-room mystery," she said. "It took place on the ocean in broad daylight." Helen threw out her arms to take in the roasting sun, the rowdy tourists and the wrinkled sea. "Ceci was killed in front of hundreds of witnesses. And they all disappeared."

"I guess that's where we start," Phil said. "We have to find someone who saw something. You go to Cy's restaurant and see if you can learn anything. I'll review those security videos of the break-in at Jim's again and see if anything was overlooked."

"From spring break?" Helen said. "You still have them?"

"I want to study them again," Phil said. "I'll also wander around the beach bars for gossip on the murder."

"You would choose a bar," Helen said and laughed.

"Hey, it's where people talk if I ply them with drink," Phil said.

"And have a few beers yourself," Helen said. She grinned at him.

"I'd look suspicious if I didn't drink, too," Phil said.

"I love how you say that with a straight face," Helen said, and kissed his ear.

"Hey," he said, "we're supposed to be undercover."

"We'll go undercover tonight," she said, and headed for Cy's on the Pier.

Cy's was decorated like every beach restaurant, with fishing nets, seashells, life preservers, and a candle on each table. At two thirty, the lunch rush was over, and only three tables had customers. Helen saw Joan, the blond server, filling a water glass at a corner table, and asked to sit in that section.

She ordered a grilled fish sandwich, fries, and a Coke. Joan brought her food quickly. The fish was fresh, but the fries were pale and greasy. Helen finished her fish and left most of the fries. The warm sun and heavy food made her sleepy. Time to get moving.

"Check, please," she said when Joan passed her, and handed her a credit card.

The server was back quickly. Helen started to leave a tip.

"Excuse me," Joan said. "I really appreciate the tip, but could you leave it in cash, please? If you put the tip on the credit card, the owner takes ten percent of it."

"You're kidding," Helen said, and pulled out a ten-dollar bill. She hoped the generous tip would pay off in information when she needed it.

"Thanks," Joan said, stuffing it into her pocket. Once again, Helen was struck by the woman's weary beauty. Her green uniform shirt brought out her sea green eyes, but there were dark circles under them.

"You left a nice tip when you had breakfast here, too," Joan said. "Lots of our customers are tourists. They figure they're never coming back here, so they don't bother tipping. I'm having a hard time making ends meet."

"You must have had a bunch of people in here when that woman drowned," Helen said.

"Most were out on the deck watching," Joan said. "They didn't eat. I saw the lifeguards taking her out of the water. I thought they would save her."

"Me, too," Helen said.

"I guess this sounds terrible, but I took a cell phone video of the accident and rescue. I was hoping to get it on Channel Fifty-four. They give viewers fifty-four dollars for photos or videos used on the air."

Now Helen was alert. "You have a video? Did you see anything?"

"A scuba diver," Joan said. "He was near the pier before the accident. I got him on video."

Joan opened her cell phone and called up the video. "Look," she said.

But before Helen could see it, she heard a man say, "Hey, Joanie, I'm not paying you to stand around and yak. Refill the saltshakers before the dinner rush starts."

"I'm just finishing up with this customer," Joan said, collecting Helen's plate and silverware.

"Sorry," she mumbled. "That's Cy, the owner."

Cy was a tubby fifty who looked like he'd been eating his own food for way too long. Joan's boss was pale as biscuit dough and just as flabby. Cy's thick hair was dyed a startling black, making his face seem vampire white. Helen wanted to check for fangs, then remembered the undead wouldn't survive daylight.

"I'd still like to see that video," Helen whispered.

"Not here," Joan whispered back. "He's in a pissy mood."

"I could look at it in the pier parking lot after you get off work," Helen said.

"He'll see us. Cy's paranoid," Joan said. "Thinks we're all talking about him. We are, too. I need lunch after I get off work here in thirty minutes. You could have a drink."

"How about the Downtowner in Fort Lauderdale?" Helen asked.

"Anyplace but Riggs Beach," Joan said. "See you there in an hour."

"JOANIE!" Cy yelled. "I said get your ass back to work."

Joan shrugged and hurried away. When Helen left, Joan was filling saltshakers. Cy was sprawled at a back table, texting on his cell phone. Helen thought he moved his thumbs fast for an older guy.

The Downtowner Saloon was in downtown Fort Lauderdale, almost under the Andrews Avenue bridge on the Las Olas Riverfront. Diners could see the yachts motoring on the New River, the skyscrapers and the jail—the city's successes and failures. The Downtowner's historic building was a series of dark connecting rooms with big-screen TVs, electronic games and an antique gas pump. Helen snagged a table outside, just as Joan arrived. She'd changed out of her uniform shirt into a peach blouse.

"Thanks for meeting me here," Joan said. "I want someone else to see that video. You seem sensible."

Helen guessed that was a compliment. "Is your last name really Right?" she asked.

"It is," Joan said. "Mom must have really loved Dad to marry him. She put up with lame 'You've finally found Mr. Right' jokes for forty years. I haven't had her luck picking men."

"You can eat lunch and rest," Helen said, "and we can pretend we're tourists."

"Do I look that bad?" Joan asked.

Helen laughed. "We depend on tourists," she said, "but we sure don't want to be mistaken for them. Why do tourists check out when they check into a hotel? They drift across A1A in front of speeding cars. They wear clothes I wouldn't put on to empty the trash. I'm sure at home they're perfectly fine, but on vacation they forget their good sense."

"And their manners," Joan said. "Maybe they know nobody from home will see them misbehaving. You've been at the beach two days in a row. Are you a sun worshipper?"

"Just a salesclerk on a staycation," Helen said. "The fun went out of my day at the beach when I saw that poor woman drown."

Joan shuddered. "I hope I never see anything like that again." A server took their orders. Joan ordered the fish tacos and a beer. "I'll have the Stranahan salad," Helen said. The prospect of grilled portobello mushrooms, mozzarella and roasted peppers on a pile of mixed greens made her feel so virtuous, she asked for a white wine.

After the server left, Joan said, "On the way here, I heard on the radio that tourist lady was murdered. I can't believe I caught it on my camera phone."

"You were going to show me the video when Cy decided to play boss," Helen said. "Don't keep me in suspense any longer."

Helen tried to contain her excitement while Joan powered up her cell phone. "Is it bloody?" she asked.

"No at all," Joan said. "Here it is. See the yellow paddleboard? It's bumping against a piling. Still wish Channel Fifty-four had bought it."

Helen could see why the station had turned down the video. She saw a yellow oblong moving against a dark blur surrounded by gray. There was no sound.

"What's the dead lady's name?" Joan asked.

"Ceci Odell," Helen said. Their drinks appeared and Helen reached gratefully for her wine.

"Right," Joan said. "You can't see her, but there's the scuba diver." She pointed at the screen.

Helen saw a roundish dark blob that could have been a dolphin, a diver's head or a shadow.

"Why would a scuba diver swim under the pier?" Helen asked.

"He wouldn't, unless he was up to no good," Joan said. "The current near the pier is dangerous. Look! Right there. See? He's swimming away from Ceci's body and the paddleboard."

Helen saw more shadows and something moving far faster than a human could swim. "Weird," she said. She sipped more wine to hide her disappointment.

"Do you think I should show it to the police?" Joan said.

"A Detective Ebmeier is in charge of the investigation," Helen said. "Maybe he could enhance the video for a clearer view."

The server brought their food. The two women watched a sleek white yacht glide past on the New River while they ate.

"I can't believe your boss takes ten percent of your tips," Helen said, "if diners put them on a credit card. That's rotten."

"That's Cy," Joan said. "He's greedy. Servers don't even make minimum wage. We only get four seventy-seven an hour, and tourists aren't big tippers. Cy helps himself to the little we do get in tips."

"Is your boss hard up for money?" Helen asked.

"He's rolling in dough," Joan said, and finished her beer. "And you're not a local taking a staycation. Your questions are too sharp. Why are you talking to me?" Joan's eyes were sharp with suspicion.

Helen decided to tell the truth. Well, some of it. "Busted. I'm a private detective," she said. "A partner in Coronado Investigations. I'm looking into the goings-on at Riggs Beach, and Cy seems to be the key."

"You want to bring down Cy for corruption?" Joan asked. "You've come to the right woman."

Helen signaled the server for another round of drinks.

"What all does Cy own?" Helen asked.

"The restaurant. It's a gold mine," Joan said. "The bait shop does well, too. He also owns the Riggs Beach T-shirt Shop and Cerise, the upscale boutique. Plus, he's got that parking lot by the pier. He charges ten dollars an hour for those spots."

"I know," Helen said. "There's no street parking."

"All the public parking was removed after Cy made generous donations to several commissioners' reelection campaigns. He has a monopoly on the beach. It's a fifty-space lot, so on a busy day he's raking in five hundred dollars an hour. But that's still not enough for the old greed head. He wants Sunny Jim's space. He figures he can cram six cars in there and make another sixty dollars an hour."

"But that will reduce the size of Riggs Beach," Helen said.

"He doesn't care," Joan said. "But Cy may not get Jim's location. My boss is in hot competition with Bill's Boards. Bill wants it for his paddleboard rentals.

"The Riggs Beach City Commission is split. Three commissioners think Cy's expanded parking lot is good for city business. Three others say it should stay beach property, but they want it for Bill's Boards. Two commissioners are on the fence: Charles Harrison Wyman and Frank Lincoln Gordon, better known as Frank the Fixer. It all comes down to who gives them the biggest payoff."

"How do you know?" Helen asked.

"They're both in and out of Cy's restaurant all the time. Commissioner Wyman—Charlie Want More—has a daughter who's getting married again. Cy volunteered to close his restaurant on a Saturday in January so Wyman could have the reception there. The commissioner is being cagey. Sometimes he says his daughter is going to elope. Wyman is too slick to take cash. Cy can't be sure of his vote and he's nervous. He wants that parking lot.

"Frank is easier to buy. He has a free lunch at Cy's every day and doesn't tip. I wait on him. Frank and Cy talk a lot. I hear things. The commissioner's kid needs new braces. We're talking about ten thousand dollars for the kid's dental work."

"That's a lot of money," Helen said.

"He needs more money and he needs it fast," Joan said. "He has this spectacular house on the water. The last hurricane damaged his seawall. Unless he comes up with cash quick, his waterfront property, his pool, even part of his house could be washed away in the next storm."

"And hurricane season starts in a month," Helen said.

"Tell me about it," Joan said. "He moans about it constantly. The pier parking lot is open twenty-four hours. The bribe is maybe one day's take."

Helen whistled. "That's twelve thousand dollars."

"That's what Frank the Fixer and the owner were talking about—how many days he should get for his support. The commissioner is holding out for a week. The owner wants one day, but I think he'll settle for a long weekend. What time is it?"

Helen checked her watch. "Seven o'clock," she said.

"I can't believe we've talked this long. I'd better get going," Joan said. "It's been fun talking to you."

"You too," Helen said and signaled the server for the check. "Dinner's on me. You've been a big help."

Joan took out her slim black wallet and said, "At least let me pay the tip."

"No way," Helen said. "That's a gorgeous wallet."

"Gucci," Joan said. "But it doesn't have those big dumb G's all over it, shouting 'I paid too much for this.' Boyfriend got it for me. Kept the wallet, got rid of him.

"Look what else I got." Joan pulled a pink ticket from the depths of the wallet. "I bought a raffle ticket for a Mercedes." Helen saw Joan's name, address and phone number scrawled on the ticket.

"My luck is turning," she said. "I can feel it." She tucked the ticket carefully back inside.

"Here's my card with my e-mail and phone number," Helen said. "Please e-mail me that video. Maybe I can have it digitally enhanced."

"I will. And I'll call you if I hear anything," Joan said. "I want Cy caught."

"Won't you be out of work if he is?" Helen asked.

"Someone else will take over that restaurant," she said, "and I'll get a better boss. I sure can't get a worse one."

CHAPTER 12

"You're working late tonight," Helen said, opening the jalousie door to the Coronado Investigations office. The only light was the pale blue glow of Phil's computer screen. Six half-empty coffee cups were scattered on his desk.

"Good. You're home," he said. "I think I've found something on Sunny Jim's security video. Take a look. I need to know if you see it."

Helen rolled her desk chair next to Phil's.

"Your eyes are red," she said. "You look like a bloodhound."

"I've been on this trail since I got back to the office about five," he said. "Look at this."

The security video, in flickering gray and black, was time- and date-stamped "1:38 AM 03/06/2013." "That's a Wednesday," Phil said. "Not many people on Riggs Beach at that hour."

Security lights cast a pale gray glow on the ocean side of Jim's Riggs Beach trailer. Two stocky men about five feet eight entered the frame from the north. Both wore black head-to-toe dive suits, gloves and hoods. Full-face dive masks covered their features.

"Creepy," Helen said. "They look like insects."

"Locusts, in Jim's case," Phil said. "Watch the destruction. It starts with that one breaking the trailer's padlock with a bolt cutter."

The other diver opened the trailer door, and both entered. Their motion triggered the inside camera. The gray illumination was fainter, but Helen had a clear view into Jim's trailer at night. The plywood desk was folded flat against the wall and the rack of paddles and boards was rolled into the trailer.

Helen watched one black-suited diver pull a paddle off the rack and smash it against the trailer wall. The other did the same. Then both men were gleefully smashing paddles in a riot of ruin.

"This looks even scarier because they're faceless and soundless," Helen said. "How many paddles did they break?"

"A dozen, at two hundred bucks apiece," Phil said.

Snapped paddle shards were tossed about like downed branches after a windstorm. Then one vandal hoisted a paddleboard off the rack. The other followed him. Helen watched them walk out of the frame with the two boards.

"Look at the man on the left," Phil said. "Is he limping?"

"I'm not sure," Helen said. "He could be adjusting his gait because he's carrying that heavy board."

"Look at it one more time," Phil said. He reversed the video until the two men were once again leaving the trailer carrying the boards, then slowed it so Helen could watch it frame by frame. Now she saw it.

"He's definitely favoring his right ankle," Helen said. "See how carefully he goes down the ramp?"

Phil sighed with relief. "We might have him," he said. "Those men are the right size to be Jim's former employee, Randy, and his buddy Buzz. They both have alibis for the time of the break-in. Each one says he spent the night with a girlfriend and the women confirm it."

"Not exactly airtight," Helen said.

"Is it too late to call Sunny Jim?" Phil said. They checked the office clock.

"It's only eight," Helen said.

Phil put the office phone on speaker and punched in Jim's cell phone number.

"You got something for me?" Jim asked.

"I might," Phil said. "Does your old employee, Randy, walk with a limp?"

"A limp?" Long pause. "No, he doesn't limp. Where'd you get that idea?"

"Just a thought," Phil said.

"Wait a minute, wait a minute," Jim said. "He doesn't walk with a limp, but he sprained his ankle this spring. Happened late January, early February."

"One of the guys on your security video has a limp," Phil said.

"That's Randy," Jim said, his voice triumphant. "You got him."

"Not really," Phil said. "Not unless he's still limping."

"No, his ankle healed up in about six weeks. He's walking fine now."

"Did he go to the ER for his ankle?" Phil asked.

"Doubt it," Jim said. "Randy doesn't have health insurance. Well, at least we know he did the break-in. But that doesn't help me."

"We'll keep at it," Phil said. "Unless you need me, I'll be tracking down the killer tomorrow."

"Go ahead. I can handle the beach rentals alone," Jim said. "Business is still slow." He hung up.

"That information may not help Jim, but it helps us," Phil said. "That was no spring break prank. Those two thieves were wearing about fifteen hundred dollars' worth of dive gear. His ex-employee probably did steal his boards and break his paddles."

"Did you hear anything in the beach bars?" Helen asked.

"Lots," Phil said. "Sunny Jim's ex wants part of his rental business.

Wilma Jane Wyman, the commissioner's daughter, actually went to a city commission meeting. Wilma told the commission she helped build Sunny Jim's business and she was entitled to a share of his profits when his lease was renewed. She's quite the looker, too."

"You met her in a beach bar?" Helen asked.

"Nope," Phil said. "The Riggs Beach City Commission meetings are taped. You can see them online. Watch."

Phil tapped more keys on his computer and called up a grainy color video. The sound was boomy, but the speakers were captioned. He fast-forwarded it until Helen could see an impressive wood-paneled room where the Riggs Beach commissioners sat in a U-shaped arrangement, with the mayor in the middle.

"That's Mayor Eustice Timmons, also known as Useless," Phil said. "Man bends with every political wind. He acts as moderator at the meetings. Petitioners come into the blue-carpeted horseshoe to talk. They have exactly five minutes to state their case; then a red light flashes on in front of the mayor's desk. Wilma will appear next."

Wilma was a curvy brunette in a tight-fitting white bandage dress that made all the male commissioners' eyes bulge—and possibly another body part. Only Wilma's father shifted slightly in embarrassment and stared at the paperwork in front of him. The commissioners let Wilma continue to state her case against Sunny Jim for nearly two minutes after the red warning light was on.

"He built that business because of me," she said. "I'm the one who risked skin cancer standing out in front of that trailer, attracting customers. I'm the one who posed for the video on the Sunny Jim Web site. I built his business, and then when our marriage fell apart, he went on working without me. When his license is renewed, I should have a share of those profits. I worked for them. Gentlemen, I stood in the sun and sweated for that man."

"Miss Wilma Jane, we've known you since you were knee-high to a sandpiper," Mayor Timmons drawled. "But, honey, we can't help you. Anything you get from Mr. James Sundusky is a matter for the civil courts and should have been settled when you divorced the man. Does your decree say you're entitled to a percentage of his future income?"

"No," Wilma Jane said. Her voice was so low, Helen had to see the two letters appear on the computer screen to be sure she'd said them.

"I'm sorry," the mayor said, "but you have no claim on Mr. Sundusky anymore. But let me congratulate you on your January nuptials. I'm glad you've found a man who appreciates your . . . um . . . intelligence."

Helen snorted.

"What's so funny?" Phil asked.

"Mayor Timmons couldn't take his eyes off her double IQ the whole time she spoke," Helen said. "Wilma may be mad at her ex, but I doubt she'd kill an innocent tourist—or hire a hit man to do the job, either. She's looking for more money, not to ruin Jim.

"I learned some things today, too, when I had a late lunch with Joan Right," Helen said. "She's a server at Cy's. Joan says there was a diver under the pier when Ceci died. She videoed it, but I couldn't see anything. Well, one thing: if it was a diver down there, he moved faster than any human I've ever seen."

"Interesting," Phil said. "Maybe I need to see if Randy or his sidekick Buzz have had a sudden increase in their income—or if any local divers have been spreading money around the beach bars."

"I guess Ceci's husband is no longer a suspect," Helen said, "now that Detective Ebmeier released Ceci's body so he could take her home."

"The detective said Daniel Odell wasn't a suspect," Phil said. "But this is Riggs Beach, remember? I want to do some checking up on Detective Ebmeier. We don't know if Ceci had any life insurance. The detective could be getting a payoff from Ceci's husband."

"And I found out Commissioner Frank the Fixer desperately needs cash," Helen said. "His kid needs dental work and the seawall around his mansion is crumbling. Why is the commissioner called Frank the Fixer, anyway?"

"He owns a TV repair shop near the beach," Phil said.

"Do people still get TVs fixed?"

"Not enough so Frank can afford a waterfront mansion," Phil said.

"So what do we do tomorrow, partner?" Helen asked. "I thought I'd check out Cy's two Riggs Beach shops. I may be forced to do recreational shopping."

"I'm looking at another day in the beach bars, knocking back beer and looking for that diver," Phil said.

"You're getting paid to drink," Helen said. "Tough job."

"It takes discipline," Phil said. "I have to drink enough to look like I'm sloshed while still being able to follow conversations. It took years to build up that kind of tolerance. Now I'm finally being paid for my expertise."

"We've done well today," Helen said, wrapping her arms around Phil's shoulders. "I think it's time for that undercover work."

CHAPTER 13

NICE STORY, BABE—NOW FIX ME A SANDWICH.

  FOR MY NEXT TRICK I'LL NEED A CONDOM AND A VOLUNTEER.

I PEE IN POOLS.

Ick, Helen thought as she surveyed the T-shirts in the window of the Riggs Beach T-shirt Shop.

Do people really wear those? Somebody must buy them, or they wouldn't be taking up expensive display space. Tourists must feel their vacation isn't complete without a tacky T-shirt.

She couldn't imagine anyone in St. Louis coming home wearing a shirt with a cartoon chef leering: TONY'S ITALIAN—IF YOU LIKE MY MEATBALLS, YOU'LL LOVE MY SAUSAGE.

More evidence that tourist brains softened in Florida's subtropical sun, Helen decided. She read the handmade sign on the shop door: NO FOOD, PETS, WET FEET. WE HAVE CAMERA SURVEILLANCE!!

Could a camera see if people's feet were wet? Helen tried to recall the grainy gray Sunny Jim's surveillance video she and Phil had examined last evening. She couldn't tell if those trailer burglars were damp or dry.

"May I help you, miss?" a pleasant brunette asked. She was holding a feather duster. Her name tag said KAREN.

"Are you the manager?" Helen asked.

"No, I only work here one day a week," Karen said. "I'm hoping for more hours. That's why I'm dusting souvenirs. I'm going the extra mile so I'll get extra hours."

"Do you know the owner, Cy Horton?" Helen asked.

"I've never met him," Karen said. "But I'm prepared. If he comes in here while I'm working, I'm going to ask him for more hours." She paused and cocked her head like a bright-eyed bird. "But maybe the store manager wouldn't like it if I went over her head. What do you think?"

"Probably not a good idea," Helen said.

"Well, let me know if I can help you with anything," Karen said, going back to shining ceramic flamingos.

Karen can't help me with information about Cy, Helen decided as she flipped through stacks of shirts, one more repulsive than another. There were stacks of shirts that said: PLEASE TELL YOUR TITS TO STOP STARING AT MY EYES. Helen couldn't imagine a woman desperate enough to date a dude wearing that. The only shirt she'd consider said REEFER MADNESS over an underwater scene.

Her stomach turned when she saw a display for Florida Gator Poop. This shop could sell the real thing. She sidled closer and was relieved when it turned out to be chocolate-nut candy. "Chocolate Lore," the package said. "To reduce calories, store your candy on top of the refrigerator. Calories are afraid of heights and will jump out of the candy to save themselves."

On her way to the door, Helen passed Karen dusting souvenir seashells and said, "Thank you." The only thing she'd learned was that the shop's T-shirts were childish.

Next door, she heard joyless pounding music. Helen held her head high when the bar rats whistled and jeered "Nice tits!" as she walked by. She wondered why more women didn't go postal when men behaved that way. She sure wasn't flattered.

This section of Riggs Beach alternated beer dives with scuzzy T-shirt shops. Helen thought there must be a kind of mathematical formula: the sleazier the bars, the nastier the T-shirt shops. At least she could enjoy the day. The sun shone in a cloudless sky, the soft sea breeze was soothing and the constant sighing surf sounded relaxing.

As Helen marched north along A1A, Florida's east coast beach highway, she passed shops promising GIANT SALES. Racks of $15.99 bargain beach cover-ups, slightly salty to the touch, were wheeled out on the sidewalk. Helen never saw anyone buy anything from the racks, but they lured in shoppers.

Boys on skateboards charged through the strolling pedestrians, rudely whistling at people to get out of their way.

When she crossed Riggs Beach Road, the stores changed for the better. Now there were brightly painted frozen yogurt shops, sophisticated wine bars and cheerful restaurants promising "fishbowl margaritas."

Helen was tempted by the pies and pastries in a case at a coffee shop but didn't stop. Cy's upscale beach boutique, Cerise, was next door. The two-story building was easy to find. It was painted cerise with a turquoise door. A window sign screamed 10% DISCOUNT FOR TOURISTS.

Helen heard more screaming inside Cerise. A stringy woman with tightly curled black hair waved a purple blouse and shrieked abuse at a slender, sheep-faced blonde.

"What do you mean, I can't have the discount?" Ms. Black yelled. "I don't live in Riggs Beach. I came here to visit on my day off. I'm a tourist and I want my discount!"

Helen noticed the blonde kept the cash register between herself and the irate Ms. Black, while she tried to placate the woman.

"I'm sorry, ma'am," she said, nervously tugging on her straight golden hair. "I can't give you the discount. You live in Hallandale Beach, right down the road. Broward, Palm Beach and Miami–Dade counties are all considered local."

"I'm reporting you to the manager. What's your name?" Ms. Black screeched, then slapped her palm on the counter. Helen jumped.

"My name is Alana, and I am the manager," she said. She seemed to grow calmer as the customer got angrier. Helen admired her professional cool in the face of the woman's shrill demands. "It's not my policy, ma'am. It's the owner's."

"Keep your blouse," Ms. Black said, throwing it at Alana. "It's locals like me who keep your shop going when the tourists go home."

She charged out of the store, knocking two skirts off a rack on her way to the door.

Helen picked up the skirts and hung them back up. Now the shop seemed unnaturally silent. She could see these clothes were a world away from the items in Cy's T-shirt shop.

Alana appeared at Helen's side. "Thanks," she said. "Sorry you had to listen to that." The store manager wasn't conventionally pretty. She had a long nose and an overbite. But her golden brown skin, gauzy gold Indian print shirt and intricate gold earrings gave her an exotic, sensual look.

Helen shrugged. "I've worked in retail," she said. "The customer is not always right."

Alana laughed. "How can I help you? What are you looking for?"

"A new blouse," Helen said. "A bright color—turquoise, pink, red. Size ten."

Alana pulled out floaty prints and cool cottons that would be comfortable in Florida's humid summer. Helen selected a sheer-sleeved turquoise blouse, a deep green tunic with melon-colored lace, and a hot pink butterfly-sleeved top banded in black. She tried them on in the dressing room and settled on the hot pink.

"Nice," Alana said, carrying it like a trophy to the cash register. "Are you local?"

"Fort Lauderdale," Helen said.

"I'm sorry I can't give you a discount," Alana said. "You also walked in on a fight. I don't want you to have a bad impression of the store. How about a coupon for a free coffee at the coffee shop next door?"

"Nice. I was eying the Key lime pie before I came in here," Helen said. "Care to join me?"

"I'm due for a break," Alana said. "Lisbeth is here now. She can mind the store and call me if any rabid customers attack.

"Order two slices and two coffees and I'll join you as soon as Lisbeth opens her register."

Helen found a table, and their pie and coffee arrived as Alana fluttered to their table in her gauzy outfit. Her coffee-colored eyes and long golden hair were a striking combination.

"Sugar and caffeine," Alana said, digging into her pie. "Just what I need after that awful woman. Cy posted all the rules on that sign, but you need a magnifying glass to read anything but the ten percent discount part. I think it loses him more customers than it brings in."

"But he's very successful, isn't he?" Helen said.

"Hell, yes," Alana said, taking a big drink of her coffee. "Cy owns most of Riggs Beach and the people who run it. Oops, guess I shouldn't talk about my boss that way." She grinned.

"I've never met the man," Helen said truthfully.

"He's not bad," Alana said, and shrugged, sending the sheer sleeves of her blouse floating on the breeze. "The pay's decent and the rent's cheap on my apartment up over the shop. There's no way I could afford an ocean view."

"Are you single?" Helen asked.

Alana nodded while she sipped her coffee.

"Must be fun living at the beach when you're single," Helen said.

"Yes and no," Alana said. "There are supposed to be plenty of fish in the sea, but I've met some real stinkers. Dudes think dinner comes with a free hump for dessert. Last one, Jordan, gave me a case of crabs, and I'm not talking about the special at Red Lobster."

Helen sat there in slightly shocked silence, which Alana interpreted as sympathetic.

"Jordan stole from me, too," she said. "I woke up the next morning, and he'd taken my TV, disk player and twenty bucks."

"Did you call the police?" Helen asked.

"Couldn't," Alana said. "I didn't know Jordan's last name. I didn't want the Riggs Beach police to know I'd been slutting around. Those boys gossip like a bunch of old ladies. Anyway, it was my own fault. I took Jordan home because I was horny. He had a fine six-pack and it wasn't Coors. The man was ripped. But that night with Jordan scared me. He cleaned me out and I slept right through it. That was my wake-up call. I was lucky something worse didn't happen. From now on, my yahoo palace is closed to strangers."

Whoa, Helen thought, way too much information. She took another forkful of pie so she wouldn't have to say anything.

Alana didn't seem to expect an answer. She kept babbling. "At least he didn't take my battery-operated boyfriend. I call him Pete, which is short for—"

"I get it," Helen said, quickly. She could feel her face getting redder and hoped Alana didn't notice she was blushing. Some tough detective she was.

"Pete's Eveready, and I don't just mean his batteries. I keep Pete in my bedside drawer."

"Ah," Helen said.

"I guess you wonder if I ever want a real man," Alana said.

No, I don't, Helen thought, but she let Alana keep talking.

"I have a nice married dude when I want the real thing," she said. "He's not much in the looks department, but he's not bad in the sack and he won't give me any diseases. He's got a kid, so there won't be any complications. He'll never leave his wife.

"Most of the time, though, I like Pete. I don't have to listen to him complain about his family. When I get tired of him, I turn him off and put him in a drawer. Pete doesn't wake me up getting dressed in the middle of the night, either."

Their server was standing at the table. "May I bring you anything else?" she asked. Helen was grateful she'd interrupted Alana's monologue.

"What time is it?" Alana asked. She checked her watch. "I've stayed too long. I should have been back at the store ten minutes ago."

"I'll take the check," Helen said. "I have a coffee coupon."

The server presented it. Helen put down a twenty and said, "Keep the change."

"Thanks," Alana said. "I hope you'll stop by the store again."

"I will," Helen said.

Alana ran lightly back to the boutique, gold sandals gleaming in the noonday sun.

Helen sipped the last of her coffee and thought, Alana is worth cultivating. Once she starts talking, she'll say anything. Next time, I hope we can talk about Cy Horton.

CHAPTER 14

"My liver may not survive this assignment," Phil said. Even on Helen's tinny cell phone, she could hear the clink of glasses and the wail of a country song in the background. "It's two o'clock and I've been to six bars already."

Now she heard the squeak of a door. Phil must be talking outside the bar. "I've talked with dozens of customers and bartenders," he said. "Nobody's heard of any scuba diver who suddenly came into money. I was sure Ceci's killer would be throwing money around in the beach bars, celebrating his windfall."

Helen sat on a weathered gray bench under a spindly palm tree and listened. She'd needed a soft ocean breeze to blow away the sour residue of Alana's confessions.

"Maybe the killer's being smart," Helen said. "He could be waiting to spend his money after the uproar over Ceci's murder dies down. Could be he's a night owl and won't be at the bars until after midnight."

"Could be he doesn't exist," Phil said, sounding slightly testy.

"Then how else was Ceci killed?" Helen said. She was in no mood to coddle him. "We don't even have another theory. Joan, the server who photographed the diver, says he was under Riggs Pier and he didn't help Ceci when she fell off the board. I'll stop by Cy's restaurant and have another late lunch. Joan might remember more details."

"Did you get any information at Cy's shops?" Phil asked.

"Too much, but nothing we can use," Helen said. "I'll tell you about it tonight. Alana, the manager at his upscale boutique, Cerise, could be useful eventually. I'm about six blocks away. I'll start walking back to the restaurant now. I love you."

"Not as much as I love you," Phil said.

They were still newlywed enough to heal a small fight with words of love. Their slight impatience with each other was quickly forgotten.

Helen kicked off her sandals and ambled along the water's edge, the surf tickling her toes. The beige sand felt warm. South Florida had few natural sandy beaches. The Riggs Beach sand had been trucked in years ago and replenished after the hurricanes. Carefully cultivated stands of round-leaved sea grape and slim, elegant sea grass helped keep it in place.

Helen's dark hair was a rippling flag in the brisk west wind. This weather felt like the weather the day Ceci died: warm, clear and windy. Helen couldn't stop replaying scenes from Ceci's death in her mind, but she never remembered anything useful.

Far off on the horizon, she saw a heavily loaded container ship stacked with wooden crates big as boxcars. Sailors called those crates "wooden icebergs." When the crates fell off the ships in storms, they bobbed in the water just out of sight, a hazard to small craft.

At last Helen saw the lifeguard towers and the gray sweep of Riggs Pier. She dropped the bag with her new blouse in the Igloo and slipped her sandals back on, ready for lunch at Cy's on the Pier.

The restaurant must have had a noontime rush. Nearly every table was piled with dirty plates, glasses and silverware. Helen saw Joan loading crockery into a gray plastic tub.

Cy sat in his booth like a pasha, eating across from a lean strip of a man in a beige suit. Cy's guest shoveled in his food like he was being paid to clean his plate. His face was long and brown. So were his teeth.

"The way I see it, Frank," Cy said, stuffing a thick chunk of meat into his mouth, "I could see my way to two days."

Frank. Was that the city commissioner Frank Lincoln Gordon, better known as Frank the Fixer? Joan had complained that Commissioner Frank dined free and never tipped.

How does Frank stay so skinny when he eats like that? Helen wondered. A thick steak covered his entire platter. The steak was heaped with onion rings and crowned with a baked potato dripping melted butter and sour cream.

"I was hoping for four days," Frank said, and somehow managed to swallow a third of his sour-cream-slathered potato.

Was Cy trying to kill the commissioner with a cholesterol overdose? Helen sneaked a peek at Cy's platter. He was eating the same food. No wonder he looked so pale and doughy. He could barely fit into the booth.

"Three?" Cy asked, and chomped an onion ring.

Frank attacked his steak. "I'll think about it. Your cook does a mean T-bone for a Mexican, Keith."

Who was Keith? Helen wondered. Frank was eating with Cy.

"The boy does all right," Cy said. "Once he tried to hold me up for a raise. I said the magic words—green card—and he forgot all about it."

The two laughed harshly. Frank crammed another bloody hunk of steak into his mouth, then said, "Wish that worked on city employees, Keith. Always wanting more money for less work."

Joan came out of the kitchen with a bottle of spray cleaner and a cloth. When she saw Helen standing at the entrance, she waved and said, "Helen! Are you here for lunch? Come sit here."

Helen sat at a freshly cleaned table and ordered a salad with grilled salmon. Joan brought it quickly and whispered, "Could you use that video I sent you?"

"No," Helen said. "We couldn't see anything."

"That's what the police detective told me," Joan said. "I e-mailed it to him. He was real nice and everything, but he sort of patted me on the head and sent me on my way. But I know that diver was there when that woman was murdered. I've got a witness."

"You do? Can you talk about it?"

"Not now," she said. "I have one other customer and I've got to clean all those tables." She waved her hand at the lunch rubble.

"How about dinner again?" Helen asked. "You like Thai food? We could try Thai Bayshore on Federal Highway."

"Across from the hospital? Love that place," Joan said. "I'll meet you there at six."

Frank was on his way out the door when a tall brunette charged out of the restroom and headed straight for Cy's table. He was dabbing his small mouth with a greasy napkin.

"Are you the owner?" she demanded, her voice icy.

Cy nodded.

"I saw a roach in the ladies' room. A big one."

"Did you say a big roach?" Cy asked. "Not a little brown one?"

"That thing is nearly two inches long," the woman said. "You could saddle and ride it. It's disgusting."

"Oh, that's not one of our roaches," Cy said. "That's a beach roach." He smiled as if that was an explanation.

"I'm never eating here again," the woman said. She threw a ten on the table and stormed out.

"Her lunch was nine ninety-five," Joan said, and sighed. "I get a whole nickel for a tip. Are you finished, Helen?"

Helen eyed the dark brown ovals in the remains of her salad and hoped they were olives. "I am now," she said.

"Look, there are no bugs near the stove or the prep table," Joan said. "It's just that sometimes a palmetto bug wanders in off the beach."

Helen found that cold comfort. "Palmetto bug" was a polite Florida name for a gigantic roach. She paid her bill and left an extra-generous tip in cash.

"Thanks," Joan said. "That makes up for the last customer. See you at the Thai restaurant tonight."

Helen swung by the Coronado and ran up the stairs to their PI office. The tiny apartment was fragrant with coffee.

Helen sniffed the air. "Coffee smells good," she said.

Phil came out of the closet-sized kitchen. "I just made a fresh pot. Would you like a cup?"

"Definitely."

Helen sat in a black-and-chrome partner's chair and said, "You've been hard at work. Your computer keys are practically steaming."

"I'm trying to shake off my morning bar tour," Phil said. "I didn't find Sunny Jim's employee, Randy, or any evidence that he's come into money, but I learned he has a record."

"Burglary?" Helen asked.

"Sea cow molestation," Phil said.

"Ick," Helen said.

"It sounds like it was worse for Randy than the manatee," Phil said. "He was a professional diver for an environmental firm, making fifty K, when he got drunk and rode a manatee. A woman tourist videoed the sea cowboy and posted it on YouTube."

"I remember that," Helen said. "I think I saw the story on the news."

"It was a big scandal," Phil said. "The video went viral and Randy was arrested. The judge threw the book at him. He said manatees were the symbol of Florida."

"Well, they are cute but kind of useless," Helen said.

"Randy's attorney argued that the manatee wasn't hurt," Phil said. "The judge didn't buy it. He said the psychological damage to the manatee couldn't be assessed and it was an endangered species. The judge gave Randy the maximum sentence—sixty days in the county jail. Randy's company couldn't have a sea cow molester working for it. He was fired. After he lost his job, his beloved Dodge Charger was repossessed and he lost his fancy apartment. Randy hasn't found a steady job since.

"His bar buddies say he's bitter. He hates tourists, especially the women. A few weeks ago Randy picked up a vacationing honey and slapped her around a bit. She didn't press charges. Didn't want her boyfriend in Massachusetts to know she'd had a fling."

"Sounds like Randy's getting dangerous," Helen said. "Think he was hired to kill Ceci?"

"He's definitely a candidate," Phil said. "I also checked out that Riggs Beach detective, Emmet Ebmeier."

"The one who cleared Daniel Odell as a suspect and said he could take his wife's body back to St. Louis," Helen said.

Phil nodded as he carefully balanced two cups. He sat in the other partner's chair and gave Helen a coffee cup and a kiss.

"Mm, extra sugar," she said. "What did you learn?"

"Ebmeier makes a modest salary for a detective who's been on the force twelve years," Phil said. "Riggs Beach is too small to have a homicide department, so Crimes Against Persons handles those. He's head of that department and makes thirty thousand a year, plus benefits."

"That's all?" Helen whistled. "I know health insurance is a good benny, but he should be making fifty thousand."

"At least," Phil said. "He's a senior person. Been on the job for years, so I would put him closer to fifty-five."

"Is he married? What about his wife? Is she well paid?" Helen asked.

"Not really. She's a Riggs Beach teacher," Phil said. "They have one son in law school—and he's not on a scholarship."

"She must be a good money manager," Helen said.

"She'd have to be phenomenal," Phil said. "Their three-bedroom house with a pool is worth about half a million dollars, even in this depressed market. They also have a thirty-foot sailboat, a Harley, and two new cars, a Lexus and a BMW."

"On their salaries?" Helen asked. "Either one inherit money?"

"Not a penny I can find," Phil said. "I pulled the Ebmeiers' credit report. Their house is paid off and their credit card debt is under a thousand dollars."

"Daniel Odell couldn't have given him a bribe big enough to buy all that," Helen said.

"No, but I think there's been a long-standing pattern of Detective Ebmeier looking the other way in Rigged Beach. That could be why he let Daniel Odell take his dead wife home."

"Are you going to investigate Detective Ebmeier?" Helen asked.

"Not our job," Phil said. "We have to find Ceci's killer. But we have another serious suspect to add to our list—Daniel Odell."

"Joan told me that she has a witness who saw that diver," Helen said. "We didn't have time to talk because she was working. I'm meeting her at six tonight."

"Good," Phil said. "Once we track down the killer, we can find out who hired him."

CHAPTER 15

Tears ran down Joan Right's face. She sniffled and blotted her face with a tissue.

"Are you feeling okay?" Helen asked. "Why are you crying?"

If the hardworking server needed a good cry, they were discreetly tucked away in a booth at Thai Bayshore. Dark wood blinds kept out the slanting rays of the evening sun and hid the approaching storm clouds.

"I'm fine," Joan said. "This restaurant isn't kidding. Their *nam sod* is spicy. It's like swallowing razor blades."

Helen eyed Joan's harmless-looking plate of lettuce and ground chicken loaded with chili peppers. "And you like that?" she asked cautiously. She preferred milder Thai food, like her chicken *satay* with sweet cucumber sauce.

"Love it," Joan said. "I asked for medium hot. This place is authentic. Good thing I have a cold beer to put out the fire." She took a gulp and smiled through her tears.

Many of the diners were Asian. Helen took that as another sign the food was authentic. She noticed several male customers had eyed

Joan. Even one or two women had glanced her way, as if studying the competition.

Helen wondered what it was about Joan that made her stand out. Her honey blond hair was pulled back in a ponytail, showing off her good bones and green eyes. Joan's slightly worn look would never make a magazine cover. But Joan had a competent, straightforward air. She was a woman who knew her own mind.

"Where did you learn to eat Thai food?" Helen asked.

"Old boyfriend," Joan said, wiping away more spice-induced tears. "Another Mr. Wrong. The only thing I got out of that romance was a love of spicy food with cold beer."

The Thai waiter brought Helen's spring rolls, and tornado shrimp swimming in chili sauce for Joan. Both plates were trimmed with small purple orchids.

Joan put her flower behind her ear and grinned at Helen. "My ideal night. I get waited on and flowers, too. Now I'd better earn my supper. What did you want to ask me?"

"That was Commissioner Frank Gordon eating lunch with Cy this afternoon, right?" Helen asked.

"Yep," Joan said. "That was old Frank the Fixer, chowing down on another twenty-dollar steak. Once again, he didn't tip—or pay for his lunch."

She took a bite of shrimp and said, "Whoa, these are even hotter." Helen could tell she approved.

"Why did the commissioner call Cy 'Keith'?" Helen asked.

Joan burst out laughing. "You don't smoke, do you?" she said, then gulped her beer.

"I don't like cigarettes," Helen said.

"I mean weed. You definitely don't smoke pot," she said. "Frank called him 'Kef,' spelled K-E-F. That's the most potent part of the marijuana plant. You smoke kef for an intense high. In the eighties, Cy brought in high-grade pot and coke. It's how he got the stake to start buying up Riggs Beach."

"Cy?" Helen tried to imagine the paunchy restaurant owner as a drug smuggler.

"Hard to believe, isn't it?" Joan said.

"And he was never arrested?" Helen said.

"Honey, we're talking about Riggs Beach in the eighties," Joan said. "One of the crookedest towns in South Florida during the days of the cocaine cowboys."

Helen felt naive. I'm not worldly enough to be a detective, she thought. Alana's confidences made me blush. Now Joan makes me feel like an ignorant schoolgirl.

Joan wolfed down several shrimp, followed by another swig of beer. "Hot damn, this is good," she said. "Cy was small-time and smart. He knew when to quit. Most dudes didn't. He never used. The statute of limitations on his drug crimes ran out long ago.

"He's Mr. Straight now. Cy married and has a kid. He has a zero-tolerance drug policy for his employees. If he so much as sees a busboy lighting a joint on break, he fires the kid. Cy was probably involved in worse crimes during his drug days, but folks around there have short memories when there's long green. Only his good friends call him Kef anymore.

"Cy needs one more commission vote to get Sunny Jim's beach spot," Joan said. "He's playing it safe, courting Frank and Want More. Cy's raking in five hundred dollars an hour during the peak times. That parking lot is open twenty-four hours a day. Frank assumes— for his negotiations—that the lot is full all the time."

"You mentioned that," Helen said. "A day is twelve thousand dollars by Frank's calculations. Four days would be forty-eight thousand."

"That's right," Joan said. "Cy's trying to chisel him down to three days. Either way, it's only a small dent in Cy's bank account, but you won't believe the poor mouthing. Cy says he's bleeding money."

"Is he?" Helen asked.

Joan laughed. "It's a self-inflicted wound. He owns a boat, Cy 4

Me. He calls it his 'yacht' but it's thirty feet long, which means it's really a cabin cruiser. A beauty, don't get me wrong, but it's pretentious to call it a yacht. You know what they say about boats?"

"They're a hole in the water you throw money into," Helen said.

"In Cy's case, 'BOAT' stands for Bring On Another Thousand. His boat always needs something. Since I've known him, he's put in new carpet, cabinets and upholstery, and upgraded the radar. The maintenance is ferocious. He just had the bottom scraped and painted and the paint cost more than a hundred dollars a gallon."

Helen whistled.

"Now he wants a new forty-thousand-dollar Zodiac tender."

"What's that?" Helen asked.

"A boat for the boat," Joan said. "A smaller boat used to get on and off the cruiser and to the dock if he's anchored offshore. Frank's money would take cash away from Cy's boat. Then there's Commissioner Want More Wyman, wanting Cy to give his daughter Wilma a wedding reception as a gift with steak, lobster and liquor."

"So he wants about the same money as Frank," Helen said.

"Exactly," Joan said. "Just not so obvious."

"That will cost Cy major money during the tourist season," Helen said.

"It will cost us servers, too," Joan said. "We won't get paid for working the reception and Wyman sure as hell won't tip us. But it's not a done deal yet. The commissioner is being cagey. Sometimes he says his daughter is going to elope. Cy can't be sure of Wyman's vote and he's nervous. He wants those extra parking lot spaces.

"Frank is easier to buy, but they can't agree on a price. I hear the same conversation every afternoon. I'm tired of listening to them."

"So Cy's whining about getting money for his yacht while helping himself to ten percent of your tips," Helen said.

"He's shameless," Joan said.

"And he didn't lift a finger to help you at the restaurant," Helen said. "Nearly every table was dirty and he didn't pick up a plate. Or seat me."

"I don't want his fingers anywhere near me," Joan said. "Cy's the original hands-on boss. He thinks the women who work for him are his personal harem—like sex with Cy is an employee benefit." She gave a derisive snort.

Helen thought of Cy's squishy-soft body and squid-ink hair. "Does anyone take him up on his offer?"

"Oh, yeah," Joan said. "He gives raises and rent breaks to the staffers who sleep with him."

Helen remembered the manager of Cy's boutique confiding about her uncomplicated married man and made a wild guess. "Like Alana at Cerise?" she asked

"You've met her, have you?" Joan said.

"She seems to be a free spirit," Helen said.

"A little too free, if you ask me," Joan said. "She gets that beach apartment over the shop for two hundred a month and all the Cy she can handle. I guess Alana closes her eyes and thinks of the ocean view. I'd sleep under a bridge before I let that man in my bed.

"At first, Cy had a habit of 'accidentally' brushing up against me. Then he outright groped me. I told him to keep his grubby hands off me or I'd tell his wife. He doesn't come near me now, and that's how I like it. His touch makes my skin creep."

They finished their food in silence. The server took their plates and brought a pot of tea.

"Have you heard any more from that detective about your diver video?" Helen asked, steering the conversation back on track.

"No," Joan said. "I'm sort of surprised he didn't talk to anyone at the restaurant. None of the tourists snapping photos of that poor woman's death caught the diver on their cameras."

"How do you know?" Helen said. "Did Detective Ebmeier tell you?"

"No," Joan said, "but the TV stations would have run a murder video *tout de suite.*"

"You really think that diver exists?" Helen said.

"I know it," Joan said. "Kevin, our dishwasher, saw the diver. He ran out on the pier like everyone else when he heard the commotion. He told me later he thought it was odd that a diver would be stupid enough to go near the pier."

"Would Kevin talk to me about what he saw?" Helen asked.

"He will if I ask him," Joan said. "He's from Nicaragua. I'm not sure he's legal, but I've never asked. That's a touchy subject for Latinos."

"Where can I talk to him?" Helen asked.

"Not at Cy's," Joan said. "My boss has a paranoid streak. He seems to be getting worse."

"With good reason, if he's trying to bribe two city commissioners," Helen said. "Would you like more tea? Dessert?"

"No, thanks. This was perfect," Joan said. "I'll take my orchid home and put it in water."

Helen signaled for the check.

"Cy is safe as long as he stays in Riggs Beach," Joan said. "But he's suspicious of outsiders nosing around in his business. A customer talking to the kitchen staff would be a red flag. Kevin works tonight till nine."

"What about his home?" Helen asked. The waiter brought the check.

"Kevin lives with his mother and five brothers and sisters," Joan said. "He doesn't hang out at bars. Every penny he makes goes to his family. He doesn't even own a car. Wait! Kevin takes the bus home. Maybe we could catch him at the bus stop. What time is it?"

Helen checked her watch. "Eight thirty," she said. "We have enough time to get to Riggs Beach and meet him at the bus stop. Which one?"

"The Seashell Drive bus stop, right off Riggs Beach Road," Joan said. "Half a block from the restaurant. Kevin lives way out west past the turnpike."

"I can drive him home," Helen said.

"I know he'd appreciate a ride," Joan said. "He sits on that bus an hour each way. The bus stop is in front of a little strip mall with a yogurt shop and a restaurant. We'll park in that lot and I'll go talk to him.

"I just hope that Cy doesn't see me with you, or I'm in big trouble."

CHAPTER 16

H elen heard the rain before she saw it, drumming on the Thai Bayshore restaurant. She opened the door cautiously and got a face full of water.

"Yuck. I like to take my shower indoors," she said.

"Wouldn't you know it? My umbrella is in my car," Joan said. "That's my little red Neon under the tree. Follow me to Kevin's bus stop. I'll have to take A1A. My car doesn't have much pickup. The big rigs try to run me down on the interstate."

Helen dashed into the warm, wet night. Needle-sharp rain sliced the humid air, danced on the Igloo's hood, and bounced on the sidewalk. Her shirt and hair were soaked in the short sprint to her car. She shivered in the first blast of air-conditioning.

The flat Florida landscape flooded quickly, but Joan's small car carefully navigated the water-washed intersections. The drive to Riggs Beach Road took twice as long as usual, and the storm intensified about halfway there. Six-foot palm fronds tore loose and scudded across the highway. Branches swayed and lightning crackled.

The Igloo's windshield fogged, but Helen wiped it with a tissue and never lost sight of the little red Neon.

At last, Helen saw the Seashell Road bus shelter, in front of a strip of beach stores. Her car lights picked out a dark figure huddled in the corner. Kevin, she thought. He must be drenched.

The rain was letting up as Helen parked the Igloo at an angle in the empty lot. Riggs Beach was deserted. The empty yogurt shop looked dingy. In the brightly lit restaurant next door, nobody wanted the $3.99 STEAK DINNER.

With a side of heartburn, she thought.

She saw an SUV slowly rolling down Riggs Beach Road, sending out rooster tails of rainwater.

Joan parked next to Helen and jumped out of her car with an umbrella. She waded through a wide puddle and splashed to the bus shelter.

Helen watched the pantomime as the server talked to Kevin. Joan pointed to Helen's car. Kevin nodded, then shrugged, then squished through the puddles behind Joan to the Igloo.

Helen opened the passenger door for him, and the interior lights shone on Kevin's and Joan's sopping clothes. Joan's blond hair was plastered to her head, showing off her gorgeous bone structure.

"This is Kevin," Joan said. "I said you'd take him home and he could trust you. He'll tell you about the diver."

Helen handed Kevin a towel from her beach bag. "Here, dry off with this."

"Thanks," Kevin said. "It's hard to talk with water in my eyes." His Latino accent was strong, but his English was clear. While Kevin vigorously towel-dried his face and dark hair, a long black Mercedes passed. Its headlights raked Helen's car.

"Oh, no," Joan said, ducking behind the door. "That's Cy's black CLS."

"How do you know it's his Mercedes?" Helen asked.

"The vanity plate is CY 4 ME," she said.

"Just like his yacht," Helen said.

"He doesn't realize that can be read two ways," Joan said. "Cy is definitely out for himself—and no woman I know sighs for him. Do you think he saw me?"

Helen thought her voice trembled with fear. "I doubt it," Helen said. "He can't see much tonight."

"I had the towel over my head," Kevin said. "I'm safe. Besides, what's he gonna do, Joan? You're his best server."

"Servers are a dime a dozen," Joan said.

A fat raindrop plopped on Helen's windshield, then another.

"The rain's starting up again," Joan said. "Good night. I'll keep in touch, Helen." She waved and ran to her car.

Kevin finger-combed his hair and handed Helen the damp towel. She tossed it in the backseat.

"Do you think Cy would hurt Joan?" Helen asked.

"I don't think so," Kevin said. "There are rumors he did crazy shit when he was young, but now he's old. He's, like, fifty and married."

Nine years older than me, Helen thought.

"Right," she said. "Old. What's the best way to your home?"

"Straight out west on Riggs Beach Road till you pass the turnpike," Kevin said. "Then take the first right turn." The parking lot lights revealed Kevin's chiseled profile. His damp hair had a slight curl. Helen envied him those long eyelashes.

The rain was hammering the car again. "Thanks for the ride," he said. "The bus is always late on rainy nights, and bus shelters don't protect you from a heavy rain."

"No problem," Helen said. "Tell me about that diver."

"I was working in the kitchen when I heard people talking and yelling. They were running outside, to the north side of Riggs Pier. The kitchen is on the south side. I went out that door. I was going to come around, when I saw a diver moving away from the pier."

"North or south?" Helen said.

"North," Kevin said. "He was about a hundred yards up from where the paddleboard was bumping against the pier pilings. Everyone was watching that board and the woman under the water."

"That explains why you saw him and no one else did," Helen said.

"Exactly," Kevin said. "It was crazy. People were pushing one another out of the way to get a better look. They wanted to see the rescue. They didn't know that poor woman was dead. Nobody did. They just liked watching the drama. You should have seen their faces. It's like they got off on it, you know what I mean?"

"I do," Helen said. "I was there on the beach. What did the diver look like?"

Kevin shrugged. "I didn't see much of him. He was wearing a black wet suit with one of those hoods that covered his head. His face was in the water. I think he had on a diver's mask."

"You keep saying 'he,' " Helen said. "The diver was a man?"

"Yes," he said. "A strong man from the size of his shoulders and arms. His body was thick. What's the word? 'Stockcd'?"

"Stocky?" Helen asked.

"That's it. He was stocky. And not too tall. About my height— maybe five seven or eight. I didn't see enough skin to tell you his race."

"You don't think the diver got lost and that's why he was near the pier?" Helen asked.

"Not with that current," Kevin said. "I've worked at the restaurant two years and I've never seen a diver near the pier. The current is dangerous and people are fishing off the pier night and day. Fishhooks can get stuck in your skin or tear your dive suit."

Helen drove under the I-95 overpass. Now Riggs Beach Road was six lanes wide and the flooded parts were easier to avoid. She stayed in the center. This section was lined with expensive one-story houses and red-barrel-tiled townhomes landscaped like small botanical gardens.

"I saw something that didn't make sense," Kevin said. "There was something yellow with the diver."

"With him how?" Helen said. "Alongside him or next to him?"

"I don't know. It was bright yellow, like a tropical fish. But it wasn't a fish or an air tank. It was underneath him. I've never seen anything like it. Anyone in that water has to fight a strong current. Even the lifeguards were struggling. But he didn't."

"Was he swimming on the surface or below it?" Helen asked.

"Below it. And he wasn't swimming. It like he was being pulled by something, but I couldn't see what it was. It was weird."

The brownish yellow glow of the turnpike lights loomed in the black night, and an eighteen-wheeler swung into the entrance lane.

"See that stoplight just past the turnpike?" Kevin asked. "Turn right. My house is the fourth one—the pink stucco with the two palm trees. Ah, Mama left the porch light on for me. That one. Pull in the driveway. And thank you so much."

Kevin waved good-bye. On the drive home, Helen pondered what Kevin had told her. He saw a diver in a black wet suit moving away from Ceci, when everyone else was fighting to see what was happening. The diver was stocky and muscular, his face was hidden, and he had something bright yellow. He wasn't swimming, either. He was being pulled along by something invisible.

Maybe Phil would have some ideas. She'd wanted to join Phil and Margery around the pool tonight when she got home, but the rain poured down like someone had opened a chute. Fog hid the houses and cars. The Cruiser's lights stabbed the thick gray blanket, but Helen could see only one car length ahead. She slowed down to twenty miles an hour and followed the yellow center line. A full hour after she dropped off Kevin, Helen pulled into the Coronado lot and sighed with relief. Home at last.

The lights were off in the office of Coronado Investigations, but on in Phil's apartment.

No point opening my umbrella, she thought. She was drenched after running to her car from the restaurant. She raced down the sidewalk, splashed in water up to her ankles near Margery's apartment, sprinted for Phil's door and let herself in with her key.

Her husband met her at the door and took her into his arms.

"I've been worried about you driving in that storm. You're soaked. Dry off and I'll get you cold wine or hot coffee."

"Wine," she said. "But I want a hot shower first."

"I could make it a really hot shower," he said, and kissed her hard on the mouth.

"Then let's not waste any time," she said. "You should let your hair down."

She yanked playfully on his prematurely silver ponytail. Helen loved running her fingers through Phil's long hair.

"Does that include a back scratch?" he asked. His eyes were the same blue as his shirt.

"Only if you scratch mine," she said.

Their hot, steamy shower led to another hot session in Phil's black silk sheets. Afterward, they ate popcorn and drank white wine in bed.

"The day has definitely improved," she said, and sighed.

"Did you find out anything?" he asked. "I got nowhere looking for the diver."

Helen told him about her interview with Kevin. "I'm convinced there was a diver and he killed Ceci," she said. "But I can't imagine what that bright yellow thing could be, or what invisible force would pull him away from the pier."

"Me, either," Phil said. "But I know who might. We need to meet with our old diver friend, Max Rupert Crutchley."

"The treasure hunter?" Helen asked. A heart problem had ended his diving days, but Helen liked the old buccaneer.

"And emerald smuggler," Phil said. "But that's all he smuggled. No drugs. I made sure of that. Maybe Max will have time for lunch or dinner tomorrow. Are you free all day?"

"Nothing else I can do right now," Helen said. "We're stuck. This case is going nowhere unless Max gives us a lead."

"He will. Max likes to flirt with you," Phil said. "He'll talk to impress you. I'll call him now."

"At ten thirty?" Helen asked.

"Max is a night owl," Phil said.

Thumbs jumped on the bed, stared at Helen with round yellow-green eyes, prodded her arm with his big six-toed paw and gave a loud, insistent meow. The big cat was a patchwork of white, brown and gray fur.

"He's demanding dinner. What year did you last feed Thumbs?" Helen asked.

"You lie, fur face!" Phil said, rumpling the cat's fur. "He had dinner at seven. Give him another scoop while I call Max."

Thumbs padded after Helen on his giant paws to Phil's kitchen. She filled his dish. "There you go, big guy," she said.

The cat plunged his face into the fishy-smelling dry food and ignored her.

"Huh," she said. "Not even a thank-you."

Phil clicked off his cell phone as Helen came back to the bedroom. "How about midnight tonight at Lester's Diner?" he said. "Is that too late?"

"Never too late for pancakes," Helen said. "Not when they come with fresh, hot information."

CHAPTER 17

L ester's Diner was a neon-and-glass temple serving divine road
food. Worshippers could partake twenty-four hours a day.
The diner was located in an industrial section of State Road
84, and even at midnight two big rigs and a smattering of trucks
were parked in the vast lot. The rain had stopped, but the lot was
dotted with puddles.

Helen saw gray-haired Max Crutchley drinking coffee in a corner booth. The old treasure hunter waved her and Phil over, his
chunky emerald pinkie ring sparkling in the light. Helen wondered
if that emerald was a smuggling spoil.

Orange tropical fish rioted over Max's blue Hawaiian shirt.
"Helen," he said, clasping her to his barrel chest. "Still with Phil.
Haven't wised up yet."

"Unhand my wife," Phil said, laughing.

They slid into the U-shaped booth, and Helen sat in the middle,
close—but not too close—to Max. Lester's red vinyl booths were as
generous as its platters of food.

The server poured coffee for three and took their orders. "I'll
have blueberry pancakes," Helen said. Phil and Max wanted Lester's

Big Deal, and it was: three eggs, three pancakes, two bacon strips, two sausage links and a patty.

Max definitely isn't worried about his cholesterol, she decided. Helen couldn't tell that he'd had heart surgery: his face was tanned and his color was healthy. Max radiated a grizzled strength, like an old lion.

"So what are you two shamuses up to now?" he said.

"We need your diving expertise for a new case," Phil said. "Did you hear about the tourist who drowned off Riggs Pier?"

"The one who went stand-up paddleboarding? Saw the story on TV," Max said. "I was surprised the medical examiner ruled that a homicide."

"We were, too," Phil said. "Helen and I were on the beach when she was killed. The victim, Ceci Odell, fell off a paddleboard. It was her second time on a board. Her instructor didn't think she was ready for the ocean, but she insisted on going out."

Max shook his head. "Mother Ocean is a deadly bitch if you don't respect her," he said. "Pardon my language, Helen."

Helen smiled at Max's old-school apology, then sipped her coffee.

"Ceci's inexperience didn't kill her," Phil said. "She was murdered and we can't figure out how."

"Who's your client? Can I ask?" Max said.

"Sunny Jim Sundusky," Phil said. "He was Ceci's instructor. Jim has a paddleboard rental concession on Riggs Beach."

"I know it," Max said. "I saw the city commissioner flapping his gums about tourist safety and pulling Jim's lease."

"Jim's a by-the-book guy when it comes to safety," Phil said. "He followed the regulations and then some. Ceci refused to wear a life jacket and ignored Jim's instructions. We saw her paddle too near the pier after she'd been warned to stay away."

"The rip current's strong next to Riggs Pier," Max said. "Any diver with a lick of sense gives it a wide berth."

"Helen found two witnesses who saw a diver near the pier at the time of the murder," Phil said. "One saw him moving away from the pier after Ceci tumbled off her board. That witness said there was something weird about the diver."

"Weird how?" Max asked.

"Helen can tell you," Phil said. "She interviewed him."

"The man works at Cy's on the Pier," Helen said. "He didn't run outside to watch Ceci's rescue when the stampede started. He came out later and saw the diver moving away from the pier. The diver wore a black suit and hood, but he had something bright yellow underneath him. The witness says it wasn't a fish or an air tank. He also said the diver didn't seem to be fighting the strong current as hard as the lifeguards. He moved like he was being pulled by something invisible. Our witness said it didn't look natural."

Max sipped his coffee and fiddled with the shark's tooth he wore on a gold neck chain. Helen could almost see Max working out the scene in his mind.

Their plates arrived. Phil poured ketchup on his eggs and sausage. Helen covered her blueberry pancakes in syrup and forked in the first bite. Mm, she thought. Pancakes might taste even better at midnight than at breakfast time. Max took the ketchup from Phil and doused his plate, but he was still staring into the distance.

Good, Helen thought. He's working out our problem.

"If the victim was in a rip current, then so was the diver," Max said, thinking out loud. "He couldn't swim against the current any more than she could. They're both at the mercy of the ocean until they're out of danger. Unless . . ."

Helen's next forkful of blueberry pancakes hovered in midair while she waited for Max's conclusion.

"Unless he had an underwater scooter," Max said. He beamed at Helen and Phil, like a professor who'd solved a difficult mathematical problem. "Yes, that's it. A scooter. Bright yellow is a common color. Even with the scooter, your diver would have to be relatively free of the current to have control of the situation.

"I used underwater scooters when I was a treasure hunter. They give you more range and extended bottom time with less effort underwater.

"You can sit on some and ride them like real scooters. Mine looked like a torpedo. A battery-powered motor drove the propeller. The propeller's in a cage so it can't hurt you. You sort of lie on top of it and steer by the handlebar."

"I don't think I've seen one," Helen said. "Are scooters new?"

"Naw," he said. "They've been around a long time. They were used way back in World War Two. Ever see that old James Bond movie *Thunderball*?"

Helen shook her head.

"I did," Phil said. "Made in the mid-sixties. A Cubby Broccoli Bond movie. *Thunderball* was set in Nassau. That's where Bond went up against Emilio Largo, the SPECTRE villain, to recover stolen nuclear weapons."

"Largo's the guy with the eye patch," Max said.

"That's him," Phil said. "The movie has this huge underwater fight."

"Right," Max said. "A whole army of scuba divers using underwater scooters, spear guns and explosives. The Bond movie used a different kind of scooter than I did, but it made for an amazing fight scene."

Phil and Max lost interest in their food while they talked about the scooter battle.

"Who was the Bond girl in that movie?" Phil asked.

"Claudine Auger," Max said, his eyes lighting up. "Gorgeous brunette. Former Miss France. Julie Christie, Raquel Welch and Faye Dunaway were considered for the part. Now, those were lookers."

"All the Bond girls were lookers," Phil said.

"Almost the equal of Helen here." Max winked at her.

Helen decided to stop this stroll down memory lane and go back to their investigation.

"So what about our diver?" she reminded him gently.

Max signaled for more coffee. "He'd need an underwater scooter and knowledge of where the rip current usually subsides," he said. "Having that information and control of his own movements, he could easily grab the victim's leg from below, pull her under and drown her."

"Actually, he stabbed her with a knife," Phil said.

"Smart," Max said. "And quicker. He'd be able to kill her and scoot back to safety without being seen. Basically, this Ceci appeared to be safe to the onlookers until she fell off the board, right?"

"Right," Phil said. "She was paddling against a strong west wind. There were some dolphins out by the reef. People ran out on the pier to see them, calling 'Here, Flipper.' Anglers threw them baitfish. It looked like Ceci was paddling over to see the dolphins when she lost her balance and fell off the board."

Max finished the last bit of sausage. "And she never resurfaced?" he asked.

"Not till the lifeguards pulled her out," Phil said. "She was unconscious and had a head wound. We couldn't see the stab wound in her back."

"If she fell off the board and then the diver pulled her under," Max said, "that would open questions as to what actually happened. Especially if there were no marks indicating a sea creature, such as a shark, had taken her down. There are sharks off that reef, but they're mostly harmless."

"Nobody saw any sharks," Phil said, "and Ceci's body had no sign of a shark attack. The medical examiner said a human stabbed her, probably with a dive knife."

"If indeed your scuba guy murdered your paddleboarding lady," Max said, "she had to have had a routine that he could count on to kill her."

Helen looked at him blankly. "I'm not tracking," she said.

"The killer had to know she'd be there at that particular time," Max said.

"Her husband, Daniel, made sure of that," Helen said. "Daniel and Ceci took lessons with Sunny Jim the day before she was murdered. Ceci wanted to go out again before they went back to St. Louis. Daniel made reservations with Sunny Jim for two boards the next morning on Riggs Beach. The couple showed up on time, but Daniel said he had a hangover and didn't want to go out. His wife went paddleboarding alone while he sat on the beach."

"Interesting," Max said. "Did the couple get along?"

"No," Helen said. "They were staying at Sybil's Full Moon, where I used to work."

"Sybil still in charge?" Max asked.

"Strong as ever," Helen said. "The hotel staff didn't like Daniel. Sybil said he and Ceci had a huge fight the night before she died."

"Hm. So it's possible the husband set up the murder," Max said. "He made the arrangements with the diver and delivered his wife to the beach at a certain time."

"Ten o'clock," Helen said. "High tide was ten twenty-six."

"So the husband delivers his wife to the location on time," Max said. "But in order for this scheme to work, the diver had to see her getting set to go paddleboarding."

"Meaning?" Helen asked.

"Meaning he'd have to know how much time it would take him to reach her. No way he could be a mile away and expect to accomplish the deed."

"He could be sitting on the beach," Helen said.

"He'd be mighty hot—and very noticeable—on a sunny beach in a wet suit," Max said. "Ditto if he hung around under that pier. But there is Sunfish Cove."

"What's that?" Phil said.

"That little inlet just before that bend in the beach, above Riggs Pier. Your diver could observe her from there and then set off to meet her at the appropriate spot. He would also have to be good with an underwater compass to get where he wanted to be when he wanted to be there."

"Do you think he owns a scooter?" Phil asked.

"He might," Max said. "You can buy some for under a hundred bucks, but they're more like pool toys. If the diver was messing around near Riggs Pier, he'd need a good scooter, and those can run more than a thousand dollars. It's more likely he rented one. I'd check the dive shops around Riggs Beach first."

"That's my job tomorrow," Phil said.

"Good luck. And don't forget, dive shop employees are very underpaid." Max grinned and rubbed his thumb and forefinger together.

CHAPTER 18

"'Dawnlight smiles on you leaving, my contentment,'" Phil howled from his shower.

Helen smiled while her husband tortured "White Room," an Eric Clapton favorite. Phil's voice was flatter than a bath mat. My man is no rock star, she thought. Except between the sheets. Good in bed and he makes me coffee in the morning. She took the last, lukewarm swallow and slipped on her satin robe.

Phil stepped out of the bathroom in a steamy cloud, his shower-damp hair the color of dull silver. He was dressed in khaki shorts and a white polo shirt. His collar was partly trapped inside the shirt neck.

Helen straightened his tangled collar, then wrapped her arms around him. "Are you sure you couldn't stay a little longer?" she said, kissing him.

"Good heavens, you're insatiable," he said in mock horror. "Twice last night and twice this morning. What more do you want?"

"Three times?" she said.

"Tonight," he said. "And that's a promise. It's almost nine o'clock. I have to check out dive shops and find out if anyone rented an underwater scooter the day Ceci died."

"Or the day before," Helen said. "I'm stalled until you make some progress. No point in me watching Sunny Jim's place. The competition can't do more damage to him."

"He's barely hanging in," Phil said. "Business is way down since Ceci's death. You might as well take the day off until you hear from me."

"I'll have coffee with Margery by the pool," Helen said. "I haven't talked to her in a while."

She kissed Phil good-bye, slipped on shorts and a T-shirt, poured herself more coffee and stepped out into the sunny-bright morning. The humid air felt soft and inviting after the chill air-conditioning, and the grass was green with promise.

Margery was hosing off the pool deck. Their landlady wore her favorite purple from her sparkly lavender T-shirt to her flip-flops festooned with mauve flowers. Her burning cigarette sent up a lazy curl of smoke.

"Morning, bright eyes," her landlady said. "How's the Riggs Beach case?"

"Phil's checking out dive shops this morning," Helen said. "It's on hold unless he finds something. We're still looking for Ceci's killer." She told Margery what they'd found so far, including their midnight meeting with Max.

"Who do you think killed her?" Margery asked, turning off the hose.

"Daniel, the husband," Helen said. "He's mean enough and he criticized his wife's weight gain."

"Doesn't make him a killer," Margery said, rolling up the hose.

"Daniel is the only one who knew when his wife was going paddleboarding," Helen said.

"Not true," Margery said. "Anyone could find out. All he had to do was call Sunny Jim and try to make a morning appointment. How many paddleboards does Jim have?"

"Eight at the beach location," Helen said.

"Then it's easy. The person calls Jim and says he wants to book a group of eight from nine a.m. till noon. If Jim said he was booked at ten, the caller would know exactly when Ceci was going out."

"Brilliant!" Helen said. "That puts Sunny Jim's competitors back in the picture."

"I have my uses," Margery said. She stashed the hose in the corner. "Are you going to hire me for part-time work?"

"There's not even work for me right now," Helen said. "That's why I'm home."

"Glad you two are still honeymooning. Twice at night and twice in the morning. Impressive."

Helen felt her face redden. "How did you know?" she said.

"Your jalousie windows leak more than your air-conditioning," Margery said.

Helen was in full blush now. Margery laughed and said, "You're young. Enjoy each other. It's better than listening to fights, like I did with some tenants.

"Right now, I hear your cell phone ringing. Is it at your place or Phil's?"

"Phil's," Helen said, sprinting for his door.

She dove through the door and grabbed her phone off the coffee table.

"Helen! It's Kathy. He called." Her sister's voice skittered with panic, as if Kathy was sliding off the edge of the world.

Helen's heart sideslipped in her chest. She sank down on Phil's couch, like someone had chopped off her legs. She didn't need to ask who'd called. She knew. The worst had happened. The black-mailer was back.

"This time he wants sixty thousand dollars," Kathy said. "In cash."

Helen tried to wrap her mind around that staggering number. She'd expected this demand. The blackmailer liked to double his demands. Last time, she'd given him thirty thousand.

"When?" Helen said. She fought to keep her voice steady. One word was all she could manage.

"He's giving us two days," Kathy said. "I'm supposed to put the money in a Schnucks supermarket bag and leave it on top of the same Dumpster on Manchester Road."

The same Dumpster where Helen had already left thousands of dollars.

"Can we do that?" Kathy asked.

"I've got the money," Helen said. Her half of the money from the sale of the St. Louis house she and Rob had owned sat untouched in the bank all the time she'd been on the run.

She could hear her sister's audible sigh. "He's giving us till tomorrow to get the money together," she said. "Helen, you have to be here this time. Last time you were out of the country and left me alone."

Helen was irritated by Kathy's whine, but her sister was right to be upset.

"Kathy, I was on a job in the Bahamas," she said. "I couldn't get to St. Louis that fast. That's why I put your name on the account, too, so you could get the money yourself."

"I did, but I was scared."

Her little sister was crying now, wrenching sobs laced with fear and regret. Kathy was two years younger than Helen, plump, pretty and placid. She loved her husband, Tom, and their two children, Allison and Tommy Junior. They lived in a house with a white picket fence. Then a blackmailer destroyed Kathy's nearly perfect life.

"I'll be there for you," Helen said. "Phil and I will fly out tomorrow."

"Phil! You can't bring him," Kathy sobbed. "You promised not to tell. You promised. For Tommy's sake."

"I also promised to love and honor my husband," Helen said. "I've already broken that promise several times. If we're going to save Tommy, we need two people to catch the blackmailer."

"You've got me!" Kathy said.

"I need a professional investigator," Helen said, "and Phil's the best. Kathy, this is it. This time, we either catch him, or we're all ruined. Tommy, too. Next time, the blackmailer will double his demands to a hundred twenty thousand dollars. I'm running out of money. It's now or never."

Her sister wailed like a war widow.

"Kathy!" Helen said sharply. "Get hold of yourself."

Kathy sniffled, gulped once and said, "Okay, you're right. I'm just so worried about my little boy."

"Tommy didn't do anything wrong," Helen soothed. "He whacked Rob with a bat, but he didn't mean to hurt him. It's not his fault. Tommy will be fine."

"How can you say that?" her sister lashed out. "How can you be so sure? He's not your son. You have no children. You have nothing to lose. I—I can lose everything."

Another burst of tears.

I was too forceful, Helen thought. She softened her voice and said, "Kathy, you're right. I don't have children. But I love Tommy and his sister. I'd never do anything to hurt them."

"Tommy did it for you. He was trying to protect you." Kathy was on the verge of tears.

"I know," Helen said. "He acted like a little man."

"I'm not blaming you," Kathy said. "It was his awful uncle Rob who tracked you down to our backyard. My Tommy saw Rob grab you and threaten me. He thought you were being hurt."

"I was," Helen said.

"Tommy hit Rob as hard as he could with his aluminum bat and knocked him unconscious. He was quite the slugger."

Even in this crisis she couldn't resist a show of motherly pride, Helen thought. But my sister does blame me—and I deserve it.

"You were smart to send Tommy to his room after he hit Rob," Helen said. "Rob revived and you begged him to go to the emergency room, but he refused." They both knew this story, but reciting it again seemed to justify their terrible decision.

"We both begged him," Kathy said. "Rob was always pigheaded. He couldn't admit he'd been knocked out by a little boy. He started laughing at us, and then he passed out again. Except this time, he didn't wake up."

"We should have called the police," Helen said.

"No! I made the right decision and I'll stand by it," Kathy said. "If we'd gone to the police, it would be in the media. My boy would be branded a killer. His life would be over before it started. No one would play with him. You don't know how cruel kids can be. You have no idea.

"I'm glad we buried Rob in the church hall basement. He deserved it." Kathy was regaining her spirit.

"We were lucky the basement hole was already dug," Helen said, scrambling back to their familiar narrative. Kathy had to feel safe enough to follow Helen's lead this time. "We rolled Rob up in Tom's plastic drop cloths and carted him to the church in your minivan. All we had to do was cover him with crushed rock. The next morning, the basement concrete was poured."

And Rob was gone but not forgotten, she thought. Nothing Kathy says can make what I did right. I never told Phil, not even when we married. I never told Margery. Rob's secret burial has weighed on me, heavier than the concrete that covered his body.

"I've kept my bargain long enough," Helen said. "Someone knows our secret. They've blackmailed me until I'm bled dry. Now we have to end it and save Tommy."

"How?" Kathy asked, her voice small.

"Did you tape the blackmail call like I asked you?"

"Yes, yes, I've got it all," Kathy said. "I practiced with the equipment you sent me until I could do it without thinking. It's a good thing, because my mind went blank when he called."

"Good girl," Helen said. "Did he use a voice changer again?"

"Yes," Kathy said. "This time he sounded like a movie tough guy. That wasn't as creepy as the time he sounded like a little girl."

"Helen, it's Rob. I know it is. I've been reading about head injuries on the Internet. They're tricky. He might have looked dead, but he could have had a small stroke and recovered enough after we buried him to drag himself out of that hole. We only buried him under a few inches of rock, and the plastic drop cloths were held with bungee cords. Rob could have escaped. You know how crooked and lazy Rob is. He'd rather torment you than turn you in to the police."

"Possible," Helen said. More than possible, she thought.

"He talked like Rob, too. He called you Sunshine. That was his nickname for you."

"That's a common name," Helen said. "It doesn't prove anything. Kathy, that blackmailer could be a neighbor, or the church guy who was cheating on his wife—what was his name?"

"Horndog Hal," Kathy said.

"Right," Helen said. "He was making out with a woman in the backseat of his car when we parked in the church lot. Didn't you say he had a bunch of kids? He'd need money."

"We all need money in this neighborhood," Kathy said. "We've got kids in school. But Hal's not a suspect. He moved to Georgia. He's gone."

"Good. One less," Helen said. "I'll book two tickets for the early-morning flight to St. Louis tomorrow. We'll rent a car. I want you to e-mail me the names and addresses of all your neighbors today. They could have seen something when we were hauling Rob's body out of there."

"We don't have to worry about old Mrs. Kiley next door," Kathy said. "She's ninety-one, and she goes to bed early."

"And never gets any visitors?" Helen asked.

"She's got a grandson who sees her sometimes."

"Get his name," Helen said. "Who else could have seen what happened?"

"The Kerchers were on vacation and no one was at home," Kathy said.

"Didn't they have a house sitter?"

"No, somebody walked their dog."

"Get that name, too. Who else?"

"There's the Cooks on the west side, but their view is blocked by our house and a big tree."

"You hope," Helen said. "Get their information, too. Call me back as soon as you have it."

"I still think it's Rob," Kathy said.

"I hope you're right," Helen said. "If it is Rob, he can't report us to the police. He's been blackmailing us and you've got him threatening you on tape."

"I do!" Kathy sounded hopeful. "Then Tommy will be free. We'll all be saved."

Except me, Helen thought. I could lose everything I care about: my home, my business and the love of my life.

She remembered Phil singing that Clapton song. *"Dawnlight smiles on you leaving, my contentment."* Her contentment left this morning.

CHAPTER 19

H elen curled up on Phil's couch, her arms wrapped around her cat like he was a teddy bear. Thumbs purred and kept his big six-toed paw possessively on her arm.

"You still love me," Helen said, hugging the cat closer. "I may lose everyone—Phil, Margery, even our PI agency, but I'll still have you."

Helen's cell phone rang and Thumbs sprang up.

"Hey, babe," Phil said. "I've got good news. I've found our friend."

She heard the sound of success in his voice.

"Who is he?" Helen said.

"I'm on my way home to tell you," he said. "You know I don't like talking on cell phones. Is something wrong?"

"I got bad news from Kathy," she said.

Triumph turned to concern. "Is she hurt?" Phil asked. "What about Tom and the kids?"

"No, they're all safe," Helen said. "But we need to fly to St. Louis tomorrow. I'll tell you why when I see you."

"Okay," Phil said. "We can investigate Ceci's husband while we're there. I'll get Sunny Jim to pay for the trip. You sure you don't want to tell me now?"

"Not on a cell phone," she said. Not ever, she thought. But I have to. I have no choice.

"Love you," he said, and clicked off.

Those two words slashed Helen's heart. Would Phil still love her after she'd told him what she'd done? What would happen to their baby, Coronado Investigations? And Margery, the closest person Helen had to a mother?

Fresh tears flooded her eyes. I won't sit here and mope, she thought, wiping them away. I can't brood on this anymore.

Helen made Phil's bed and wondered if they'd ever make love on those black silk sheets again. She rinsed her coffee cup and put it in the dishwasher. Would he bring her coffee in the morning anymore? Or make popcorn and wine snacks?

She wiped away more tears, then went online and made reservations for their flight, a rental car and a hotel near her sister's home.

Her cell phone rang and she checked the display. Kathy.

"I've e-mailed you the information about the neighbors," Kathy said. "Do you need me to pick you up at the airport?"

"No, thanks. Just booked a rental car and a hotel," Helen said.

"What will I tell Tom?" Kathy asked.

"The truth," Helen said.

"I can't," Kathy said. "He'll hate me when he finds out I've lied to him."

"I meant the truth about Phil and me," Helen said. "We're coming to St. Louis to investigate a murder. Do you know a Daniel and Ceci Odell? They live at . . . let me look it up"—she checked her case notes—"225 Clafin Drive in Kirkwood. Ceci was the tourist killed while paddleboarding in Riggs Beach."

"I saw that on TV," Kathy said. "I don't know the Odells, but I have friends who live on Clafin. I'll ask Maureen Carsten if she'll talk to you."

"Thanks," Helen said. "We'll be working most of the time we're in town. You'll have to find some excuse to get away for the money drop tomorrow night."

"Already have it," Kathy said. "I'm on the church's Summer Fest committee. Those meetings last late. I've told Tom there's one tomorrow night.

"We can at least have a barbecue when Tom comes home from work, right?"

"As long as we're free by eight," Helen said. "I'll read your e-mail now."

Kathy's e-mail was a glimpse into that perfect picket-fence life. Kathy said old Mrs. Kiley's grandson was seventeen-year-old Matt Madley. He went to Parkway West High School and stopped by his grandma's house two or three times a week to do little chores. "He even mows the lawn," Kathy wrote. "Find another kid who does that for his grandma. She pays him in chocolate chip cookies."

The Kerchers, who lived behind Kathy, always hired Nan Siemer to walk their dog, Benji. Nan was fifteen, on the honor roll, and lived two doors up from the Kerchers. The dog was a cute white twelve-year-old bichon.

Not sure why we need the dog's info, Helen thought, but I asked for information and she delivered.

The Cook family on the other side of Kathy included the father, Lee Boyd Cook; his wife, Sharon Osborne Cook; and their two daughters, Chloe Madison Cook and Cassidy Mason Cook. Cassidy was a sophomore and Chloe a senior at Webster High. "I gave you their middle names because there are so many Cooks," Kathy added.

"Thank you," Helen said to the computer screen.

She checked the time, then brushed her hair and put on fresh lipstick. Might as well look my best when I ruin my marriage, she thought. I wish I could fix this gut-wrenching fear, but there's only one cure for that.

She heard Phil's key in the lock and pasted on a smile. He burst through the door, picked her up and waltzed her around the room. Thumbs took refuge from their flying feet under the coffee table.

"I found him!" he said. "I found the diver!"

"Who is he? Where is he?"

"Randy," Phil said, kissing her soundly. "Randall." *Smack.* "Travis." *Smack.* "Henshall." *Smack.*

These may be the last carefree kisses I'll ever get, Helen thought. She pulled herself together and asked, "The same Randy lured away from Sunny Jim's by more money at Bill's Boards?"

"And the same one who probably trashed Jim's paddles and helped steal his boards," Phil said. "The manatee molester who hates women tourists."

"Way to go," Helen said and tried a lopsided smile. "Where did you find him?"

"Well, I didn't exactly find Randy himself," Phil said. "I showed his photo around the dive shops."

"What photo?" Helen asked.

"I made one from that video you took of him lurking around Sunny Jim's. The dude at Riggs Beach Dive Shop identified Randy as the diver who rented an underwater scooter about eight o'clock the morning Ceci was murdered. He returned it at three."

"The time fits," Helen said.

"Randy signed the rental agreement 'John Smith,'" Phil said.

"Original," Helen said.

"And paid cash," Phil said. "I asked why Mr. Smith didn't use a credit card. The dude said Mr. Smith was paying down his debts and had cut up his credit cards. He left a five-hundred-dollar cash deposit instead."

"Isn't that a little irregular?" Helen said.

"Irregularities at that shop can be cured with a cold cash compress," Phil said. "This information cost me fifty bucks. I stopped by Bill's Boards looking for Randy, but the employee said Randy up and quit."

"Let me guess," Helen said. "The day after Ceci was murdered."

"Wrong. The day before," Phil said.

"Think Randy called in rich?" Helen asked.

"That's my guess," Phil said. "He hasn't been seen in any of his usual haunts. Randy's been heading downhill since he wrangled that sea cow. He lives in a dump off Riggs Beach Road and drives a junker. His landlady says he left for a vacation the day after Ceci died. He didn't say when he was coming back, but he paid a month's rent in advance."

"Sounds like he's playing it smart," Helen said. "He's gone off somewhere else to celebrate."

"He'll turn up soon," Phil said. "Otherwise, he wouldn't have paid more rent on his apartment. Meanwhile, I've convinced Sunny Jim we should fly to St. Louis to check out Daniel Odell."

"Good," Helen said.

"Hey, can you show a little more enthusiasm? We're getting a free trip to see your sister. Why do you want to go to St. Louis, anyway?"

"Uh," Helen said. She was standing on a crumbling ledge, staring into a bottomless lake. She had to take the plunge, and it might be fatal.

"Sit down," she said.

Phil plopped on the couch. Helen studied the face she loved: his long, slightly crooked nose, those blue eyes, that silver hair haloing his young face. She sat next to him, took his hand and gently touched his wedding ring. Would he pull it off when she finished?

"You look pale," Phil said.

Here goes, she thought, and stepped off the ledge.

"Remember when Mom died and we went to St. Louis for her funeral?" she said, still holding his hand.

"Of course," Phil said. "That was a hard trip home for you, but I got to spend some time with my in-laws. I love your family. I have a cool brother-in-law. Tom and I ran out of beer and you and Kathy sent us off for guy time at Carney's Bar."

"While you and Tom were at the bar, Rob turned up in Kathy's backyard," Helen said.

"You never told me that," Phil said.

"It gets worse," she said. A whole lot worse, she thought.

"Rob was drunk. He demanded fifteen thousand dollars. Then he said you got his secondhand goods."

"Why, that no-good SOB," Phil said. "I'll punch his face in."

"I tried to," Helen said. "That's when the trouble started. Rob grabbed my arm and bent it back. He hurt me so bad, he forced me to my knees."

Phil tensed and gave a slight growl.

"Then he sat next to me on a lawn chair, all the while twisting my arm. My nephew, Tommy, saw that lowlife threatening me and hit Rob with his bat as hard as he could."

"Good," Phil said.

"Not good," Helen said. "He knocked out Rob. Kathy sent her son to his room; then we threw water on Rob and revived him. He refused to go to the emergency room. He laughed and demanded to talk to me alone.

"This time, I sat down in a lawn chair with the bat. Kathy gave me her cell phone and went upstairs to see Tommy. I told Rob I wasn't going to pay him. He didn't answer me. I thought he'd fallen asleep. I shook him but—"

"He was dead," Phil said. He spoke slowly, as if trying to absorb the words, then said, "Little Tommy killed Rob." There was wonder in his voice. Wonder and something else Helen couldn't identify.

"Yes," she said. Now she rushed to finish her story, to get this horror over with. "So Kathy and I wrapped Rob's body in plastic and hauled it to Mom's church. They were building a new hall and the concrete floor was going to be poured the next morning. We buried Rob under the crushed rock."

"And you never called 911?" Phil asked.

"Kathy begged me not to," she said. "I said Tommy was defending me. I said I'd take the blame. She refused. She said Tommy would be ruined, like KK."

"Who's he?" Phil voice was ominous. He pulled his hand away from Helen's grasp.

"A boy we went to school with who accidentally killed his baby brother. It wasn't his fault, but everyone called him a killer. KK's in jail now. His life was never the same. Kathy was afraid that would happen to Tommy. I offered to take the blame myself and say I hit Rob with the bat, but she said Tommy would step up and confess the truth to save his aunt Helen."

"And you didn't bother calling Tom and me, even though we were a block away?" Phil's eyes crackled with electric blue fire.

"I couldn't," Helen said. "She wouldn't let me."

"Your little sister, a marshmallow suburban mom who sits on church committees, wouldn't *let* you?" His lips twisted into an ugly smile. Phil stood up and paced his living room. "Yeah, I can see why you couldn't. Kathy's one tough customer."

Helen winced as if he'd hit her.

"Not calling the police, I might understand. Might. It's a stupid move, but I could at least follow your reasoning. But not telling me, your own husband? What's your excuse, Helen?"

Phil shouted at her for the first time ever. Thumbs came out from under the coffee table and stared.

"I don't have an excuse, Phil. I was wrong."

"Damn right you were!"

He took a deep breath, then said slowly, "So now, after all these months, you suddenly trust me. Why the big change?"

"Because Kathy and I are being blackmailed," Helen said. "He says he'll make sure Tommy is known as the Killer Bat Boy. He doubles his demands each time. Last time, he wanted thirty thousand. Now he wants sixty thousand tomorrow night at nine. I don't have much more money."

"And where the hell are you getting this money?" Phil slapped his forehead dramatically. "Oh, wait, I know. You're giving him your share of your house sale, aren't you?"

Helen nodded, not daring to speak.

"Kathy still didn't want me to tell you, but I said I had to," Helen said. "I need you, Phil." Her voice quavered.

"Now you need me," he said. "I'm so honored. Do you even know who's blackmailing you?"

"He uses a voice changer. I think it's one of Kathy's neighbors," Helen said. "Kathy thinks Rob is blackmailing us."

"I thought you said Rob was dead."

"He was. He is. But head injuries are tricky."

"Not as tricky as you, sweetheart," Phil said, his eyes angry. There was no love in that last word.

"There is one bit of good news," Helen said. "Kathy taped the last blackmailing demand. In Missouri, only one party has to consent to a taped call."

"Perfect," Phil said. "You've got a tape of someone with a voice changer."

They sat in shattering silence for a long moment.

When Phil spoke, his voice was hard and low. "Here's what we're going to do, Helen. We're going to St. Louis tomorrow. I assume you've already booked the trip."

She nodded, too afraid to speak.

"Do you have the information about the other blackmailer suspects?"

"Yes, Kathy e-mailed it to me."

"Then send it to me, along with the reservations. I will help you and Kathy catch the blackmailer. You will help me investigate Daniel Odell."

"Kathy knows a woman who lives on their street," Helen said.

"Good. These are Coronado Investigations' last two cases. Now, get out."

"Out?" Helen said.

"Go to your own apartment. Give me your key to this one. We're through, Helen. It's over."

"That's not fair," Helen said. "You would have done the same thing."

"I don't think so," Phil said. "I'd like you to leave."

In a daze, Helen found her cell phone and purse, then picked up her cat.

Thumbs struggled to get away, raking her arm with his razor claws. He jumped to the floor and slid under the couch, leaving Helen bleeding and alone.

CHAPTER 20

Helen stumbled out of Phil's apartment, dazed as a shipwreck survivor, and nearly fell over Margery. Their landlady was weeding the orange-and-yellow coleus plants along the walkway.

"You're dripping blood on my concrete," Margery said. Her cigarette was carefully balanced on the walkway's edge so the ash fell into the flower bed.

"You heard," Helen said.

"Every word," Margery said. Her smile could have frostbitten those plants.

"Phil's furious," Helen said, trying to hold back her tears.

"He's got every right to be," Margery said. "And stop dripping blood on my walk. It's hard to clean up. Did that cat scratch you?"

"Yes," Helen said. She moved to the grass and watched the red drops fall on the thick green blades as if the blood belonged to someone else—someone she didn't like much.

"So Thumbs is mad, too," Margery said. "I hate cats, but I agree with that one."

"Was I so wrong?" she asked. All the pain she couldn't feel came out in that agonized question.

"Yes," Margery said. Her response was a slap. "You promised to love and honor that man. Instead you betrayed him."

"But I didn't," Helen said.

"Oh, really?" Margery said. "You didn't trust Phil—the man you married—enough to ask for his help? I call that a betrayal. Why didn't you call him? He was what? A block away?"

"I wasn't thinking," Helen said.

"That's for damn sure," Margery said.

"You don't know what it was like," Helen said. "You weren't there, either. It was one shock after another. Rob stormed in drunk, Tommy knocked him out, he came to again and then he was gone like that."

Helen snapped her fingers.

"We couldn't believe he was dead. Kathy and I did every test we could think of to make sure."

"How could you two figure out if he was dead?" Margery said. "Even the best doctors can't do that unless someone's hooked up to a zillion machines in a hospital."

"We did our best," Helen said. "And then we realized we were in a suburban backyard with houses all around. My sister was frantic to save her son. Kathy swore me to secrecy. I had to keep quiet."

"You *had to*?" Margery's scorn scorched the grass.

"Yes," Helen said. "I wasn't thinking of anything but saving that boy. So we hurried up and got Rob out of there and buried him."

"Did you really think Phil would betray your nephew?" Margery said through clenched teeth. "He loves Tommy and you know it. Little Allison, too."

"I don't know what I thought," Helen said, staring at the blood-spotted grass. "I guess I just wanted to bury the whole awful episode, like we buried Rob, and never think about it again. Except it didn't work out. Somebody started blackmailing us and I've paid a fortune to stop him."

"How many demands for money did you get?" Margery asked.

"Three," Helen said. "No, four. I can't remember if this is the third or the fourth demand." The harder she tried to remember, the more confused the facts became.

"Why didn't you tell Phil when you got the first blackmail demand?" Margery asked, tearing out a weed by the roots. "Why did you lie to him and fly back to St. Louis?" Yank. Another weed was out.

"I don't know," Helen said. "I tried to tell him more than once, but it got harder and harder to tell him."

"And what about me?" Margery asked. She wrapped her old fingers around a vine clinging to a bush and pulled. "I've been here for you from the first—even before you knew Phil. You told me you were on the run from Rob. I could have called the cops and had you hauled back to St. Louis. But I kept that secret."

Margery pulled on the vine. It refused to give.

"When Rob came sniffing around," she said, "I lied and said you didn't live here. Hell, I even set him up with the Black Widow. I was sure he'd have a fatal accident, like all her other husbands." Another fierce tug on the vine. It held.

"I risked being an accessory to his murder for you. How could you do that to me?" Margery wrapped both hands around the vine, braced her legs and pulled. It came free and she staggered backward.

"I don't know," Helen said. "I don't."

She was crying now, her tears falling hard and fast. She tried to stop and save some of her dignity, but she couldn't. The sun beat on her without mercy, while she wept for her lost love and ruined friendship. She wanted Margery to gather her into her arms. Instead, her landlady wiped her muddy hands on her shorts and folded her arms.

"Is there anything I can do to make this right?" Helen asked.

"You've got one hope and one hope only," Margery said. "Phil agreed to fly to St. Louis to catch the blackmailer. You also have to find the killer of that tourist. That means the two of you will be working together at least a little longer. Maybe while he's working those two investigations he'll calm down and forgive you."

"I was going to e-mail him the information my sister sent me about possible suspects," Helen said.

"Then go do it," Margery said. She yanked out one last stubborn weed with such ferocity that Helen fled to her place.

The cozy apartment had been Helen's refuge since she'd lived at the Coronado. Now it seemed empty. Five years ago, if someone had told Helen she'd be living in two rooms in Fort Lauderdale, she would have laughed. Then she'd been on the corporate fast track, living in yuppie splendor in a twelve-room home. Those rooms had been furnished by a decorator. The huge windows were draped with sixty-dollar-a-yard fabric. Everything in that house had been perfect— except her husband, Rob.

That same decorator would have drooled over the midcentury antiques that came with Helen's apartment: the boomerang coffee table and the turquoise lamps shaped like nuclear reactors. The turquoise Barcalounger looked inviting, but Helen couldn't afford to curl into a ball right now. She had work to do.

She sat on the couch and powered up her laptop. A fluff of cat hair made tears start in her eyes. She missed her cat already. She missed Phil. If she was going to get him back, she had to start working.

This time, she tamped down the tears.

She forwarded Phil her sister's e-mail about the suspects, as well as their travel plans. They had to leave tomorrow around five a.m. to catch the first flight to St. Louis. That would give them the day to work on Sunny Jim's case, have dinner with Kathy and Tom, catch the blackmailer, then fly back to Fort Lauderdale the next morning.

Helen checked the time. Nearly nine o'clock. She called Joan's cell. The server was home from Cy's on the Pier.

"How did the interview go with Kevin?" Joan asked.

"He was extremely helpful," Helen said. "I'll be out of town until tomorrow night, but you can reach me by e-mail or at this cell phone number."

"Just as well you don't come by the restaurant right now," Joan said. "I think Cy is getting suspicious. He saw me at Kevin's bus stop and asked why I was parked in the shopping plaza on Seashell Road. I told him I liked frozen yogurt."

"How long should I stay away?" Helen asked.

"He'll forget about it in a day or so," Joan said. "He's still got the two commissioners in here, those bloodsuckers. Wyman nearly reached a deal with him, but then he upped the ante."

"Still angling for Cy to host his daughter's reception?" Helen asked.

"Yeah," Joan said. "And Cy's howling like every dollar is being stripped off his hide. Commissioner Wyman wants the restaurant for a Saturday night, steak and lobster on the menu, an open bar and now—get this—free parking. Cy is balking at the free parking and making our lives sheer hell."

"Now I'm really glad I'll be gone," Helen said.

"If I hear anything useful," Joan said, "I'll call or e-mail."

Helen hung up, then checked her e-mail. She had two new ones. The first was from Kathy:

"Hi, Helen. Hope this is okay," it said. "I've set up two interviews for you and Phil tomorrow morning. You're supposed to talk to Maureen Carsten. She's my friend who knows Daniel and Ceci. She lives next door to them in the white house with the red door. I think Maureen will be more comfortable talking to you. She likes to gossip, so be prepared to sit and drink coffee.

"Soames Welch lives on the other side of the Odell house. Yes, that's really his first name. He's about eighty and lives in the two-story brown shingle with the white porch. Soames is a nonstop talker, retired and kind of lonely since his wife died. He knows everything that happens on that street.

"I told Soames that Phil wanted to talk to him. He's really impressed to talk to a real private detective. Sorry, Sis, but I thought a man his age would take Phil more seriously.

"Your e-mail said your plane gets in about eight thirty. Your interviews are both at eleven o'clock. I figure that gives you plenty of time to pick up your rental car and check into your hotel. I've included their addresses and phone numbers if there's a problem.

"Looking forward to seeing you. Love you, Big Sis."

Helen forwarded Kathy's e-mail to Phil with a little note: "Dear Phil, Looks like Kathy has made some contacts for us. Okay with you? Love, Helen."

Phil's e-mail was painfully curt:

"Got trip info. Meet me at the Jeep tomorrow at 5 a.m."

Each word felt like a small stab wound. Helen shut off her computer and tried to read an old Agatha Christie mystery. Miss Marple and her well-ordered world were literary comfort food. Even a murder at a vicarage could be explained and the criminal caught. If only my mysteries could be solved so easily, Helen thought. She waded deep into the story as if it was a warm pool.

Helen must have fallen asleep. She was awakened by pounding music. Was that "I Shot the Sheriff"? She listened a moment longer. Yes. Phil was blasting Clapton's version. Helen could feel the wall behind the couch vibrating.

She beat on the wall and pleaded, "Phil! Phil, turn that down, will you?"

No response. Maybe he couldn't hear her.

No, wait. He turned Clapton up even louder. Now the skinny glass slats in the jalousie door were rattling. She needed her sleep. She had to get up at four thirty. To hell with crawling to that man. Yes, she was wrong to hide what she had done about Rob, but by damn, she wasn't malicious. And she wasn't a doormat.

Helen marched outside and slammed her fist on his front door.

"Phil!" she said. "I asked you to turn that music down."

He turned it up again.

"Turn it down!" she screamed.

Still louder.

"Keith Richards is a better guitar player than Clapton," she shouted.

That was childish, but it felt good. Helen had just committed the ultimate heresy, as far as Phil was concerned. So what? It was true, she thought.

Phil turned the Clapton song up another notch, and the lights popped on in Margery's apartment. Their landlady came flying out her kitchen door, tying the belt on her purple robe. She pounded on Phil's door until he poked his head out.

Helen saw her man in the moonlight, that strong, noble nose, those sculpted lips, his hair like spun silver.

"What are you two idiots doing?" Margery said. "It's eleven o'clock at night and you're blasting music like a teenager, Phil Sagemont. And you, Helen Hawthorne, are howling like a fishwife."

"But—" Helen said.

"She—" Phil said.

"Shut up!" Margery said. "Both of you. Phil, turn off that music now. Helen, shut up and go to bed. What time are you two leaving tomorrow?"

"Five o'clock," Helen said.

"Go to bed, both of you," Margery said.

They went to their rooms like sulky children.

CHAPTER 21

Helen didn't see a glimmer of dawn at five o'clock the next morning. She felt smothered by the heavy, humid air and dark sky as she rolled her suitcase down the sidewalk of the now-silent Coronado Tropic Apartments. All the apartment lights were off, including Phil's.

He was waiting in his Jeep. Helen threw her case in the back and climbed in, weary after a sleepless night.

"Is Margery watching Thumbs?" she asked.

"Yes," Phil said. His one-word answer bristled with such anger and contempt, Helen didn't dare say anything else. They rode in black silence to the airport.

Phil parked the Jeep in the long-term lot. Helen saw a few early travelers moving toward the shuttle bus shelters like the walking dead. He yanked out his suitcase and slammed his door. Helen grabbed her case. Phil locked the Jeep and they rolled their bags to the bus shelter.

Helen saw headlights pierce the graying darkness. "Is that our bus?" she asked.

It was, but Phil said nothing. He ignored Helen and lugged his bag onto the bus. The driver helped Helen hoist hers onto the luggage rack. She sat next to Phil and he flinched when her arm brushed his.

Helen fought hard not to cry.

By the time they got through security, their plane was boarding. Southwest Airlines did not have assigned seats. Phil chose a middle seat between two other flyers. Helen took a window seat behind him, pulled down her shade and pretended to sleep for the next two and a half hours.

Except she did sleep. When she woke up, sun was streaming into the cabin and the plane was making its final descent into St. Louis. She could see the sun gleaming on the silver skin of the Gateway Arch and the yellow-brown Mississippi River.

Helen was comforted by these familiar sights. St. Louis would never be home again, but she no longer felt so alone.

She pulled her suitcase out of the overhead bin and rolled it to the rental car shuttle. Phil was already standing in a thicket of sober-suited business travelers. She tried not to admire his lean good looks or the casual cut of his blue shirt. He wore her favorite shirt. Was that a good sign? Or was it the last clean shirt in his closet?

Their rental car was a white PT Cruiser. Helen knew it was absurd, but she took that as a good sign, too. They completed the paperwork and tossed their bags in the back.

"I'll drive," Helen said, "since I know the city."

"Fine," Phil said.

He didn't sound quite so angry. She gathered her courage and asked, "Did your Internet search turn up anything about Kathy's neighbors?"

"A little," he said. "Nan Siemer, the dog walker, is in the clear. She's a bright schoolgirl who wants to be a journalist. She'll probably get a scholarship and her parents have a good college fund for her.

"Mrs. Kiley, the old widow next door, lives off her Social Security, has a comfortable nest egg and no debts. She lives frugally and gives ten percent of her income to the Church.

"Her teenage grandson, Matt Madley, is a piece of work. He knows how to charm Grandma Kiley out of her cookies, but he crashed his car last summer and was charged with DUI. He broke his leg in the accident and lost his part-time job, which may be why he has time to help Grandma. He still owes his lawyer major money."

"How much?" Helen said.

"Seven thousand dollars," Phil said.

We're having an actual conversation, Helen thought. Phil is so cold, we don't need the Cruiser's air-conditioning, but at least we aren't screaming at each other.

"Kathy's other neighbors, the Cook family, are desperate for money," Phil said. "Lee Boyd Cook was one of the six thousand people who lost his job when Chrysler closed its St. Louis plant in 2009. He found another job, but not with the same salary or perks. He just had knee surgery and his new insurance didn't cover it because it's a preexisting condition. Their older daughter, Chloe, is going to Mizzou in September and she didn't get a scholarship. Their credit cards are maxed. The Cooks still owe sixty thousand on their mortgage."

"Exactly the amount the blackmailer is demanding," Helen said. "We're here. This is our hotel."

In their room, Helen eyed the big bed hopefully. A king bed would be a good place to make up.

"What time is it?" Phil asked, parking his suitcase by the couch.

"Ten o'clock," she said. "I want to check in with my sister. We won't get to talk with her alone tonight at the barbecue."

Phil shrugged and went into the bathroom. Once the door was shut, Helen called Kathy. Her sister answered on the second ring. She could hear her niece, Allison, shrieking in the background.

"Allison," Kathy said to her daughter. "Quiet, please. I'm talking to your aunt Helen.

"Sorry about that," Kathy said. "Excitement is running high because Aunt Helen and Uncle Phil are coming. How is Phil? Did you tell him?"

Helen glanced at the closed bathroom door. She could hear water running.

"Yes," she said, lowering her voice. "He's furious. He threw me out. He says when we solve these two cases, we're through."

"Divorced?" Kathy sounded shocked.

"He hasn't actually said the D word," Helen said, "but it's definitely in the air."

"You see why I didn't tell Tom?" Kathy asked.

Helen was irritated by her sister's smug tone. "No, I don't. If we'd called Tom and Phil right away, we wouldn't have these problems."

"We'd have worse ones," Kathy said. "Maybe I can talk to Phil. If he understands why I insisted, he'll feel differently."

"He won't," Helen said. "Don't." She didn't hear the water running, so she changed the subject. "Phil found out some interesting things about your neighbors. The Cooks are hard up for money."

Phil was out of the bathroom, rummaging in his suitcase.

"But Lee found another job within three months," Kathy said. "We were at the barbecue to celebrate."

"He got the job, but not his old salary," Helen said. "Or the same perks. Phil says his health insurance didn't cover his knee surgery."

"They just bought new storm windows," Kathy said. "Those are supposed to save them a fortune in utility bills. The utility bills are killing them, just like everyone else here. But Lee Cook wouldn't blackmail me."

"Really?" Helen said. "Phil found out that sixty thousand dollars would pay off his mortgage."

"I still can't believe it," Kathy said. "The Cooks go to our church."

"Well, Mrs. Kiley's grandson doesn't. Matt is jobless and he crashed his car. He owes his lawyer thousands."

"I still think it's Rob," Kathy said.

"We'll find out tonight," Helen said, her voice sharper than she intended. Why did she fall back into sisterly squabbling so quickly? "Kathy, honey, thank you for setting up those interviews for us. Phil and I are going to them now. We'll see you tonight about six."

"Helen, do you have the money?"

"I'll get it after the interviews."

She clicked off her cell phone and said to Phil, "Shall we go?"

He nodded.

On the way to Clafin Drive, Helen had a chance to admire her hometown. The Odells lived in Kirkwood, an old suburb with big houses and broad, shady streets. The trees were still a tender spring green, and the gardens were bright with flowers. The houses on Clafin Drive were about a hundred years old. The Odells had a two-story white house with black shutters and a walkway lined with old-fashioned flowers: fragrant lavender, purple phlox, lilacs and iris. Purple-blue hydrangeas banked the foundations. Helen wondered if Ceci had planted them.

"Margery would love all those purple flowers," Helen said.

"Hrmph," Phil grunted.

Okay, he doesn't want chitchat, Helen thought as she parked the car in front of Soames Welch's brown-shingled house. The old man was outside, digging in his yellow day lilies. He stood up slowly, laid his trowel on a porch step, then carefully came toward the car.

"You that detective fellow?" he asked.

"Yes, sir," Phil said, getting out of the car.

"Pleased to meet you. Soames Welch. You want a beer or iced tea?"

"Beer," Phil said.

"Good," Soames said. "A man's drink. Sit on the porch and I'll fetch us both one."

Sounds like Kathy sized up Soames correctly, Helen thought.

Maureen Carsten lived in a two-story brick home with a generous white-painted porch. Helen was halfway up the stairs when a trim woman in her late thirties opened the door.

"Helen?" she asked, and smiled. "I'm Maureen. Come on in."

Helen followed Maureen into a pleasant blue living room with Colonial-style furniture. The room smelled of cinnamon and lemon polish. A braided rug warmed the hardwood floor. Maureen's brown hair had bounce. In her sneakers, shorts and T-shirt, she looked athletic. Helen wondered if she'd played soccer in school.

"Are you really a private eye?" Maureen asked. "It must be exciting."

"Sometimes," Helen said, following her into the kitchen, a shining showcase.

"Coffee or tea?" Maureen asked.

"Black coffee, please," Helen said. She sat at a round maple kitchen table with a cinnamon coffee cake in the center. Maureen cut them both generous squares, then sat down and leaned forward a little, in the "girl talk" pose.

"What can I tell you about Ceci?" she said. "She was my best friend."

"I'm sorry for your loss," Helen said.

"It is a loss," Maureen said. "Ceci and I ran in and out of each other's houses a dozen times a day. She told me everything."

"Was her marriage happy?" Helen asked.

"It was until Ceci put on weight. She turned thirty-five and dieting became torture. Poor Ceci was hungry all the time. She lived on lettuce and grilled chicken. She gave up her favorite desserts— like that coffee cake. But she'd gained forty pounds and she couldn't shake them.

"Daniel nagged her constantly, and that didn't help. She'd be dieting and dieting and he'd say something like 'You used to have a cute figure. Now you're a fat slob.'

"She'd get so mad. She'd wait till he went to bed and then sneak downstairs and eat a quart of Ben & Jerry's. But Daniel caught on and padlocked the fridge after dinner.

"Daniel was old-fashioned. He didn't want Ceci to work. She said if she had a baby she'd have something else to think about besides food. Daniel wouldn't hear of it. He didn't want a baby. He said they couldn't afford one."

"Is that true?" Helen asked.

"They were in debt," Maureen said. "Like all of us."

"Was either Daniel or Ceci having an affair?" Helen asked. "Did they want to divorce?"

"No," Maureen said. "Ceci still loved Daniel. She wanted things to go back the way they were. Daniel's family is very rich and very Catholic. They would have been unhappy if he'd divorced."

"Did Ceci have life insurance?" Helen asked.

"Yes," Maureen said. "He didn't want to pay for that. Daniel said she was just a housewife and it wasn't worth the payments. You can imagine how that made Ceci feel. Eventually he took out a policy for a million dollars. Ceci joked that Daniel made her feel like a million bucks. She was proud of that policy, even if the premiums were high.

"This trip to Florida was supposed to be a second honeymoon," she said. "Instead my best friend was killed. And you want to hear the worst part? Daniel had her *cremated*."

"That wasn't her wish?" Helen asked.

"No!" Maureen said. "Ceci was Catholic. The Church doesn't forbid cremation, but most Catholics prefer burial. Ceci could have been buried next to her parents at Calvary Cemetery. Instead, she's sitting on the mantel in their house. It's disrespectful. Well, I'll tell you one thing—she's a hell of a lot thinner now."

Helen said her good-byes soon after that, and walked around the block while she waited for Phil to finish interviewing Soames Welch. She reveled in the May sunshine. It felt less punishing here than in Florida. People in Kirkwood sure liked their gardens, she thought.

She enjoyed the quirks of the houses, so much older than most South Florida homes—an odd gable, a stained glass window with a beaux arts vase, flower boxes overflowing with pink petunias.

On her third circuit, Phil stumbled out of Soames's house, looking slightly dazed. She waved and ran for the car, then honked the horn.

Wispy-haired Soames followed Phil, talking all the way. "Say, that's some dame you got for a driver," he said. "You private eyes." He winked at Phil. "Was I any help?"

"You were a big help, sir," Phil said. He shook Welch's liver-spotted hand and slid into the car.

"Drive away," he muttered. "Quick."

"Did he really help?" Helen asked as she turned onto Kirkwood Road.

"Oh, yeah," Phil said. "He said that Daniel and Ceci were in debt, and Daniel was mean enough to kill his wife. But he says Daniel never went diving and knew nothing about it. Also, there was a big life insurance policy on Ceci."

"That's also what Maureen told me," Helen said. "A million dollars. Plus Ceci wanted a baby and Daniel didn't."

"Here's the best part," Phil said. "Mr. Welch said that Daniel was having an affair—with Maureen."

"What!" Helen was stunned. "But she was Ceci's best friend."

"Happens more than you think. Mr. Welch caught Daniel and Maureen together," Phil said.

"At a hotel?" Helen asked.

"No, at a Home Depot," Phil said. "Mr. Welch went there to buy a new ceiling fan. He's quite the DIY dude. He parked at the far end of the lot because he wanted the exercise. There was only one other car that far away from the store. It was dark—about eight on a winter night—and he started hiking to the store, when who does he see drive up but Maureen. The passenger door opened, the light flashed on, and Mr. Welch saw Daniel in the car with her. Maureen parked next to his car—the lone car in the far corner of the lot. He got out, ran to his car, waved and drove off."

"So?" Helen said. "Maureen gave Daniel a ride to his car when she met him in the checkout line. It's dangerous to walk around an empty parking lot."

"Mr. Welch says Maureen never went to Home Depot, not even for plants. They had their kitchen remodeled—"

"I saw it," Helen said. "Beautiful job."

"It should be," Phil said. "Cost thirty thousand dollars, according to Mr. Welch. He says Maureen can barely change a lightbulb and her husband isn't any handier. They hire all their work out. Daniel loves Home Depot. It would be the perfect place for him to leave his car for an assignation with Maureen. No one would be surprised to see Daniel's car there. Ceci would never question Daniel spending a couple of hours at his favorite store."

"So Daniel had a million reasons to kill his wife," Phil said.

"A million and one, if you count Maureen," Helen said. "She lied to me. She made Daniel sound like a terrible person."

"What better way to deflect attention away from their affair?" Phil said.

"She told me Daniel's family is very Catholic and they wouldn't approve of a divorce."

"I'm sure," Phil said. "But that doesn't mean Daniel won't run off with Maureen once he gets his million in insurance. He definitely goes to the top of our suspect list. When we get back to Lauderdale, I'll have to figure out how he contacted that diver."

We're having a normal conversation, Helen thought. Maybe he's forgiven me.

"Doesn't the city look good?" Helen said. "I love driving on a sunny day."

Phil ignored her attempt at conversation. "What's next?" he asked.

"I have to stop by the bank and pick up the money for tonight."

"You know that's risky," he said. "A withdrawal that big will be reported to the authorities."

"I still have to do it," she said.

"But not with me," he said. "Drop me off at the hotel first."

The sun vanished behind a cloud.

CHAPTER 22

As she pulled into Tom and Kathy's driveway, Helen thought their house could be a picture in a family magazine. Her sister waved from her gingerbread front porch, gleaming with its new white paint. Rambler roses tumbled over the picket fence. Allison and Tommy Junior scrambled out of the backyard, yelling, "Aunt Helen! Uncle Phil!"

Helen inhaled the meaty perfume of barbecue. Pork steaks! She was still St. Louisan enough to identify the city's favorite barbecue.

Tom prodded pork steaks with his barbecue fork at the grill. Helen could read his sauce-smeared apron: THIS IS A MANLY APRON FOR A MANLY MAN DOING MANLY THINGS WITH FOOD.

For the first time since her fight with Phil, she smiled.

This homey scene is a relief after my tense time at the bank, she thought. I was nervous as a cat burglar at a police convention when I withdrew the blackmail cash. Then I had to endure four hours of Phil's sullen silence in our hotel room. He reread that free copy of *USA Today* until I thought he'd wear the newsprint off the pages.

"I'm so glad you're here, Aunt Helen," Allison said as she hugged Helen's legs. "I got a present for you." She stepped back and solemnly handed Helen a drawing of a butterfly with red and turquoise wings. The butterfly's black feet gripped a bright purple flower.

"I love it," Helen said. "I'm going to frame it and hang it in my kitchen."

"Really?" Allison said, her eyes widening.

She looks so much like her mother did at that age, Helen thought. "Really," she said, and kissed her niece's dark curls. "You're much taller than the last time I saw you."

"I'm older," Allison said. "I'm four years, eight months and one week."

Oh, for the days when I proudly counted each week so I'd be older, Helen thought. "Let's put your pretty drawing in my car so it doesn't get dirty," she said, and carried it to the PT Cruiser.

Tommy, nearly eleven, was too old for a hug. Helen smiled when he greeted Phil with a handshake and a man-to-man "How are you, Uncle Phil?"

"How's the future Albert Pujols?" Phil said.

"He left," Tommy said.

Phil, who didn't follow the finer points of baseball, seemed confused. "Left what?" he asked.

"Albert Pujols abandoned the Cards for bigger bucks in Los Angeles," Kathy explained.

"So who do you want to be now?" Phil said.

Tommy shrugged. "David Freese is okay. So is Jason Motte, the relief pitcher. He can hit." Helen smiled. Tommy's boyish enthusiasm was turning into cool teen indifference.

"I'm not sure kids idolize players anymore like in the old days," Kathy said, as if in apology.

"But I still want to play for the Cards," Tommy said.

When he smiled, he looked like his father. They had the same dirty blond hair and broad shoulders, Helen thought, though Tom Senior had the beginning of a paunch.

"How about some batting practice?" Phil asked.

"No time," Kathy said, halfway up the back stairs to the kitchen. "Dinner's in five minutes. I have to leave at eight, and so do you and Helen. Phil, get a beer out of the cooler and talk to Tom. Both you kids wash your hands. Then, Tommy, put the plastic knives and forks on the picnic table. Allison, I need you to put a napkin by each plate."

Helen followed her sister into the kitchen, noting sadly that Kathy's dark hair had more silver and she'd put on a few pounds since her last visit.

Kathy's kitchen was no showcase, but it was livelier and more lived-in than Maureen Carsten's. Bowls of potato salad, baked beans, and coleslaw and a huge platter of corn were lined up on the table.

"I'll start carrying these out," Helen said.

"Quick!" Kathy said, her voice low. "While the kids are washing their hands, did you get the money without any trouble?"

"The teller made me see a bank manager, but he was so busy I hope he'll forget to report the transaction," Helen said. "The money's in my car, packed in a cloth Schnucks bag. We'll all leave here together at eight."

"How will I get the money?" Kathy said. Helen heard her distress at this small complication and felt sorry for her little sister—and guilty for the worry she caused her.

"Pull into the convenience store on Lindbergh on the way to the drop-off," Helen said.

"Good," Kathy said. "I always buy a lottery ticket there."

"You do?"

"You know what they say: 'You can't win if you don't play.'" She grinned at Helen.

"That's the spirit, Sis," Helen said. "And you won't seem out of place if anyone spots you there. We'll transfer the money in the parking lot. Then Phil and I will leave first in our rental car and park in the lot next to the drop-off spot."

"Good choice," Kathy said. "That drugstore is always crowded. You'll blend in."

"You wait at the convenience store until ten minutes before nine," Helen said, "then make the drop-off and go."

"Go where?" Kathy asked. "I can't go home. I'm supposed to be at a meeting."

"Go back to the convenience store and really buy a lottery ticket," Helen said. "Or wait there for me to call your cell phone. Don't be alarmed if you don't hear from us right away."

"What are you going to do?" Helen heard the fear in her sister's voice.

"Phil and I may have to confront the blackmailer," Helen said.

"Will you call the police?" Kathy asked.

"We'll try not to," Helen said. "Do you have the recording?"

Kathy nodded, then reached into a kitchen drawer by the phone for a slim metal recorder. "Here," she said. "The recording is on it."

"If we tell the blackmailer he's been recorded, that should scare him away permanently," Helen said, crossing her fingers that Kathy didn't realize a recording with a voice changer was useless. "Hopefully we won't have to go to the police, but I don't know how long it will take. It could be a while."

"You know what I'm going to do?" Kathy said. "I'm going to Cyrano's on Lockwood Avenue."

"The dessert house?" Helen said.

"You haven't been there in a while," Kathy said. "It has food and a bar. I'm going to sit in the nice dark bar and have"—she paused for a moment—"a raspberry cosmo in a real glass glass. That kind that breaks if the kids even look at it. For one hour, I'll pretend I'm mysterious and sophisticated. I'll even wear my black pants and new black blouse."

"And Tom won't notice when you walk out all dressed up?" Helen asked.

"I have my ways," Kathy said, and giggled.

Helen hugged her sister. "Good plan."

She carried the potato salad outside just as Tom was putting the pork steaks and burgers on the picnic table. Kathy followed with a basket of hamburger buns and the coleslaw. Two more trips and all six were seated at the picnic table, piling food on their plates.

Tom waited until Helen and Phil had their first bites of pork steak, then asked, "Well, how is it?"

"Awesome," Phil said.

"Perfect," Helen said. "It's been way too long since I've had a good pork steak. Florida doesn't appreciate the special delights of the pork shoulder. I can tell you've used Maull's barbecue sauce, like a true St. Louisan, but there's more in this."

"My secret ingredients are mustard, brown sugar and beer," Tom said, grinning proudly. "Some for the cook and some for the sauce." He waved at a man in the next yard who was slowly climbing down his back stairs. "Hi, neighbor!" Tom said. "How's your knee?"

That must be Lee Cook, Helen thought. And I can definitely see him from Kathy's backyard. So much for her theory that the Cooks' view was blocked. Lee was fortysomething with thinning mouse-colored hair and a round face with the features smushed in the center.

"I'm better," Lee said.

A chubby woman with short brown hair and a thin, sharp nose stuck her head out and said, "He's so much better he's going bowling tonight, against doctor's orders." She smiled fondly at her husband.

"Aw, I'm just going to shoot the breeze with the boys," he said. "Sunshine here has me on lockdown since I had knee surgery."

Kathy turned white when Lee said "Sunshine." Helen raised an eyebrow. She'd told her sister that was a common nickname. Phil and Tom were oblivious to the sisters' silent communication.

"Lee and Sharon, these are my in-laws, Helen and Phil, all the way from Florida," Tom said proudly.

Helen waved. Phil stood up and said hello.

"Pleased to meet you," Lee said. "Don't let me interrupt your dinner." He limped to his car and waved good-bye.

"What time is it?" Helen asked.

"Ten till eight," Kathy said, and started piling up paper plates.

"You go ahead and get dressed, sweetie," Tom said. "The kids and I can clean up."

Kathy didn't hesitate. She flew up the stairs to change.

"Will we get to see you before we leave tomorrow afternoon, Tom?" Helen asked.

"No such luck," he said. "I'll be at work. But thanks for stopping by tonight. Kathy's been so jumpy lately. She's much calmer since you got here."

Tom gave her a slightly beery kiss on the cheek. Helen and Phil said their good-byes. Kathy honked the horn on her minivan. She'd slipped out the front door and was ready to go.

They met two miles down the road at the convenience store. Phil stayed in the car while Helen handed Kathy the cloth Schnucks supermarket bag.

"Watch it," she said. "It weighs a ton."

Kathy carefully placed the heavy bag in the minivan's passenger seat.

"You look chic in your black outfit," Helen said. "How are you?"

"Nervous," Kathy said. She tried a small smile. "I hope Lee isn't the blackmailer. He's such a nice neighbor."

"I hope so, too," Helen said. "We'll be drinking cosmos before you know it."

"You promise?" Kathy's lip trembled.

"Trust me, Little Sis," Helen said. "You're dealing with pros now."

CHAPTER 23

8:58 p.m.

Helen and Phil were parked at the edge of the drugstore lot, facing the empty strip mall on Manchester Road. Only two feet of grass divided the blacktop lots. Cars streamed in and out of the drugstore lot.

The strip mall's parking lot was empty and had been for two years. Once, the low redbrick building had housed four struggling businesses: a bridal resale shop, a discount shoe store, a dog groomer, and a pretzel store. All were empty now, their dark, dusty windows plastered with sad FOR LEASE and GOING OUT OF BUSINESS signs.

Across the street was Jackie's Fine Eats. The homey restaurant lived up to its name. Helen had had a first-rate meal there and still remembered the luscious gooey butter cake. Only two cars were parked in front of Jackie's, both anonymous silver. Inside, Helen saw a man eating at a table in the far corner while a waitress hovered nearby. The chairs at the front tables were upended on the tabletops and a man mopped the floor. Jackie's closed at nine o'clock, she remembered.

Helen checked again to make sure the Cruiser's headlights were off. The drugstore lot had more than enough light for Helen to see the rusty blue Dumpster where Kathy would drop the blackmail money.

Any car traveling west on Manchester could turn into the strip mall's short potholed drive, continue past the Dumpster, go around the back and come out on the other side.

Manchester was six lanes wide here, divided by a concrete median. Even at this hour, the road was clogged with traffic. Eighteen-wheelers barged through on their way to major highways. Small cars zipped past. Nobody drove the speed limit.

Phil drummed his fingers on the dash.

"Nervous?" Helen asked.

"Mrx," he said.

Okay, buddy, if that's the way you're going to be, she thought, I won't tell you about my secret weapon in the backseat. But if this goes sideways, you'll be damn grateful I brought it. Buying that aspirin at this drugstore was brilliant. You'll see. You need me and you know it. And so does Coronado Investigations.

Helen checked the Cruiser's dashboard clock again. 8:59. Was that clock broken? she wondered. She glanced at her watch and the same time taunted her.

Finally, the dashboard clock flipped over to nine o'clock. Helen tensed. Phil looked more alert.

Where was Kathy?

She checked her watch again. That time was still 8:59. When her wristwatch clicked over to nine o'clock, Kathy's minivan slowed and approached the strip mall drive. The tubby blue vehicle lumbered onto the pitted driveway, then stopped beside the blue Dumpster. The engine sounded like a sewing machine. Kathy rolled down her window.

Helen waited, hardly daring to breathe.

What's taking my sister so long? she wondered. Does she need help lifting the heavy money bag?

Helen forced herself to remain in her seat. Finally, she saw the bag shoved through the driver's window. It landed on the empty Dumpster with a booming thud.

Helen breathed a loud sigh of relief. Phil's face twitched.

Kathy drove slowly around the back of the strip mall, flipped on her blinker and eased into the traffic.

Enjoy your cosmo, Little Sis, Helen thought. It was 9:02.

Where was the blackmailer? How long would he leave that much cash sitting out in the open? A homeless man could have the luckiest find of his life. A curious shopper at the drugstore could wander over and check out the bulging bag on the Dumpster. The pale, sturdy cloth bag glowed like a beacon in the dark.

Helen wanted to tell Phil she was worried, but after a look at his grim face, she didn't dare. Instead, she studied the scene behind the sparkling windows at Jackie's Fine Eats.

The lone diner at the back table signaled the server for the check, put down some bills and stood up. The server hurried over to take his money, counted the bills and shook her head. Then she cleared the table. The mopping man made his way to that section.

It was 9:04.

Now the last customer was outside. He walked with a limp. Helen still couldn't guess his age or see his face, just his pear-shaped body in khaki pants and a dark T-shirt. His hair was conventionally short and either very thin or receding.

The man limped past the two silver cars in the restaurant lot to the curb, then looked both ways. He waited for a break in the traffic, then limped awkwardly across the first three lanes of Manchester, dragging his right leg. He barely made it to the concrete median before the next rush of traffic.

"Phil!" Helen said. "Look! I think that man standing on the median is heading this way. Is he our blackmailer?"

Phil craned his neck.

"Could be," he said. "Or he might be a diner who parked at the drugstore because he couldn't find a spot at the restaurant."

It was 9:07.

"The blackmailer has to pick up that bag soon," Helen said. "That much money can't just sit there."

"The blackmailer's probably parked in this lot," Phil said. "That would make more sense. Manchester is dangerous to cross, especially if you have trouble walking fast."

He peered at the man on the median. "Maybe that is the blackmailer," he said. "He may not want to risk driving into the strip mall. That cash has been sitting on the Dumpster a long time."

There was a short break in the stream of traffic. The limping man stepped off the median, then hurriedly tried to hop back on it. A passing Honda honked angrily as he landed safely on the concrete.

"That was close," Phil said. "That last car nearly flattened him."

"I can't see his face yet," Helen said. "But I think it's Lee Cook, the neighbor who had knee surgery. They're both built like bowling pins."

"Could be the grandson who broke his leg," Phil said.

"No, he looks too fat to be the grandson," Helen said. And we're having a real conversation, she thought, but tamped down that hope.

"You didn't see Matt's class photo," Phil said. "He's been porking out on Grandma's cookies."

"And drinking beer," Helen said. "Don't forget that DUI."

Suddenly, the three eastbound lanes were empty. Helen saw the man step off the curb and run across Manchester. He wasn't exactly running. It was more like a limping lunge. But he made it across before the next fleet of cars barreled down.

He limped faster now that he was safe and hop-limped up the drive.

"It's the blackmailer!" Helen said. "He's heading straight for the Dumpster."

His head was turned so Helen couldn't see his face. Phil cracked his door, ready to pounce.

"Careful," Helen said. "He'll see us when you open your door."

"No, he won't," Phil said. "I unscrewed the dome light while you were getting dressed this afternoon."

Just then, the man turned toward them.

"Oh. My. God," Helen whispered. "It can't be."

But it was.

"Rob," she said.

"A badly damaged Rob, overweight and crippled," Phil said.

"Look how he's favoring his right arm," Helen said. "That whole side seems partly paralyzed. Tommy's crack on the head with his bat did some serious damage."

"Unless it was the premature burial," Phil said.

"Rob's sick, too," Helen said. "His color is bad. He's pale as lard."

"Sh!" Phil said. "Get ready. It's time."

They both eased out of the Cruiser and silently stole across the short strip of grass as Rob clumsily grabbed the money bag off the Dumpster with his left hand. The bag was so heavy, Rob staggered under its weight.

He scuttled down the drive with his prize. Rob reminded Helen of a fish hawk she'd seen, trying to fly off with a fat, struggling fish. The bird nearly drowned trying to hang on to its prey.

Rob could hardly walk, but he wasn't going to let go of his prize.

Phil stepped out in front of Rob. "Can I help you with that?" he asked.

Helen came up beside him and grabbed the bag.

"I'll take that," she said. "It's mine."

Rob looked stunned. He stood there, staring. Helen couldn't pry the bag out of his fingers, but she had a good grip on the handles.

Then her ex seemed to recover from his shock. His small eyes lit with malice. "Well, well," he said. "If it isn't Auntie Helen and her new squeeze."

His voice was flat and hard. "Hey, Phil, she still make that little moan when you stick it in her? I would have dumped her years ago, except for that sound. It was a real turn-on.

"But you won't be getting any once she's in jail, will you? And dear little Tommy will be motherless. The ugly sisters are going to jail for attempted murder."

"No, they're not," Phil said, his voice cool.

"What?" Rob said.

"You lose, loser," Phil said. He smiled, as if he was explaining something to a slow learner. "If you'd called the cops when you crawled out of the church hall basement, they'd both be in jail. But you got greedy. You had to blackmail Helen for the rest of her money. Well, the game's over. Beat it."

"Beat it?" Rob said.

"Git. Go. Vamoose," Phil said. "You've got nothing to go to the police with."

"It's not my fault I didn't call them right away," Rob said, his voice unnaturally high. "I was unconscious. Do you know what that bitch and her fat sister did? They buried me in a basement. Wrapped me in plastic and then covered me with crushed rock and drove off. Drove off and left me to die.

"I woke up sometime after midnight—I heard the church bells; that's how I knew the time. They stole my watch, too. I woke up and found myself under the rocks in the church hall basement. I was panicked and in pain. If I hadn't crawled out of there, I'd be buried under concrete by now."

"Gee, what a loss to the world," Phil said.

"I suffered," Rob said. "Look at me."

"You never were much to look at," Phil said.

"She ruined me," Rob said. "I can't move right anymore. I think I had oxygen deprivation when she buried me. Or a small stroke caused by that little bastard. But I'm going to tell the police and ruin them all."

"No, you're not," Phil said. "You can't prove a thing. You should have called the police after you escaped. Now it's too late. You made it worse when you tried blackmail. Didn't the Black Widow give you a million bucks to go away? That was one desperate woman."

"I spent it," Rob said. "So what?"

"Looks bad," Phil said. "An ex-millionaire blackmailing a hard-working suburban mom and a little kid. Even for you, Rob, that's low."

"You can't prove I blackmailed anyone," Rob said.

"Yes, we can," Phil said. "Kathy recorded you the last time you called."

Rob's face turned another shade of pale.

"Got the recording right here," Helen said, and pulled the digital recorder out of her pocket.

"Give me that!" Rob grabbed for it, stumbled, missed and caught Helen by the arm.

"Ow!" she cried. It felt like Rob was trying to squeeze the bone out of her flesh.

"I said, give it to me."

Helen slid the recorder into the money bag with her other hand. Rob wrenched Helen's arm so hard, she screamed louder, but she didn't let go of the bag.

"Phil, call 911," Helen shouted, hoping that would scare Rob away.

It worked. Rob pulled harder on the bag, but Helen hung on to it. Phil produced his cell phone, and Rob's eyes were frantic.

"No!" he said. "No, don't. You can't." He threw Helen into the Dumpster. She hit it face-first and got a long, ugly slice on her forehead from a sliver of rusty metal. Her face throbbed and her arm ached, but she was still clutching the bag.

Rob scrabbled away, dragging his right leg. He'd given up the cash fortune. Now he tried to flee across the street to keep his freedom.

"Phil!" Helen said. "He's running for his car across the road. Don't let him get away."

Phil was already after him. He looked up, saw the approaching traffic, and stayed at the curb.

Rob kept going. He hobble-hopped across the first lane, then the second, to a braying chorus of horns and squealing brakes. An air horn bellowed as an eighteen-wheeler in the third lane tried to stop. Helen heard shouts and screams, then screeching brakes and a sickening thump.

She hid her face.

There was a shocked silence. Helen looked up from the Dumpster, her face burning from the ragged scratch. Handprint bruises were already blotching her arm.

Traffic had stopped on Manchester, all six lanes. The truck's driver leaped out of his cab and ran toward a broken figure on the road.

Helen saw a long red-gray smear on the truck's gleaming radiator, then heard the driver say, "He's dead."

She dropped the money bag in the Dumpster.

"He's dead," the driver wailed. "Sweet Jesus, save me. I've killed a man."

Thank God, Helen thought. Her knees buckled and she slid down onto the cracked pavement.

CHAPTER 24

"Miss, are you okay?" the woman asked.

Helen stared at her young, kind face. Her startling flamingo-pink hair was oddly pretty with her creamy complexion.

"Your face is bleeding," she said. "And I can see the bruises on your arm already. My name is Kirby, and I caught the whole thing on my iPhone."

"What whole thing?" Helen said. She wasn't as woozy as she pretended. How much of the confrontation with Rob had Kirby videoed?

"I was coming out of the drugstore when I saw the fight," Kirby said. "I saw that weird dude try to steal your grocery bag and twist your arm."

"He hurt me," Helen said. "My face hurts, too."

"I'm not surprised," Kirby said. "The dude threw you against the Dumpster."

Helen was almost afraid to ask the next question. "Did you get audio, too?"

"No, my mic's busted," Kirby said. "Should have never bought a refurbished one."

"I feel dizzy," Helen said. She was. Dizzy with relief. Kirby hadn't caught the whole scene. Just the right part.

"Where's Phil?"

"The dude who attacked you?" Kirby asked. "He's dead. Seriously dead."

"No, the man with the silver hair. He's my husband." Helen moved her face slightly and felt blood trickle down her neck. She saw Phil in a small knot of people clustered around Rob's body on Manchester Road.

Let's hope he's doing damage control, she thought. She tried not to look at the mangled mess that was her ex-husband. Suddenly, she was shaking all over.

"I think you're in shock," Kirby said.

"I need to get to my car and sit down a moment," Helen said, pointing to the Cruiser. "It's right there."

"You need to go to the hospital," Kirby said, "but I'll help you to your car. The police and ambulance are on their way. About a zillion people called 911, but I think I'm the only one who videoed the fight."

She held up her iPhone proudly. The pink case matched her hair. "Think the police would like to see my video?"

"I'm sure they would," Helen said. She stood up slowly, holding on to the rusty Dumpster. She couldn't stop shaking.

Kirby was shorter than Helen, but sturdy. "Here, lean on me," she said.

"I don't want to get blood on your T-shirt," Helen said.

"Hey, it will be something good to show my mom. I sneaked to the store to buy ice cream. She's always on me about my weight. The chocolate swirl is melting." She held up a dripping plastic bag.

"I'll get you more," Helen said, limping toward her car.

"No, don't," Kirby said. "The universe is saying I don't need more ice cream. It sent me to this store for a purpose, and that was to help you. Do you believe that?"

"Oh, yes," Helen said. "You're exactly what I need now. I'm still light-headed. I want to stretch out in the backseat."

"The police are here," Kirby said. "And a couple of ambulances. I'll make sure they find you—and show them my video." She ran off into the night.

"Thank you, Kirby," Helen said. Her voice sounded weak. She didn't have to pretend to be dizzy now. She stretched out on the backseat and wrapped her hand around her secret weapon. Emergency lights flashed on the strip mall, bleaching the brick bone white, then bloodred.

Rob is dead, she thought. Really, truly, finally dead. He can't hurt me or Kathy or Tommy anymore. I wish I could feel sorry for him, but I don't. He's killed my marriage.

Maybe, she thought. Memories of the good times she'd had with Phil rushed back—their long afternoons of lovemaking, their hot honeymoon in the Keys, working together on cases, even the first time she'd met him, when she was undercover at a wild party. Well, not totally undercover. She'd been hired as a topless bartender. She'd tried to cover her chest with two one-liter soda bottles.

Usually, that memory made her smile. Now tears started in her eyes. She wiped her face with her hand and it came back smeared red.

Maybe Phil will forgive me now that Rob is dead and I've been hurt. Where is Phil? Did the police arrest him? Would Kirby's video get them off the hook? Or did someone else video the whole incident—with sound?

Helen heard Kirby say, "She's over here in her car. I think she feels pretty sick and she's all bloody."

"Helen!" Phil said. "You're safe. You're bleeding. How bad did he hurt you?"

"It's just a scratch," Helen said. She remembered that line from a movie and hoped it really was a scratch. She'd hate to have her face scarred.

What am I doing? she thought. A man was killed—no, my ex-husband was killed—and all I can think about is my face.

Phil opened the passenger door on the driver's side, sat beside Helen and cradled her in his arms. She inhaled his comforting scent of coffee and sandalwood and leaned her bloody face on his chest. Maybe everything will be all right after all, she thought.

Then a uniformed officer knocked on the window. "Sir, I understand you witnessed this accident?" he asked.

Helen saw that his name tag said GRIMES, but she couldn't see his department's name. Officer Grimes looked like a sandy-haired, freckled farmboy, but there was nothing friendly in his manner. He was all business.

"Yes, I did," Phil said. "And so did my wife. She's been injured."

"Please step out of the car, sir," the officer said. "Was your wife also hit by a car?"

Helen sat up and Phil opened the back door and climbed out. "No, she was attacked by the man who died," he said. "The dead man is Rob—"

"We have his driver's license, sir. I need your information."

Phil opened his wallet and pulled out his license and PI credentials. "I'm Phil Sagemont and this is my wife and business partner, Helen Hawthorne. We're Florida private eyes, up here to investigate the death of a St. Louis woman, Ceci Odell, who was murdered in Riggs Beach."

"That the Kirkwood woman who was paddleboarding?" Officer Grimes asked. "I saw that on TV."

"That's the one," Phil said.

"How did your wife come in contact with the victim?" Officer Grimes asked.

"We think he followed us here," Phil said. "Helen and Rob divorced a couple of years ago, and it wasn't friendly. He hounded my wife, even followed her to her new home in Florida."

Fairly true, Helen thought. He left out the part where the court said I owed Rob half my future income. But he did come to Fort Lauderdale looking for me.

"He even watched her sister's house," Phil said. "Kathy lives in Webster Groves. We were at a barbecue there tonight, and Rob must have seen us. We left to go to the drugstore."

Half-true, Helen thought. Rob was definitely watching Kathy. But now it's time for my secret weapon.

She spoke up quickly. "Officer," she said. "I needed some aspirin from the store here." She held up the plastic drugstore bag.

"I also bought groceries," she said. She pulled out her secret weapon, a cloth Schnucks shopping bag packed with bulky boxes so it resembled the money bag.

"My ex attacked me and tried to take my shopping bag. Why he'd want crackers and cookies, I have no idea."

She wished she could see Phil's face. Then she reminded herself not to get too clever. "He grabbed the bag and twisted my arm," she said. "I tried to get away, but he threw me against the Dumpster and I hit my face."

"I can see that, ma'am," Officer Grimes said. "I'm calling the paramedics now. They can't do anything for the victim."

The uniform spoke into his shoulder mic, and two hulking paramedics trotted over. "Are you able to walk, ma'am?" one asked. He was twentysomething and heroically ripped. "I'd like to look at your wound in the light. If you're not able to walk, we'll wheel you to the ambulance parked over there."

"I can walk," Helen said firmly, and she did, escorted by the strapping pair. Now she could see Manchester's snarled traffic and the cops diverting cars to detour routes. A dozen police cars and official vehicles were parked haphazardly in the strip mall lot. A CSI team was photographing Rob's mangled body. Helen looked away.

The brawny brown-haired paramedic opened the ambulance doors and said, "Sit here."

Helen was grateful to escape into the brightly lit interior. The paramedic dabbed gently at her bloody face with clean, damp gauze. "When's the last time you had a tetanus shot?" he asked.

"I don't remember," she said.

"Then you'd better get a booster. That Dumpster's rusty. This wound doesn't look too deep, but it's on your face. I'd suggest you have a doctor look at it. We can take you to the ER."

"Will you tell my husband, please," she said, "so he can follow in our car?"

If I wasn't fighting with Phil, I'd ask him to drive me, Helen thought. But a little drama might help my marriage.

The paramedic jogged off to find Phil. Helen saw Officer Grimes wave to another police officer, a lanky man with graying hair. They met for a quick conference next to a police car.

"The two married PIs—Sagemont and Hawthorne—made statements that corroborate what the witnesses saw and that pink-haired girl's video," Officer Grimes said. "It's a traffic fatality, Ray. An idiot ran into the street after striking his ex-wife. Neither PI pushed the victim into the path of the oncoming vehicle.

"Sagemont, the husband, wants to know if he and his wife can leave town tomorrow."

"Don't see why not," Ray said. "The victim ran into the street of his own accord. If he hadn't died, we'd be arresting him for coercion and battery. Record their statements, then the other witnesses'. Did you get the video?"

"The girl with the pink hair gave me the whole phone," Officer Grimes said. "Said the mic was broken and she didn't want it. Said it was her civic duty."

"Good," the other cop said. "Let's wrap this up. It's an accident. Hawthorne, the wife, is in the ambulance. Better record her before the paramedics take off. I'll get the husband."

Officer Grimes respectfully asked Helen for her statement, and she talked into the digital recorder, keeping to the bones of her story.

"Which town is this?" she asked. The St. Louis area was a confusing tangle of some ninety municipalities and she saw no sign saying which one she was in.

"Froxbury Heights," Officer Grimes said. Helen relaxed. Froxbury was a West County millionaires' ghetto. The residents didn't like publicity. The police would wrap up Rob's death swiftly and efficiently and hustle Helen and Phil out of town.

"Does your face hurt?" he asked.

"It's starting to throb," she said.

"The paramedics will take you to the hospital right away. As soon as my partner records your husband's statement, he can join you. Good-bye and feel better."

Helen heard the big-shouldered truck driver crying. He leaned against a car and twisted a Cardinals ball cap in his hands while saying, "He just darted out in front of me before I even saw him. I couldn't stop."

A woman in a server's uniform patted his hand. "I know you couldn't," she said. "There was no way. We saw the whole thing from the restaurant. It's not your fault and I told the police officer myself."

Was that Rob's waitress? Helen wondered. Her words had no effect. The driver said again, "He just darted out in front of me . . ."

Helen felt a stab of pity. That poor man would carry the weight of Rob's death. She wished she could tell him he'd done her and her family a favor, but she knew that wouldn't comfort him, either.

Then she realized this man was the only person who would cry for Rob. His parents were dead. She wasn't wasting any tears on her ex, and neither would the Black Widow. Sandy, the woman Helen had caught him with on their back deck, wanted nothing to do with him, either.

Helen watched a stretcher with a black body bag being rolled onto the street. Four men reached down to pick up Rob's body. That's when Helen noticed the accident had knocked off his shoes.

Rob's barefoot body was zipped into the bag. The sound had a horrible finality, worse than earth tossed on a coffin lid. An attendant found one of Rob's shoes in the street and dropped it on the bag. He didn't see the other.

But Helen did. The last bit of Rob was lying on the concrete median—a loafer.

CHAPTER 25

H elen was marooned in a hospital cubicle not much bigger than a Dumpster, but a lot cleaner. She eavesdropped on the man in the next cubicle while an ER nurse took his history. Mr. Burke said he was fifty-one, diabetic and weighed three hundred twenty pounds. "Guess I should lose some weight, huh?" he joked.

The nurse didn't laugh. "I'm going to take your blood pressure now, Mr. Burke," she said. "Mr. Burke? Mr. Burke?"

She stuck her head out the door and screamed, "He's not breathing. Call a code!"

Helen saw a crowd in scrubs pile into the cubicle. One woman's voice was unnaturally calm. "I'm the code nurse," she said. "Get the crash cart next to the patient here. Ready the pads."

Helen heard frantic thumps, rips and tearing sounds, while a distant siren wailed.

"Continue CPR," said the code nurse. "Let's start the ventilations here. You help her ventilate. Continue ventilations one every ten."

I'm here for a long wait, Helen thought. This is life-and-death.

The fight intensified.

"One milligram of epi in," the code nurse said. "Flushed."

"I'm gonna open up an airway," another voice said. "He's got a lot of secretions."

That's when Phil rushed in, carrying her black purse. Now she was in the middle of another struggle to save her dying marriage.

"Nice purse," she said. "But you don't wear black with brown shoes." She tried to smile, but her face hurt too much.

Phil didn't bother. "The nurse said you'll be okay," he said. "She doesn't think you'll need stitches. I'm happy to hear that."

Happy? Helen thought the cubicle's white walls showed more emotion. He might have been talking to a stranger in the waiting room.

"I want you to know this doesn't change anything between us," he said.

"What!" Helen said, then realized she was shouting. The walls were thin. She lowered her voice to a whisper. "After I produced that substitute bag? And the aspirin to justify why we were sitting there? I saved you."

"That was clever," he said, a judge permitting a technical point. "I'll give you a good recommendation when you look for another job. You'll make a good private eye."

Helen felt something cold reach in and freeze her heart. "I am a good private eye," she said, each word carved in ice. "I don't need your recommendation. But you need to remember I kept us out of jail tonight. You saw what Rob was like. How mean and sneaky he was."

"Oh, yeah," Phil said. "Rob's a real master criminal. That's why I could bluff him into thinking I was going to call the cops and tell them we had a recording. The dumb-ass forgot he'd used a voice changer. He wasn't smart enough to hijack a kid's Hershey bar, but you were terrified of him."

"Oh, I get it," Helen said. "This isn't about me. It's about you. You hate Rob."

"So do you," he said. "But you invested that nitwit with brains and style and even—sex appeal."

Sex appeal? Helen thought. Where did he get that antique phrase?

"You let him have power over you," Phil said.

"He's dead," Helen said. "He has no power over anyone. And until he limped across Manchester, I had no idea I was dealing with Rob. Or did you forget that, Mr. Big Brain? We had two other good suspects: a drunken kid and a desperate family man. Both could be dangerous when they were cornered. Kathy and I had good reason to be frightened. We were worried about her boy, your nephew. What the hell's wrong with you?"

"Nothing," Phil said. "It's you. I thought I could trust you and now I can't. I can't have a partner I can't trust. Cops know that. If you can't trust your partner, you're dead. Sometimes, you're really dead."

His whisper was a snaky hiss. So was hers, Helen realized. They'd been hissing at each other like a nest of snakes.

"There's no point in talking to you when you're this pigheaded," she said. "Please leave. I'll call my sister, Kathy. She can drive me to the hotel when the doctor finishes here."

Helen heard a voice from next door say, "That's it. TOD ten thirty-two."

"No, I'll stay," Phil said, his voice grudging. "I'll be in the waiting room." He slammed the cubicle door so hard, its glass window rattled. A passing nurse frowned at him.

Now she heard a tentative voice ask, "May I spend a little time alone with my husband?" The new widow, Helen thought, as her heart-wrenching sobs tore through the wall.

She took a deep breath to calm down. I will not cry, she told herself. She pulled out her cell phone and called her sister. Kathy answered on the second ring, and Helen heard the soft hum of restaurant noises in the background.

"Helen!" Kathy said. "How are you? Where are you? Did you catch him?"

"I'm fine," Helen said. "That man will never bother us again. You and Tommy are safe."

"Thank God. Who was it? What happened to him?" Kathy asked.

"He's been put away," Helen said. In a body bag, she thought. "It's complicated. I'd rather tell you in person."

"Too bad you can't join me for a raspberry cosmo," Kathy said. "Cyrano's is closing. I only had one drink." She giggled, but Helen didn't think it was a tipsy giggle, and her sister wasn't slurring her words.

"But you took so long, I ordered a Cleopatra," Kathy said. "I haven't had one since Tom and I were dating. That was our favorite dessert: French vanilla ice cream with bananas, strawberries, rum sauce—"

Helen stopped her sister before she listed all the ingredients. "Kathy, I couldn't join you even if I wanted to," she said, her voice serious.

"Why?" Kathy asked. "What's wrong?"

"I'm at the emergency room, but it's minor."

"No, it's not," Kathy said. "You don't go to the ER because you scraped your knee. I'm coming over now."

"It's not much worse, I promise," Helen said. "I'm at Webster General. If you see Phil in the waiting room, we're not speaking. He's still furious."

"Oh, no. I'll be there in twenty minutes," Kathy said.

She was in Helen's cubicle in eighteen minutes. "What happened?" she asked. "You're all bloody."

"It's just a scratch," Helen said. "No permanent damage."

"It looks painful," Kathy said.

Helen shrugged. The cubicle next door was empty now. She quickly scanned the hall, then whispered, "No one's listening. You won't believe who the blackmailer was."

Kathy plopped down on the hard plastic chair when Helen told her, mouth gaping. After she finished her tale, Helen said, "Rob is really dead this time. He can't hurt anyone anymore."

"It's the best possible outcome for all of us," Kathy whispered back.

"For you and Tommy," Helen said. "Phil won't forgive me."

"Is there anything I can do to change his mind?" Kathy asked again.

"No," Helen said. "I just hope he'll eventually forgive me."

"What happened to the money?" Kathy asked.

"I dropped it in the Dumpster when everyone else was watching Rob get flattened," Helen said.

"Do you want me to swing by and get it tonight?" Kathy said.

"No, stay away from there," Helen said. "I'll pick it up tomorrow."

"Will it fit in your suitcase?" Kathy asked.

"I can't carry on that much cash, and I'm sure not going to pack it," Helen said.

"I could deposit it back in your St. Louis account," Kathy said.

"I'd rather you didn't call attention to yourself at the bank, now that our troubles are over," Helen said. "I'll FedEx it home. I might need it to start a new life in Fort Lauderdale."

With that, her voice broke, and she started weeping. Kathy hugged Helen while she cried on her shoulder. "Sh," she soothed. "Phil still loves you. He'll come around. I know he will."

Helen wasn't sure at all, but she said nothing.

While she wiped her eyes, Kathy asked, "What if someone steals that money?"

"I can't make myself crazy over that money when this turned out so well," Helen said. "I expected to lose it. If I get it back, wonderful. But if anyone takes it, that person will still be more deserving than Rob."

The door opened and a blond doctor breezed in, so pale he looked newly hatched. He checked Helen's forehead with his gloved hands and said, "That cleaned up nicely. You're lucky; the cut's not deep. You won't need plastic surgery. Don't wear makeup and keep your hair off your forehead until it heals. The nurse will be in shortly with a booster shot and your instructions. I'll give you an antibiotic ointment. Do you want anything for pain?"

"I have aspirin," Helen said.

"If you need something stronger, ask your internist. Your arm may be sore for a few days after the shot. Okay?" He bustled out before Helen could answer.

After an endless half hour, Helen was discharged. Phil gave Kathy a good-bye hug. Kathy hugged her sister, then took their hands and said, "Thank you both. I can't tell you what a relief it is to have my family safe."

She looked years younger. Helen and Phil watched her walk to her car with a light step.

Phil drove back to the hotel. The oppressive silence made Helen's head ache—or maybe it was the battle with Rob. She dry-swallowed two aspirins and was grateful when she was back in their room. The big bed looked inviting.

"I'll sleep on the sofa," Phil said, grabbing two pillows and the bedspread.

He's going to have fun sleeping on that short, hard sofa, she thought.

The next morning, Helen was awakened by her cell phone ringing. She fished it out of her purse and answered with a groggy "Hello."

"Helen, it's Joan. Joan Right, the server at Cy's on the Pier," she said. "I sneaked out on my break to tell you. Cy's going to give the bribe to the commissioner at the restaurant tonight, at closing time. In cash. Frank has settled for four days. Can you be here tonight about eight thirty?"

"We're flying home today," Helen said. "If there are no delays, we should make it."

"Wear a disguise," Joan said. "Cy's acting real jumpy. Don't take any chances."

"You, either," Helen said.

She hung up the phone and checked the time on her watch. Eight thirty a.m. That would make it nine thirty in Fort Lauderdale. They didn't have to leave for the airport for nearly three hours. Phil was sitting at the round table near the window, reading the *St. Louis City Gazette* and drinking coffee.

"Phil," she said. "Joan says that Cy's going to bribe Commissioner Frank Gordon tonight at the restaurant with cash. We have to be there. If we catch Cy buying the commissioner's vote, we can save Sunny Jim. Joan said I should wear a disguise. I'll buy a cheap blond wig here and some tourist clothes at the Lauderdale airport. We should have Margery at the restaurant, too. I can call her now."

"I'll get Valerie Cannata at Channel Seventy-seven," he said. "She'll want to know Frank the Fixer is involved in a bribery attempt."

"This is a primo setup for an investigative reporter," Helen said.

Phil set down the *City Gazette*.

"Are we mentioned in today's paper?" Helen asked.

"We caught a break," he said. "The paper says Rob darted into traffic and was a pedestrian fatality. The truck driver wasn't charged and no one else is mentioned."

"This operation has gone incredibly well," Helen said.

Phil grunted, dialed Valerie's number and put her on speaker. "I'm in the editing suite," she said, sounding slightly breathless. "Make it quick."

Phil did.

"Shut up!" she said. "I've been watching Frank the Fixer for four months. I'm itching to catch him in the act. When and where?"

Phil told her.

"I'm in, but don't meet me at the station," Valerie said.

"There's a Target on Riggs Beach Road near I-95. I'll meet you there at eight tonight," Helen said, "and we can go in your car. I think Cy knows mine. I'll dress as a tourist in loud clothes and wear a wig."

"Me, too," Valerie said. "I have a really ugly T-shirt I got as a gift. Ooh, I smell another Emmy."

Next, Helen called Margery on the room phone. "We've got a job for you tonight," she said. "Are you free?"

"The big question is, Are you? Are you two still an item?" Margery asked.

"I'm still hoping," Helen said, guardedly. She was glad Phil wasn't listening in. "How do you feel about . . . things?"

"About you?" Margery said. "I've decided you were dumber than a box of hammers, but I may forgive you if you take that yowling fur ball off my hands. He gorped on Phil's floor and I'm not cleaning it up. I assume you aren't calling me from jail. Did you catch the black-mailer? Who was he?"

"Rob," Helen said, and told her the story.

"So he's dead for real?" Margery asked.

"Had to scrape him off the road," Helen said.

"Couldn't happen to a nicer guy," Margery said.

"Good old Margery," Helen said.

"Don't expect me to cry crocodile tears," she said. "What do you want me to do?"

"Be at Riggs Pier tonight at eight thirty and go fishing."

"And what am I catching?" Margery asked.

"A crook," Helen said.

CHAPTER 26

"Valerie Cannata, are you really wearing pink Crocs?" Helen said.

The woman in the gray sweatpants and supersized T-shirt was the same size and shape as the investigative reporter. But Helen was sure Valerie had never been in a Target parking lot, unless she was on assignment. She locked the Igloo and ran toward her.

Valerie looked worried. "Quick!" she said, sliding into the driver's side of the shiny black Mercedes. "Get in before someone sees me."

"I never thought I'd use 'Valerie Cannata' and 'Crocs' in the same sentence," Helen said. "Are they more comfortable than your usual sky-high Manolos?"

"My feet shriveled when I stepped in these things," Valerie said, and shuddered delicately. "The sacrifices I make for my profession."

Helen had barely buckled her seat belt when Valerie roared out of her parking spot toward the exit.

"Which designer did your T-shirt?" Helen teased. "Nice cat. Love the glitter."

"It was a gift from a sweet fan," Valerie said. Her long nails were stripped of polish and her chic dark hair was hidden under a frizzy gray wig.

Valerie dodged a woman pushing a shopping cart and was out on the street and over the speed limit.

"We're okay for time," Helen said, hoping Valerie would slow down. "It's only eight o'clock. We'll have no problem getting to Cy's restaurant by eight thirty."

"I'm not worried about time," Valerie said. "One of our satellite trucks is two blocks over. I don't want anyone from the station to see me. I'm sneaking out to tape this." She sounded giddy with excitement.

"Your boss doesn't know?" Helen said.

"He knows I'm working on the Riggs Beach story," Valerie said. "But he doesn't know I'm taping the commissioner."

"Valerie, is that a good idea?" Helen asked.

"I'm silent taping—video but no audio," she said. "That's legal in Florida. My boss has been in meetings all day. It's sweeps. He'll be thrilled when I bag another exclusive."

"Did you bring the hidden camera?" Helen asked.

"I borrowed it," Valerie said.

"Borrowed it how?" Helen asked.

"Sneaked it out without authorization," Valerie said. "But don't worry. All is forgiven for a good story. This will work out, won't it?"

"It has so far," Helen said. "We've done risky stories before."

"And the ratings made them worth it," Valerie said.

"Where's the camera?" Helen asked.

"Check out the bag in the back," Valerie said.

Helen saw a frumpy brown vinyl purse as big as a gym bag. "I cut a hole in the vinyl near the clasp for the lens," Valerie said. "Hideous, isn't it?"

"That purse will age you twenty years," Helen said. "Speaking of hideous, what do you think of my outfit?"

"You look different as a blond," Valerie said.

"I look awful," Helen said. "This blond wig makes my skin look jaundiced. I stuck with the classic tourist look: an 'I Heart Florida' shirt and polyester pants."

"What happened to your face?" Valerie asked. "Your forehead is bruised and that cut looks nasty."

"It looks worse than it feels," Helen said. "I've got a floppy fishing hat in my purse that will hide it."

"Will the person who gave you the tip be at the restaurant tonight?" Valerie asked.

"Nowhere near," Helen said. "Cy set this bribery scheme up in advance so only one server will be on duty. The kitchen staff has been ordered to leave at nine, even if their work isn't finished. I'll meet my source for coffee late tomorrow morning."

"Think she'll talk to me? I can disguise her voice and hide her face for the interview."

"She'd still be too scared," Helen said.

"Does she work for Cy?" Valerie asked.

Helen searched for an answer and couldn't think of anything.

"You don't have to say it. She's right to be afraid," Valerie said. "Cy is a big deal in the Riggs Beach Chamber of Commerce, but he played rough when he ran drugs in the eighties."

"You know about that?" Helen said.

"I've heard rumors," Valerie said. "No proof. But two of his associates disappeared in 1986. Cy claimed they left the country. All I can find out is they've never been seen again. That's why I'm going out on a limb to tape this tonight. It may be the only way to get Cy."

She turned into the pier parking lot. "Okay, Helen. From now on, we're tourists. Where are you from?"

"St. Louis," Helen said.

"I'm from Oyster Bay in New York." Valerie reached in back for the ugly bag. "Keep talking tourist." She locked the Mercedes while Helen clapped the floppy beige fishing hat on her wig.

"So what's the weather like back home?" Helen asked as they walked toward the main entrance to Cy's on the Pier.

"I called my sister," Valerie said. "She says it's drizzling. I always feel like I get my money's worth if it's yucky back home."

Helen scanned the pier, which was lined with anglers. She spotted Margery about halfway down. Their landlady had rented a fishing pole and bought bait. She didn't bother with a disguise. She blended in well wearing a purple shorts set and lavender tennis shoes.

Good, Helen thought. Margery can run if she has to.

The restaurant looked almost romantic at night. The low lights mellowed the corny fishing nets and dusty seashell decor. Each table had a thick white shell with a lit candle.

"Isn't this cute?" Valerie said. "I love the candles."

"How's your kitty now that you're gone?" Helen asked.

"The cat sitter says Fluffy is sulking," Valerie said. "Looks like I'll get the cold shoulder when I get home."

"Thumbs does that to me," Helen said, "for about ten minutes. The closer we are to dinnertime, the sooner I'm forgiven."

"Cats are so cynical," Valerie said.

"They're practical," Helen said.

Inside the restaurant, Phil was eating a burger at a table by the door. He had on his redneck disguise. His distinctive hair was hidden by a gimme cap with its own curly brown hair. He wore a SILENCE IS GOLDEN—DUCT TAPE IS SILVER T-shirt and disreputable jeans.

He snapped his fingers at the lone server, a generously proportioned woman with a sweet, plain face. "I'll take some more coffee, darlin'," he drawled.

The server fought hard to conceal her distaste. "As soon as I seat these ladies," she said.

"Please," Helen said in a low voice. "Not near him."

"I've got a nice table for you ladies here with a view," the server said. Her name tag said she was Bridget.

"Perfect," Helen said.

Their table for four had a splendid view. It was in a direct line with the booth containing Cy Horton and Commissioner Frank

Gordon. They could also see a small strip of the pier and the ocean. Just past the booth was the door to the pier.

"I love the view," Valerie said, and plopped her purse on the chair facing the booth, the clasp aimed at the two diners.

"Do you ladies want time to study the menus, or do you know what you want?" Bridget asked. "The kitchen closes at nine tonight."

"I'll have a turkey burger and black coffee," Helen said.

"Mixed green salad with the dressing on the side," Valerie said, "and black coffee."

Bridget buzzed over to the booth and took Frank's nearly empty platter. Once again, Frank the Fixer was a stellar member of the Clean Plate Club. His steak platter was bare except for a T-bone without a shred of meat and an empty sour cream container. He must have eaten the baked potato, skin and all, plus his vegetables. The roll basket was empty, too.

"How about a slice of Key lime pie and coffee?" Cy asked the commissioner.

Frank nodded.

"Two pies and two coffees," Cy said.

"Yes, sir," Bridget said.

Both men studied Helen and Valerie while they talked like tourists. "Thumbs did the cutest thing when I was packing for my trip," Helen said. "He jumped in my suitcase and refused to leave. I had to carry him out of the room. He really didn't want me to go."

"My Fluffy sits on the case and looks sad," Valerie said. She switched to baby talk. " 'I'll be back, widdle kitty,' I tell her, 'and I'll bwing you a nice big tweat.' "

"Did you get her a treat this time?" Helen asked.

"I want to buy some wild salmon tomorrow at the pet store on A1A," Valerie said.

The two women discussed cats until the men's eyes glazed over and they went back to their conversation.

Helen felt something nudge her foot and realized Valerie wanted her attention. "My cat can take over the whole bed, and she only weighs ten pounds," she said, and spread her arms wide, her index finger pointing toward the booth.

Helen shifted her eyes. Cy was handing Frank the Fixer a big, heavy carryout bag. Valerie adjusted the purse for a better view.

"Here you go," Cy said. "Four days' worth."

"That should keep me happy," Frank said, and winked.

Cy didn't smile back. He jumped up and said, "Wait a minute. These broads aren't babbling about their cats. They're watching us." He pointed to Helen. "I know you!" he said. "You're no tourist. You're that bitch who's been hanging around here, causing trouble with my staff. And you're no blonde, either."

He flicked off Helen's hat and ripped off her wig.

"And I know your voice," Frank said to Valerie. "I hear it every day on TV. You're that reporter for Channel Seventy-seven."

"How dare you!" Valerie said.

"I'm right. You wouldn't be caught dead with that ugly purse," he said. "Everything you wear has a designer name on it. What's in there?"

He lunged for the bag and unzipped it. "A hidden camera!" he screamed. "The bitch has been videoing us." Commissioner Frank stuffed the bag under his arm like a football and charged out the pier door. Helen saw him toss the bag over the pier railing.

"No!" Valerie screamed, running after him.

Frank laughed at her. "You want it? Go get it."

Valerie tore off her wig, kicked off her Crocs and leaped into the strong current.

Helen tried to run after her, but Cy swung at her. He missed. She picked up the heavy shell on the table and hit Cy on the head. Hard. He flopped down hard on the floor, dazed.

Meanwhile, the lean, long-toothed commissioner leaped over the dazed restaurant owner, snatched the carryout bag of bribe money and charged toward the main door. Phil blocked his way.

The commissioner threw the nearest shell at Phil, winging him in the shoulder. Phil wrestled him to the ground and knocked over another shell. Its candle slid across the table and landed on the dry fishing-net wall decoration. That caught fire; then the cork floats and a stack of paper napkins began to burn. A bottle of olive oil in a salad set spilled, splashed and ignited.

The fire spread to the cash register, where a rack of potato chip bags burst into flame. The room was filling with smoke. Helen choked and tried to find Phil.

The commissioner fought free of Phil, abandoned the bribe money and sprinted out the other way, onto the fishing pier.

"Fire!" Helen shouted.

Phil pulled the wall alarm and rushed back to the kitchen, where he led the server, cook and dishwasher onto the pier to safety.

Cy tried to run out on the pier, but Helen hit him with a chair, and he was out cold. By now the fire was crackling and two walls were burning. She pocketed Cy's cell phone and dragged him outside on the pier. Phil was chasing the commissioner. Frank ran past Margery on the pier, and she whacked the commissioner with her fishing pole. That slowed him down, but he was up and running again. Phil jumped on him and slugged him. He fought back, and Phil had a hard time subduing him. The commissioner was surprisingly strong. Helen ripped a fishnet decoration off the wall by the door and threw it over the commissioner. That stopped him.

"We caught ourselves a big fish," she said.

CHAPTER 27

"Why were you at Mr. Horton's restaurant, Miss Hawthorne?" Detective Emmet Ebmeier asked.

Helen had lost track of how many times he'd asked her that. The Riggs Beach detective looked as bad as Helen felt: He had a five o'clock shadow at two in the morning, his scrawny body was jittery as a junkie's, and his weary eyes were buried in dark bags.

His thin slit of a mouth opened like a trap. "I asked you a question. Why were you at Cy's on the Pier?" His words were soft and menacing.

Helen fought to remember the story she and Phil had cooked up before the Riggs Beach cops shoved them into separate patrol cars, then stuck them in two smelly, barren police interrogation rooms. They'd agreed on three things: They wouldn't mention they were PIs, say why they were at the restaurant or ask for an attorney.

All three decisions were risky, but the last one was downright stupid, Helen thought. "I told you. I was having dinner with my friend Valerie Cannata."

"And both of you were wearing wigs?" the detective said.

"No law against that," Helen said. She felt like a stuck DVD. She couldn't go forward or backward and the picture was breaking up.

"But there is a law against assaulting a restaurant owner," Ebmeier said. "And slugging a city commissioner."

"I didn't hit the commissioner," Helen said.

"You started a fire," he said. "That's arson."

"No, I did not," she said. "A candle was knocked over when the commissioner ran away. Did he tell you why he ran?"

"Any smart person runs from a fire," he said. "The fire chief tells me Mr. Horton's restaurant is a total loss."

Helen noted the respectful "mister" and "commissioner" titles. Phil said the detective was a crook. Ebmeier would serve the men who let him take bribes.

"The fishing pier's saved," he said. "Good thing all those innocent fishermen escaped, or I'd be charging you with murder. You're damn lucky."

Why do people always say "You're lucky" when something unlucky happens? she wondered. I've answered these same questions for four hours straight. Sorry, Phil. I've had enough.

"I'm not saying another word," Helen said. "I want my lawyer, Nancie Hays. Either charge me or set me free."

There was a knock on the door. Detective Ebmeier cracked it. Helen heard mumbled conversation; then the detective stepped into the hall, leaving her alone. She must have nodded off. She started when he reentered the room. Her eyelids felt heavy and crusted.

"I'm supposed to let you go," he said. "Commissioner Gordon and Mr. Horton have decided not to press charges. Your husband is in the lobby, along with that reporter. And don't thank me. If I had my way, your ass would be in jail."

Helen staggered out of the room, so tired she had trouble focusing. She saw a bedraggled Valerie and Phil, huddled like castaways on a bench in the lobby.

Valerie's usual straight dark hair hung in stringy clumps and her glitter cat shirt was wrinkled, stained and baggy. She'd lost the Crocs and the wig.

Under the fluorescent lights, Phil looked vampire white with fatigue. Still in his lowlife disguise, he fit right in as a cop catch of the day. Margery, pacing near the door, was the only one who seemed alert. The nerve-wracking evening had energized her.

"We need to talk," Margery said.

"Valerie will have to drive me to my car," Helen said.

"We'll collect it in the morning," Margery said. "You'll all fit in my car. I drove here."

"We can talk while you drive me to my car at the pier," Valerie said. "I have to be at the station at five tomorrow." The night was moonless, sticky and unnaturally still. Margery had parked under a streetlight across from the police station. She lit a cigarette and took a long drag while Phil and Helen slid into the backseat. Helen moved close to her husband, but he scooted away. Okay, she thought, if that's the way you want to play it. She slid back toward the window and crossed her arms.

Valerie didn't notice this domestic drama. She collapsed in the front seat, put her head back and closed her eyes.

Margery crushed out her cigarette and climbed into the driver's seat, bringing a whiff of cigarette smoke. "I needed that," she said.

When the landlady's white Lincoln Town Car was headed toward the pier parking lot, Helen asked, "How are you, Valerie? The last time I saw you, you were diving over the rails for your camera. Did you find it?"

"It's gone," Valerie said, her voice flat and tired. "I was nearly swept away, too. The current was so strong, I had to hang on to the pier pilings. I'm lucky I was able to pull myself out of the water. I'm just glad you're not in jail." She yawned. "Keep talking, please. I'm exhausted. I want to listen for a bit."

"I don't understand why the police didn't arrest us," Helen said.

"I do," Phil said. "Cy and the commissioner didn't want to call attention to themselves. Where there's smoke, there's fire—in this case, for real."

"That's how this city has always operated," Margery said. "They can hush things up in Riggs Beach, but they don't like outsiders poking around. In the sixties, they voluntarily desegregated to keep the feds away."

"We owe our freedom to Margery," Phil said. "She showed up at the station and demanded the police take her statement as a witness, then waited for us."

"I thought I'd be camped in that lobby all night," Margery said. "They wouldn't let me smoke. By two o'clock, I was desperate. I told the desk sergeant I was calling Channel Fifty-four to tell them the news. He laughed and said every major station was covering the fire.

"I said, 'Maybe, but they don't know about the big fight with Commissioner Frank Gordon. That TV station will love a story about Seventy-seven screwing up.'

"The desk sergeant still didn't get off his duff, so I pulled out my cell phone and said, 'I saw Cy Horton hand Commissioner Gordon a bag of money disguised as restaurant carryout. I'll be happy to show Channel Fifty-four where I last saw it.'

"Never saw a fat man move so fast." She grinned.

"It worked," Phil said. "Ten minutes later, the cops let me go. They set me free right before Helen."

Helen saw Valerie shivering in the front seat. "Is the air-conditioning too cold?" she asked.

"I'm fine," Valerie said. "Just tired, like I said."

"What's going to happen to you?" Helen asked.

"I'm in trouble," Valerie said. Helen could tell the normally bold reporter was frightened.

"Will you have to pay for your lost camera?" she asked.

"That's the least of my worries," Valerie said. "I wasn't authorized to be there tonight, taping."

"I thought two-party taping was illegal in Florida," Phil said.

"I was silent taping, video only," Valerie said. "I do that all the time. But I need permission and I didn't have it. I could get fired. Cy told me he's going to sue the station."

"He won't do that," Helen said. "He'd call attention to himself."

"People sue us all the time," Valerie said. "Most viewers have no idea. It's not something we broadcast on the news. But when he files suit, word will get out among the courthouse wonks and the rumor mill will go into overdrive."

"That lawsuit is frivolous," Phil said. "It will never get past a judge."

"Cy can threaten, though," Valerie said, "and there's nothing a TV station hates more than paying a lawyer to defend someone—unless it's having to actually pay a judgment.

"This is the worst possible time. My contract is up for renewal. I'm very, very nervous, because the last thing you want to do is cause trouble before contract renewal, and trouble especially means costing the station money. Just the threat of a lawsuit is a terrible thing. Even if you know you're right, a lawsuit never feels right. Besides, I'm forty. That's old for TV."

"Old?" Margery said, and snorted. "You're a baby."

"You don't look forty," Helen said.

"You've got a huge following," Phil said. "You're the face of the station."

"Which means I make the big bucks," Valerie said. "The station may decide it's time to find a newer, cheaper face. They could hire three or four twentysomethings for what I make."

"Do you really think you'll be fired?" Helen asked.

"I don't know," Valerie said. "If I'm lucky, they'll put me on probation. Which means I'll have to come up with something good soon. Please, please, promise you'll call me if you get something. I need a good story to save my career."

"You know we will," Phil said. "You're our first choice. We owe our success to you."

A success you want to throw away, Helen thought. "We'll come up with something for you," she said. "Wait! I do have something. I snagged Cy's cell phone during the fight." She rummaged in her purse and pulled it out. "He loves to text."

"Check his messages," Margery said.

Helen thumbed through them. "I see six from his wife and three from Commissioner Frank Gordon. His wife wants him to pick up a loaf of bread when he stops by Publix."

"Helen!" Margery and Valerie shouted. "Read the commissioner's messages."

"The oldest one says, 'Must have four days,' " Helen said. "My tipster told me 'days' is their code word for the amount of the bribe. It's twelve thousand dollars, one day's take on the pier parking lot."

Phil whistled.

"The next one says, 'Carryout tonight at eight forty-five.' He's talking about picking up the bribe in that carryout bag."

"Except the bag burned up in the fire and the video was swept away by the current," Valerie said. "We have no proof."

"We might," Helen said. "My tipster's a server at the restaurant. Maybe I can talk her into an interview with you. She was afraid of losing her job, but it's gone now anyway."

"Oh, could you?" Valerie said. "If she'll talk, I'll be forgiven everything. You know I protect my sources. I'll go to jail before I'll talk. When are you meeting?"

"The day after tomorrow at the Brew Urban Cafe," Helen said.

"Is that the coffeehouse on Southwest Second Avenue near the railroad tracks?" Phil asked.

"I've been there," Valerie said. "It's the hippest coffeehouse in Lauderdale. Call me as soon as you talk to her." Now she was alert, awake and hopeful. Even her hair looked better.

Her elation was catching and the mood lightened in the big white car.

Until Margery turned on Riggs Beach Road. The street was blocked about a quarter mile from the pier. Through the thicket of police, fire trucks and TV vans, they could see the devastation. Only the charred bones of the restaurant remained. Firefighters in turnout gear guarded the blackened ruins. The burned restaurant smelled good, as if someone had lit a huge campfire.

"Oh. Sweet. Jesus," Valerie said, her words like a prayer. "Look at all the media. How am I going to get to my car without someone recognizing me?"

"You can have my Billy Ray cap," Phil said. "The hair is attached." He whipped the cap off his head, and the fake brown hair dangled like a dead rat.

"Thank you, Phil," Valerie said. She jammed her hair under it. Now she looked like a miscreant on the TV show *Cops*.

"I'll make sure you get it back," she said.

"Don't wash it," Phil said. "You'll ruin it. I'll walk you to your car. My Jeep is parked there, too."

Helen started to slide out with him, but Phil turned on her. "Ride with Margery," he said coldly. "We'll meet in the office tomorrow."

"Oh, Phil," Margery said sweetly. "May I speak with you a moment?"

Valerie loitered out of earshot near the car bumper while Phil jogged over to Margery's window.

"I see you haven't come to your senses yet," she said, all sweetness gone.

"I can't trust her," Phil said. "She's wrong."

"She is," Margery said. "She's guilty of criminal stupidity. But if you dump her and dissolve Coronado Investigations, what are you going to do? Your last PI job blacklisted you. You need a female operative. And don't look at me. I have an apartment to run. You need someone younger who can work full-time.

"So if you ask me, you should swallow your pride."

"Thank you, Margery, but I didn't ask you," Phil said. Helen felt the chill in the backseat.

He left. She was alone, staring at the smoldering ruins.

CHAPTER 28

"Found something. Meet me in 2C 11 a.m.," the e-mail read. Phil sent that at nine twenty-two the next morning, and the tiny *ding!* of his new e-mail woke up Helen. She'd fallen asleep with her laptop open on her bed. Her vast, empty bed.

Eight words. That's all Phil wrote, Helen thought. He didn't even sign it, or ask if I'm free at that hour. He just assumed I'll show up. I won't play games. I'll finish this case and get on with my life. And stop sounding like a self-help article.

Her anger burned away her grogginess. She'd slept late in her apartment. No husband woke her whistling in the shower. Helen had always found Phil's early-bird cheer annoying. Now she missed it. She even missed Thumbs demanding breakfast at seven o'clock.

Neither one missed her. The weight of last night's failure came crashing down. Her tiny apartment felt huge and lonely.

She fought back with a pep talk. Time to pick myself up and start over, she decided. I did it before and I can do it again. After coffee.

She set up the coffeemaker and noticed her hair smelled of smoke. She'd been too tired to shower when she got home. She'd do it while the coffee was brewing.

Her closet-sized bathroom was deliciously steamy. She started a bold song about washing that "man right outta my hair," but her voice wobbled and her tears mingled with the shower water.

Enough with the waterworks. Helen turned off the tears and the shower, poured some coffee and blow-dried her hair. It seemed to take forever to dry in the humidity. The scratch on her forehead was healing. She draped her bangs to cover the wound, then dressed extra-carefully in her black pencil skirt and the fluttery-sleeved pink-and-black blouse she'd bought at Cerise.

Helen checked herself in the mirror: glossy dark hair with a bit of curl, touch of pink lipstick and dark mascara. The skirt and blouse weren't bad, she decided. No, they were stunning. Eat your heart out, Phil.

She slipped on her black sandals, opened her door to a glorious sunny day, then marched across the Coronado yard and straight up the stairs to 2C. Helen didn't knock. It was her office, too.

She opened the door exactly five minutes late.

Phil was at his desk. Her heart melted. Almost melted. She hardened her aching heart, sat in her black partner's chair and said nothing. He'd called the meeting. He could speak first.

Phil fiddled with his coffee cup but didn't offer her any. Last night took its toll on him, Helen thought. He's ashen and the lines around his eyes look deeper.

He cleared his throat and said, "We still have to find out who killed Ceci and save Sunny Jim's business."

She nodded. He shifted in his chair. Her silence made him uneasy. Good.

"Her husband, Daniel, is still a suspect," he said. "We have a good motive—the insurance policy and Daniel's affair—but I can't find any Florida connection. I'll show his picture around the dive shops and beach bars and see if anyone remembers him."

Helen broke the next uncomfortable silence with "What if Cy hired Randy the diver to kill Ceci?"

"The restaurant owner didn't know her. Why would he kill Daniel's wife?" Phil asked.

"To ruin Sunny Jim's business," Helen said.

"Max told us the killer had to know what time Ceci started paddleboarding," Phil said. "He couldn't hang around the pier in a black dive suit with an underwater scooter. Why would Cy buy the commissioner's vote if he'd already hired a killer? He'd be spending double the money for the same result."

"Makes sense," Helen said. She didn't bother hiding her doubts. "I can ask the staff at the Full Moon Hotel if Daniel went anywhere except the usual tourist places."

"No need," Phil said. "He used credit cards. I've already checked his bill online. He and Ceci only went to tourist spots. I've been looking into Bill Morris Bantry, the owner of Bill's Boards. That's what I wanted to tell you. Turns out Sunny Jim's rival is a killer."

"He went to jail for murder?" Helen asked.

"He was tried for manslaughter," Phil said, "but not convicted. Bill used to live in the Florida Panhandle, in Pensacola, with his fiancée, a twenty-year-old named Tiffany. She disappeared ten years ago.

"Bill was questioned by the police. He kept to his story: The couple had argued after a long night at the clubs. Tiffany wanted out of the car so she could watch the sunrise on the beach. Alone. She was never seen again.

"Bill claimed he let her out, went for breakfast and spent the day at his mother's house, repairing her roof and gutters. Two days later, Tiffany's family reported their daughter missing. Bill didn't bother to call the police and he didn't help search for her."

"And she was supposed to be his fiancée?" Helen asked.

"That's why her family said Bill murdered Tiffany," Phil said. "No point in joining in the search if he knew she was dead. Her body was never found and there was no forensic evidence that she was dead.

"The cops arrested Bill. At the trial, his lawyer tried Tiffany, dragging her name through the mud. She'd been a wild child, charged with possession and prostitution. Bill's lawyer said Tiffany was killed by a drug dealer or a former pimp. Bill was acquitted. After his mother's death a year later, he sold her house and moved to Riggs Beach to start over. His beach rental business is struggling, like Sunny Jim's. Maybe more so, since Bill isn't a local."

"You agree with the family and the cops?" Helen said.

"Bill's a killer," Phil said. "He killed Tiffany and got away with it. Now maybe he's getting away with murder again. He's bold. He challenged Sunny Jim on his own turf, setting up his rental business next door to Jim on the beach. He's worried about his business. He hired his employee, Randy, to wreck Jim's business at spring break. When that didn't work, he paid Randy to kill a customer and ruin Jim's business permanently. Bill knew and trusted Randy."

"Makes sense that Bill would go one step further and kill Ceci," Helen said. "But why not do it himself?"

"With his past?" Phil said. "Bill barely avoided a murder conviction when his fiancée disappeared. The last thing he wants is more police attention, even in Riggs Beach. Besides, I can't find any evidence that Cy ever talked to Randy. The diver sure didn't eat there. Cy's restaurant is too upscale."

"But how did Randy know what time Ceci went paddleboarding?" Helen asked.

"Easy," Phil said. "I asked Sunny Jim if he'd had any odd calls lately. Jim remembered one. The day before Ceci was murdered, a tourist called wanting to book boards for a big group—a party of eight—from ten to noon. Jim said he didn't have eight boards because he had two reservations at ten o'clock. Most of Jim's group bookings are for three or four people. Eight is unusual.

"Bill and Randy know exactly how many boards Jim has. When Jim said he had two ten o'clock appointments, that tipped them off when his customers were going out."

"That's what Margery said the killer would do," Helen said. "Turned out Sunny Jim only had one paddleboard rental that morning. Ceci went paddleboarding alone, which made her even easier to kill. That theory is plausible, but you can't prove it."

"I need to find Randy, the missing diver who rented the underwater scooter," Phil said. "I got a tip he's back and hanging around in the Riggs Beach dives along A1A. I'll go there this afternoon."

"I don't meet with the server, Joan Right, until tomorrow morning at seven," Helen said. "I have to persuade her to talk to Valerie so our TV friend can save her job. Joan is terrified."

"She can't be worried about losing her job," Phil said. "It went up in smoke." He didn't seem aware of the pun.

"I think she's afraid of Cy," Helen said. "Valerie says she should be. Some of his smuggling buddies disappeared in the eighties. Did you hear from Valerie yet?"

"No. I watched Channel Seventy-seven, but she wasn't on. That doesn't necessarily mean anything."

"I feel bad that things went south last night," Helen said.

"We got too used to good luck," Phil said. "We started counting on it."

I wonder if that was a royal "we," she thought. Or did Phil mean himself and me? Or is Valerie the second person? Phil and Valerie were lovers long before he met and married me. They both moved on. Didn't they?

Helen tried to push that thought out of her mind, but she knew Valerie was rich, famous and glamorous.

"I still think Cy is up to something," she said. "He's greedy and desperate. I'll talk to Alana, the manager at his boutique, as soon as I leave here. She knows Cy way better than I ever want to."

"She sleeps with him to get cheap rent, right?" Phil said.

"And doesn't hesitate to tell me," Helen said. "Alana is the original Miss TMI."

"Let me know what happens," Phil said. He made no move toward her. She left, head high.

All the way to Riggs Beach, Helen replayed their conversation in her mind. She didn't know how to react. Was Phil being professional or was he thawing slightly?

As she approached the pier parking lot, Helen heard the wildcat screams of power saws and furious hammering. Workers were constructing a temporary wooden walkway to the pier. A mobile sign flashed: FISHING PIER OPEN AT 5 PM TODAY! YES, WE SELL BAIT!

Riggs Beach didn't waste time recovering.

A knot of gawkers watched a growling backhoe bite into the blackened restaurant rubble and drop it into a construction Dumpster that took up five precious parking spots. Helen was lucky to find an open slot.

She breathed in the soft, salty ocean air, slightly tinged with wood smoke. Helen swung by Sunny Jim's on her way to Cerise. His yellow banners and canopy made a brave show, but Jim was staring glumly at the restaurant ruins.

"My business fell from zero to below zero," he said. "People aren't even stopping by to ask how much it costs to rent a paddleboard. I've been entertaining myself watching that tourist."

A sunburned man in lime board shorts gingerly carried a big bluish crab to the water. The crab, big as a saucer, wiggled its hairy legs and waved its claws dangerously close to the man's thumbs.

"That crab looks angry," Helen said. "I mean, if crabs get angry."

"That one's pissed, all right," Jim said. "It's a land crab. They don't like salt water once they're adults. Buncha land crabs live in burrows by that sea grass there. This is the third time he's thrown that poor creature in the water. I better tell him before that crab takes a hunk of his hand.

"Hey, dude!" Jim said. "Dude in the green! Drop that crab."

"You talking to me?" the man asked. He was in his twenties, with buzzed brown hair and small features scrunched together in his red face.

"Yeah. That's a land crab," Jim said. "You aren't doing it any favors dunking it in the ocean. It hates salt water."

"Can I, like, eat it?" the man asked.

"You can," Jim said. "It can eat you, too. Watch your hand!" The crab's sharp claw lunged for the tourist's thumb. He dropped the crab and leaped back before it attacked his bare toes. The crab scuttled across the sand to the sea grass. The tourist waved at Jim and ran into the ocean.

"How's the investigation going?" Jim asked.

"Our trip to St. Louis helped. We found Ceci's husband had a good motive for wanting her dead," Helen said, "but we have other suspects. We're both interviewing today. I'm on my way to Cy's boutique."

Helen enjoyed her stroll to Cerise in the warm afternoon sun. The boutique was empty at one o'clock. Alana greeted her with a big smile.

"Helen! I'm glad you came by," she said. "This place is deader than disco. I've got some new things I know you'll like." Her dangly gold earrings jingled cheerfully as she plucked blouses off the racks. "This white blouse looks simple, but it's dynamite on. This tie-dyed turquoise silk is fabulous. Try them on."

In the dressing room, Helen liked both but decided to buy the silk tie-dye. She'd come back for the white blouse if she needed to talk to Alana later.

Alana's gauzy red print top set off her golden-brown skin and long blond hair. She should have been homely with her long nose and overbite, but they made her more attractive.

She wrapped Helen's purchase with swift, deft fingers, then rang it up, talking nonstop. "I guess you saw what happened to Cy's last night," she said.

"It's totaled," Helen said. "I parked my car at the pier lot."

"Cy is beside himself," Alana said. "He came by my apartment at two this morning. Didn't even call. Said he lost his cell phone in the fire."

"Really?" Helen said. "What started it?"

"Some clumsy customer knocked over a candle and those stupid fishnets caught fire."

Cy wasn't talking about what really happened, Helen thought. Good to know.

"I warned Cy not to use those crappy shells with candles stuck in them," she said. "They're too easy to knock over. But he's too cheap to buy decent candles. His cheap ways cost him big-time.

"He came by my place looking for sympathy. I should get workers' comp for repetitive motion injury. He said he was horny, but he couldn't get it up with a derrick. My hand still hurts."

She used that hurting hand to give Helen her shopping bag—and way too much information.

"If he wants anything else this month, he's going to have to give me this."

Alana held up a sheer peach paisley dress.

Helen whistled. "That's perfect for you," she said.

"Retails for sixteen hundred," Alana said. "I'm worth every penny. He spends too much on that damned boat of his. Oh, I shouldn't complain. I do have an apartment with a fabulous ocean view."

But what you have to see to get it, Helen thought, and hoped her face didn't show her disgust. A customer came in, and Helen waved good-bye, promising, "I'll be back."

Helen checked her cell phone. Phil had sent her this message: "Found diver at Beached. Meet me at the ice cream shop on A1A near Riggs Beach Road."

Beached was a nasty little hole-in-the-wall in a strip of grungy T-shirt shops and bars along the ocean. She was glad Phil didn't want to meet in the bar, but when she reached it ten minutes later, she peeked inside the open door. It was so dark, she could only make out two customers slumped over their beers and a nearly life-sized framed photo of a hairy naked man on a toilet. "Only one here who knows what he's doing," it said underneath.

Ew.

"Hey, baby, come on in," someone shouted from a dark corner. "Sweet cheeks, don't leave," said another. "You look like you could use a real man," shouted a third. Helen escaped in a chorus of whistles and catcalls.

The ice cream shop seemed sweet, clean and innocent after the dingy bar. Phil was at an outside table, eating rocky road in a waffle cone. Helen ordered a scoop of chocolate chip and joined him.

"I found Randy," Phil said. "He was easy to track down. He's been spending money in the beach bars since he got back. He was sloppy drunk and said he didn't have anything to do with Ceci's murder.

"I asked him if he'd been hired by Bill's Boards or Cy to kill Ceci. He said, 'I ain't talking. I don't want to get killed, too,' and started to leave.

"I gave him my card and said, 'Contact me if you want to make a deal before it's too late.' I doubt he was sober enough to know what I was saying, but he stuck the card in his pocket."

Helen told him about her encounter with Alana.

"I think her apartment is worth staking out tonight," she said. "Cy may be seeing more of her now that he's in trouble. Do you want to do the stakeout, or should I?"

"I'll take tonight," he said. "You need to be in good shape for tomorrow. Joan will take all your persuasive powers at seven in the morning. I'll walk you back to the parking lot."

They parted on what Helen thought were good terms. She took the faster route back to the Coronado, except this time, it wasn't. A traffic accident kept her stuck on Federal Highway for thirty minutes.

As she pulled into the Coronado parking lot, she saw Phil's Jeep and a locksmith's truck. Was someone new moving in? she wondered as she crossed the courtyard and stopped dead.

A uniformed locksmith handed Phil two keys and said, "If you need more, call this number."

Phil had had the locks changed on his door. She felt like she'd been stabbed. Helen hurt so bad, she could hardly walk to her apartment. She wanted to be alone, like a wounded animal.

CHAPTER 29

B rew Urban Cafe opened its door at seven o'clock, and Helen was nearly trampled by a trio of coffee fiends. She stepped aside to let them order. She was jittery, too, but not because she needed caffeine. She had to find the words to persuade Joan to give Valerie an interview.

Helen plunked an alternative paper on a table hugging a wall of colorful art. After the rush was over, she stepped up to the counter for a caffe latte, made with espresso.

The barista's white fern in the velvetized milk was so pretty, she almost didn't want to drink it, but the rich roasted coffee was too tempting. The espresso jolted her brain after the first sip.

What was Joan doing now that the restaurant had burned? she wondered. Was she working somewhere else? Collecting unemployment? Cy wouldn't pay his staff while he rebuilt. Maybe that would help Valerie.

Valerie protects her sources, Helen thought. I know from personal experience. I'll tell Joan this interview will be safe. But she remembered some anonymous TV interviews she'd seen. Undercover cops speaking from deep shadow. Disgruntled employees with digitized screens over their faces. She could always pick out a distinctive feature—a nose or ear shape. Even if the voices were disguised, most people had favorite phrases. Cy would be able to identify Joan.

Promises of confidentiality wouldn't pay Joan's rent once Cy knew she'd blabbed to a reporter. He could blacklist her at other Riggs Beach restaurants.

But Valerie knew everybody in Lauderdale. Joan was a good server. If the TV reporter could get Joan a job at a better restaurant with big tippers, Joan wouldn't have to worry about Cy.

At 7:12, Helen called Valerie on her cell phone. The TV reporter answered on the second ring. "Helen," she said, her voice quick and telegraphic. "On my way to meet with management."

"How are you?" Helen asked.

"On probation," Valerie said. "Scared. Watching a parade of younger, prettier women come in for interviews. I'm dead if I don't come up with a scoop. Did you talk with your source? Will she talk to me?"

Helen heard her desperate hope and hated to crush it. "Not yet. She's on her way. This interview could kill any chance for a job in Riggs Beach. Do you know a good Lauderdale restaurant that's hiring? She's an experienced server."

"I'm dating Ben, executive chef at Fresh Ocean," Valerie said. "It's a business restaurant. Ben complained one new staffer is showing up hungover. I'll put in a word for her."

"Thanks," Helen said. "I'll call you as soon as we talk. Hang in there."

Helen tried to relax, but she jumped every time the cafe door opened. The TV screen perpetually played black-and-white films with the sound off. Helen didn't know which classic this was, but she saw a British courtroom and recognized Tyrone Power's dark good looks. *Witness for the Prosecution?* Phil would know. He's good at movies. He's locked me out of his life.

A mournful train whistle from the tracks alongside the cafe underscored the movie's noir feel—and her own loss.

Helen checked her watch: 7:17. No Joan. She must have gotten stuck in rush-hour traffic. Helen opened the free paper but couldn't concentrate enough to read it.

Next time she looked, it was 7:32. Maybe Joan couldn't find the cafe. It was on Southwest Second Avenue at Southwest Second Street, one of those loony Lauderdale addresses that locals insisted were logical.

Scratch that theory. Joan had suggested the cafe because she didn't like the big coffee chains.

Helen called Joan's cell phone at 7:43. *"I'm not here to take your call. Please leave a message,"* Joan's voice said. Helen left an anxious message. Of course Joan isn't answering the phone while she's driving, she told herself.

Helen looked up hopefully when the door opened but saw a red-eyed young man with a plaid shirt and fashionable stubble. He winced at the sound of the door shutting. A refugee from last night's revels?

Lauderdale's hippest coffeehouse was in Himmarshee, a historic area with low, flat-fronted buildings. At night, the streets were packed with twentysomethings searching for a party. At eight in the morning, most of those party-hearty types were sleeping off their good time. Except for this molting early bird.

It was now 7:58. Joan got the time wrong, Helen decided. She thought we were meeting at eight. She'll come through the door any second.

On cue, the door swung open.

And two women in suits walked in.

I need more caffeine, Helen thought. It will save time when Joan shows up. She'll order her coffee, and sit down, and I'll make the case for Valerie.

This time, she upped the caffeine dose with a double espresso. While the barista worked, Helen idly read the drink menu. She loved the names on the menu: Rogue Dead Guy ale, Old Russian dark imperial stout, and the Bolshevik Revolution—Old Rasputin stout and espresso. She bet the chocolaty taste of stout went well with espresso. Phil would like that. Again, she felt a sharp pang of loss.

I haven't heard from Phil, she thought. He staked out Alana's apartment last night. Will he call or e-mail me? I'll be the adult and phone him after I talk to Joan.

Her thoughts slid painfully toward the possibility of divorce. Our marriage will be easy to dissolve. We have separate cars, apartments and bank accounts. My cat's already sided with Phil. On paper, it's a clean, simple cut. So why does my heart feel like it's been skewered with an ice pick?

Her double espresso was gone. Already? What time was it? She checked her watch again: 8:26. Joan isn't coming to Brew Urban Cafe. I should quit kidding myself and track her down. My nerves are sputtering like a broken neon sign.

I can't ask Cy where Joan is. I'll see Sunny Jim. He's so bored, he's rescuing land crabs. He may know where Joan lives. If Jim can't help me, I'll drive to Kevin's house, out past the turnpike. He's Joan's friend at the restaurant. He'll trust me.

Once she'd decided to act, Helen felt better. Outside, she squinted at the bright sunshine and slipped on her sunglasses. She was too rushed and worried to appreciate the day's perfection.

She drove to Riggs Beach in ten minutes on nearly empty roads.

That kills my theory that Joan's caught in traffic, she thought. As she turned toward the pier, Helen was snarled in the only traffic slowdown that morning. Riggs Beach Road was blocked by police, ambulances, crime scene vehicles and a Channel 54 news van.

Helen parked at a strip mall two blocks from the pier, bought sunscreen at a T-shirt shop to justify her parking spot and tossed it in the car.

The pier was thronged with anglers. A makeshift bait shop had opened under a beach umbrella at the entrance. But no one was fishing or buying bait. They were watching the drama on the beach.

Helen sprinted toward Sunny Jim's, passing paramedics unloading a stretcher from an ambulance. They were in no rush. The ominous black plastic on the stretcher said why. It was a body bag.

Oh, no. A drowning victim? One more death would be the end of Sunny Jim's business.

She loped toward the crowd clustered near his yellow canopy with the brave banners. A uniformed officer stopped her. "Sorry, miss," he said. "Police investigation."

"I work for Sunny Jim," Helen said.

The officer hesitated. His pale face was covered with peach fuzz and his button nose and red lips made him look tough as a teddy bear.

"Please?" she said and smiled, hoping she looked harmless.

"Well, all right. Since you have business there. Stay away from the investigation," he said.

"Thanks," Helen said, and ran awkwardly across the sand, which had been trampled into little hills. A breeze off the ocean blew sand in her face. Jim was watching the scene on the beach, his bronze, muscular arms folded protectively across his chest. The wind whipped his frizzy blond hair, and his sun-lined, leathery face looked sad.

Men and women in uniforms were gathered around a woman's body. The dead woman wore a wet pink T-shirt and white shorts. Her feet were bare. In life, her long legs had probably been handsomely tanned. Now they had an odd greenish cast. Her long blond hair was flat against her skull. Helen couldn't see her face.

"Jim!" she said. "Who is it? Who died?"

"Joan," he said. "Joan Right. The waitress at Cy's. She committed suicide. Dammit! Why didn't she call me if she was in trouble?"

Helen stumbled into Jim's yellow beach chair as if someone had kicked her legs out from under her.

"Not Joan," she said, hoping to deny the awful truth. "No." She felt sick. "We were supposed to meet for coffee this morning, but she never showed up. I came here because I thought you might know her."

"I do," Jim said. "I mean, I did. Joan was a little older, but we went to the same high school. Good-looking woman. Nice, too."

"Who found her?" Helen said.

"Couple of tourists, about an hour ago. They were looking for shells. Her body washed up under the pier and they dragged her out on the sand there."

Now Helen could see the drag marks, partly erased by the stampede of first responders. At the edge of the crowd, a silver-haired woman with a crumpled face sat shivering, wrapped in a blue blanket. A thin older man held her as if a rogue wave might wash her away, while a stern-faced police officer lectured them.

"That couple with the cop find her?" Helen asked.

"They got a vacation they'll never forget," Jim said. "The cop is ripping them a new one for moving the body. They were afraid the current would carry her away. The cop's wrong, and if I get a chance, I'll tell them."

"How do you know . . ." She stopped. *If I say this, then she's really dead.* But she watched the paramedics zip the body bag with that sound of terrible finality. *Face it,* she told herself. *Joan is dead.*

"How do you know Joan killed herself?" Helen asked, getting the words out in a rush.

"Cy told everyone on the beach," Jim said, "including the reporters scavenging for a story."

"I thought deaths aren't announced until the next of kin are notified," Helen said.

"They aren't, if you have a shred of decency," Jim said. "Cy's using Joan's suicide to promote his damned restaurant. I swear, when he rebuilds, I'll torch it myself. You won't believe his disgusting, self-serving display. Vulture." He spat on the sand.

"Look!" he said. "Watch it yourself. Channel Fifty-four is going to interview him. He wants his burned restaurant as the backdrop. Cy doesn't walk. He slithers."

He did, sort of, Helen thought, if a fat man could slither. His lardlike complexion shone in the sun. He crossed his hands protectively over his paunch. Helen wanted to slap that satisfied smile off his face.

She didn't get a chance. When the TV camera swung his way, Cy assumed the expression of a high-class undertaker in a long-sleeved shirt.

"Joan Right was my best waitress," he said, as if he owned her. "I saw her about eight last night. She'd been walking along the newly opened pier. Joanie was very depressed."

Joanie? Helen thought.

"She had financial problems," Cy said. "When my restaurant burned down, she didn't know how she was going to make it. I understood. I've known hard times myself. I'm fortunate my restaurant was fully insured. I assured her that when the new, improved Cy's on the Pier reopened, she'd be the first waitress rehired. I can't afford to let good help drift away.

" 'But what will I do in the meantime?' Joanie asked. 'I'm no lady of leisure. I can't sit around for a year doing nothing.'

" 'It won't be a year,' I told her. 'Cy's will be up and running by February. I'm taking reservations for Valentine's Day 2014. Joanie, if you're worried about your bills, I'll loan you the money, no interest, no strings. You can pay it back at five dollars a week. That's the kind of person I am. Cy's will come back better than ever, and so will you, Joanie.' I gave her a hug and said, 'When you're back working at the new Cy's on the Pier, you'll get a nice big bonus.'

"Joanie was so grateful, she hugged me back. The last time I saw her, she was smiling. She waved good-bye. I went to check on our new, temporary bait stand and got distracted because we were selling out of baitfish.

"I didn't think about her the rest of the night. I thought Joanie's problems were settled.

"I blame myself for her death. After I left, she must have had a relapse. Maybe she was staring at my poor burned building. That's like standing by a grave. She'd spent so many hours working there, she had to feel like a member of her family had died. She must have given up and jumped.

"I should have come back and checked on her. I should have given her money right then and there. I could have saved her. Joanie would still be alive if I'd used my common sense.

"Instead, I came by this morning to check on the progress. You can see how quickly the site's being cleared." The camera panned the blackened rubble. "That's when I learned . . ." He paused dramatically, as if swallowing his sobs. "Poor Joanie was gone." He hung his head dramatically.

Helen was tempted to clap. Hollywood lost a great actor when Cy took up restaurant running.

Jim was angry. "That revolting creep, using Joan to publicize his restaurant. If Joan needed money, I would have given her some. I should have gotten in touch with her. She didn't have to crawl to that man. No wonder she killed herself."

"She didn't," Helen said. "Joan didn't commit suicide."

"How do you know?"

"Joan would never, ever hug Cy. She loathed him," Helen said. "She hated how he hit on the staff and went out of her way to never be alone with him. He's lying."

CHAPTER 30

J oan Right's body, a mournful mountain range, rolled past on a stretcher.

Helen and Sunny Jim bowed their heads when the stretcher trundled by the canopy. Even the insensitive Cy ceased blathering while the photographer recorded Joan's sad cortege.

"She was a damn fine woman," Jim said.

A fitting epitaph, Helen thought. Poor Joan. She thought her luck was changing. It was. For the worse.

I will find your killer, she vowed silently. I will track him down and he will pay. And then I hope I can forgive myself. You paid for my overconfidence with your life.

They watched the ambulance doors slam shut on Joan's life.

Jim broke the silence first. "You say Joan didn't kill herself, and she sure as hell didn't fall off that pier. That means she was murdered. Who did it?"

"Cy," Helen said. "She was helping us with your investigation. Remember that heavy rain a few nights ago? Joan told me that Kevin, a dishwasher at Cy's, saw something in the water when Ceci was killed."

"The Latino guy?" Jim asked.

"Nicaraguan," Helen said. "Kevin wouldn't talk to us at the restaurant, but Joan helped me meet him at his bus stop on Seashell. Joan introduced us and told Kevin it was safe to talk to me. That's when Cy's Mercedes went by."

"The one with that stupid CY 4 ME plate?" Jim asked.

"That's it," Helen said. "Kevin was in my car, drying his drenched hair with a beach towel, so his face was hidden. But the passenger door was open and the dome light was on. Joan was upset. She thought Cy saw her face. She said he was paranoid about outsiders finding out his business."

"You know he ran drugs," Jim said.

"I've heard the rumors," Helen said. "But there's no proof, and that statute of limitations ran out long ago. I heard he murdered two of his associates. Again, no proof. I knew he had a dangerous past. But I didn't take her fears seriously. Phil and I should have protected her."

"I could have, too," Jim said. "I feel even worse now that I know she died trying to help me."

"She wanted to help," Helen said. "She wanted to put Cy in jail for good. She tipped us off that he was going to bribe Commissioner Frank Gordon."

"So I was right," Jim said. Helen heard the satisfaction in his voice. "Frank the Fixer was selling his vote. I knew it."

"Phil and I were at the restaurant with a female operative when it happened. So was Valerie Cannata, the Channel Seventy-seven investigative reporter." Helen wished Margery was there. She'd love being called a "female operative."

"Valerie's smokin' hot," Jim said.

"She wasn't hot in her disguise," Helen said. "No, that's wrong. She didn't look like her glamorous TV self in a cat T-shirt, but Cy recognized her. She had a hidden camera in a big old purse to silent-tape the bribery. Cy handed Frank a restaurant carryout bag stuffed with cash. Valerie caught it on tape."

"And you didn't tell me this!" Anger made Jim's leathery skin even redder and his frizzed hair bobbed with impatience.

"It failed," Helen said. "We failed. Cy recognized Valerie despite the disguise. He saw through my disguise, too. He knew I'd been hanging around his restaurant, talking to Joan.

"The bribe attempt went sideways: Frank the Fixer tried to run away with the cash out one door. Cy tried to escape out the other. Phil tackled Frank and they fought. The restaurant's phony nautical decor caught fire from those cheap candles. Frank and Cy got away, the bribe cash burned and Frank threw Valerie's camera into the ocean."

"Was Joan there?" Jim asked.

"No. But he not only recognized me that rainy night," Helen said. "He saw Joan talking to me when I was in my white PT Cruiser. She'd arranged a meeting with a key witness."

"It's pretty distinctive," Jim said. "I haven't seen another white Cruiser on the beach. Cy's no dummy."

"Cy was afraid Joan would tell Valerie about his deal to bribe the commissioner," Helen said. "He was absolutely right."

"Cy's got a sixth sense for his own survival," Jim said. "He's as crafty as he is crooked."

"Our plan blew up in our faces," Helen said. "Now Valerie's on probation at the station and Cy is threatening to sue her. The Riggs Beach cops are protecting him, and Cy's lying about what started the fire. Phil and I can't say anything or Valerie's career is over. It may be ruined anyway. There's no proof Cy bribed the commissioner or killed Joan."

"So what's Plan B?" Jim asked.

"We keep searching for Ceci's killer and save your business. We have some leads on another suspect. We're interviewing people. Cy has a girlfriend."

"The chick who runs Cerise?" he asked. "Big deal. I knew that."

"Phil staked out her place last night."

"What did he find?" Jim said.

"Don't know. He was out all night," Helen said. "I'm calling him now." She started strolling down the beach.

"Hey, don't walk away," Jim said. "I want to know what's going on. I hired you two because you were supposed to be the best and you're running around tripping over your di—your shoes."

"We are the best," Helen said. "This case is impossible and you know it. Nobody but us believed your story about the bribery. Even the cops are on Cy's side. It's best you don't know what we're doing."

"Hell, that's easy," Jim said. "You don't know what you're doing, either. You got one more week. I'm not wasting more money. I'll need it to live on while I rebuild my business. Or start a new one."

Helen walked into the wind. The air smelled clean and salty, and the sun beat down on her head, but nothing lightened her dark mood. Joan was dead. Her marriage was dead and her career was dying.

She saw two guys in gray college T-shirts and black board shorts playing catch on the beach. The crew-cut college boys were throwing a small pink football with a tail.

A tail?

Helen looked closer. That wasn't a football. It was a fish. A red snapper was gasping and flopping as it arced through the air.

"Hey!" she shouted. "Stop that!"

"What?" said the short one. He had heavy shoulders and slitty eyes and wore his arrogance like cologne. "It's just a fish."

"Then eat it or throw it back in the water. Don't torment it. It's alive."

She glared at them both.

The taller boy with the lean runner's body had the grace to look ashamed. He cupped the wriggling fish in his hands, carried it to the ocean and gently lowered it into the water. The fish lay on its side for a long moment, then righted itself and swam slowly away.

"Thank you," Helen said. She walked another quarter mile, practicing how she'd tell Phil the news about Joan's death and Jim's warning. She sat under a palm tree and speed-dialed her partner with trembling fingers.

"Hello," he said.

"She's dead!" Helen blurted and her voice broke. All her carefully rehearsed words fled.

"Who?" Phil said.

"Joan Right," Helen said.

"No! That's terrible. How'd you find out? It wasn't on the TV news."

"She didn't show for our meeting at the coffeehouse this morning," Helen said. "I went back to Riggs Beach to ask Jim if he'd seen her since the fire. A couple of tourists found her body this morning under the pier. Cy said she'd committed suicide, but I knew he was lying."

"Because his lips were moving?" Phil said.

"No jokes," Helen said. "Cy made up some story that she was depressed and worried about money, and he'd offered her a loan. He said she was so grateful, she hugged him. Joan would never touch that scumbag. She hated him."

"So how did Cy get close enough to murder Joan?" Phil asked.

"I don't know," Helen said. "Someone she trusted lured her down to the pier after dark and Cy ambushed her. Maybe the autopsy will give us information. How did the stakeout go at Alana's apartment?"

"It was a long night," he said, and sighed. "Alana got home about eight thirty. Looked like she'd been going for a long walk, possibly along the beach. Her hair was windblown and she had a beach bag but no purse.

"Cy showed up at her place at eleven. I took photos of him leaving her apartment at two a.m. It might be enough for a divorce. It certainly establishes a connection between Alana and Cy."

"Which everyone knows anyway," Helen said. "That's not enough to crack the case. I'll take her to lunch today and see if I can learn anything new."

"Be careful," Phil said. "If she catches on, we'll break our last link to Cy."

"I have time to think of ways to approach her," Helen said. "It's not even ten o'clock. I wanted to ask you about Daniel."

"Ceci's husband? What about him?" Phil said.

"He may have put their vacation on credit cards," Helen said, "but that doesn't mean he paid for everything that way. He's a liar, Phil. He betrayed his wife with her best friend. That tells me he's used to sneaking around. I want to talk to the staff again at the Full Moon Hotel."

"Fine with me," Phil said. "I'm going to catch up on my sleep."

"Phil," Helen said, "I think we're responsible for Joan's death."

"What? Where did you get that crazy idea?"

"We've had two major failures—the disaster at Cy's restaurant that may have ruined Valerie's career, and Joan's death. Both times, we weren't talking things over enough. Our lack of preparation showed.

"We should have gotten Joan protection," she said. "We should have made her stay with someone who'd watch her. I could have put her up in my apartment until Cy was in jail. She'd still be alive."

"Helen, the only one responsible for Joan's death is her killer. Even if we'd warned her, she wouldn't have believed us."

"Yes, she would," Helen said. "She was afraid of Cy—with good reason."

"Look, Helen, I'm sorry Joan is dead. She seemed like a good woman. But you'll go crazy blaming yourself. Sometimes, we fail. It happens. We learn to live with it."

"I still say our agency is failing because we're not communicating."

"I don't know what you mean." Phil sounded surly.

"When Joan said Cy was suspicious, I should have told you. We

should have sat down with Joan and discussed the best ways to protect her. When we taped the bribe at Cy's, we should have talked
about what to do if Valerie was recognized. She's one of the most
famous people in Fort Lauderdale. If we'd had a fallback plan, we
could have saved her camera."

Phil kept a stony silence.

"Oh, I forgot to tell you something," Helen said.

"Perfect," Phil said, sourly. "What now?"

"Sunny Jim says we have one week to get results or he's firing us."

"Well, well. Looks like the rest of the world agrees with me," Phil
said, his voice unnaturally cheerful. "The agency is failing. It's time
to go our separate ways."

He hung up without saying good-bye.

CHAPTER 31

"Did you catch the bastard yet?" Sybil asked. The owner of the Full Moon Hotel exhaled a ferocious cloud of cigarette smoke, as if she was burning to drag Daniel off to hell.

Helen had trouble breathing in Sybil's dark, smoky cave. How did her bright, sunlit hotel have such a black heart?

She smothered a cough and Sybil waved one wrinkled hand in a useless effort to banish the smoke. "Take a seat and tell me what you've got," she said.

Helen's leather chair felt slightly sticky with nicotine residue. She leaned forward in the seat and told Sybil about the diver who'd killed Ceci and what she and Phil had learned about Ceci's husband in St. Louis. "Daniel took out a million-dollar life insurance policy on Ceci," she said. "He was having an affair with her best friend."

"Disgusting," Sybil said. "Shouldn't surprise me, though, after more than half a century in the hotel business. How can I help you nail him?" Her smile showed sharp yellow teeth that would make a shark shudder.

Why is this scraggy little woman so endearing? Helen wondered.

"Phil, my partner, says Daniel put his whole vacation on a credit card," she said. "He saw the statements. But Daniel's sneaky. I think he used cash to buy things and hide them. Things that will connect him to hiring Ceci's killer in Florida."

"You're right," Sybil said. "My night clerk, Jackie, told me that the day Daniel checked in, he waited till his wife was out at the pool, then asked where he could buy a phone card. No, he *demanded* to know. Barged right up and interrupted Jackie when she was checking in a couple."

"Sounds like Daniel made friends from the first day here," Helen said.

"Oh, he was a beauty," Sybil said. "That move got me wondering: Why would a cheapskate like Daniel make calls from a pay phone?"

Sybil answered her own question. "So the police wouldn't find them on his cell phone, that's why."

"Like contacting the diver who killed his wife," Helen said.

"Exactly," Sybil said. "He could have bought a second cell phone or a throwaway phone. But that could be traced back to him. The store would have the receipts and videos of him buying it. The prosecution loves those videos at murder trials. But a pay-phone call— that's harder to track."

"Is there a pay phone near your hotel?" Helen asked.

"Used to have one right here in my parking lot. Had it taken out," Sybil said. "It was an old rotary dial. Drug dealers get callbacks on those phones. I wouldn't have anyone selling drugs near my family hotel, so I had the phone company get rid of it. But a nasty little convenience store on Federal Highway has a pay phone."

"I think I know the place," Helen said. "Cinder-block cube painted pink a long time ago. Next to a liquor store. Scary-looking guys hanging around it."

"Lots of riffraff around that place. Crack dealers, some of them," Sybil said. "That store sells phone cards, too. Jackie sent him there. She didn't care if he got mugged or not. Wish he had been. His sweet little wife would still be alive. Guess there's no chance you'll come back and work for me?"

"You never know," Helen said, and thanked Sybil.

She felt vindicated when she walked to her car. Next time she talked to Phil, she'd tell him about Daniel's phone card, paid for in cash. Phil had a phone company contact who owed him. He'd give Phil the numbers dialed out from that phone on the dates Daniel was in Lauderdale. They'd have the link that would tie Daniel to his wife's murder.

That's damn good detecting on my part, she thought. Not that Phil will say so.

All the way back to the beach, Helen brooded about her painful conversation with Phil. He seems eager to destroy Coronado Investigations as well as our marriage, she thought. Why won't he forgive me?

Yes, it was wrong to hide the fact Kathy and I were being blackmailed. Just as wrong as burying Rob in the church basement. But I did it to save my nephew. I was stupid, not malicious. Now my mistake could ruin my life. Our life—and our business.

Riggs Pier, bristling with anglers, appeared on the horizon. The restaurant's blackened ruins were smaller. The hardworking backhoe had nearly cleared the rubble. A new restaurant would soon rise on the same spot. Without Joan.

Helen felt a stab of sadness and guilt. She could almost see Joan, with her tired blond beauty, hurrying to clear tables and waiting on customers who didn't tip. She's dead because of me, she thought. Because Cy knew she'd talk to Valerie. Now I have to prove that he killed her. I owe her that much.

Why would Joan meet Cy alone at Riggs Pier? She wouldn't. She'd never do anything so risky. But Joan knew Alana at Cy's boutique. She wouldn't see her as a threat.

Maybe Alana is the key.

Helen parked her car in the pier lot, made Cy ten dollars richer, and barged through the throngs of strolling tourists toward Cerise, impatient to talk to the boutique manager.

"Hey, girlfriend!" Alana greeted her with a smile. "I'm having a terrific morning. Want to join me at that coffee shop for a chicken wrap and Key lime pie? My treat. I'm celebrating."

"Glad to," Helen said.

"Shelly, I'll be at the coffee shop," Alana called. The short, brown-haired woman gave her a big lipsticked smile and waved good-bye.

Alana seemed to glow with success today. Her golden hair was shiny and her sheer bronze top caught the sun. The customers at the coffee shop stared at her as she sat at a table with a view of the water.

"This sun matches my mood perfectly," Alana said and stretched like a long-limbed golden cat.

For a beach business that catered to tourists, the coffee shop operated with stunning efficiency. Helen and Alana had their food and drinks minutes after they sat down.

"So tell me your good news," Helen said, nibbling at her chicken wrap.

"Cy gave me that outfit I showed you," she said. "I didn't even have to do anything disgusting."

"Very generous," Helen said. Cy? Giving a sixteen-hundred-dollar gift to his girlfriend? What have you done? she wondered.

"It gets better. Today, the tourists are buying everything I set out—even the ugly sale stuff that's been cluttering up the racks all season."

"You are having a good day," Helen said.

"You aren't. You look sad," Alana said. "What's wrong?"

Helen thought this was the first time Alana had ever asked how she felt. "I was on the beach this morning when they found Joan, the server at Cy's restaurant," she said. "I liked her."

"So I heard," Alana said. "She committed suicide."

She used the tone that someone might use to say, "She took an aspirin." No sympathy and even less interest.

"Joan didn't seem the suicidal type," Helen said.

Alana shrugged. "Who can tell? Kef said she'd been depressed for a very long time."

Kef? Helen was startled. Joan had told Helen that only Cy's close friends from the old days called him by that drug nickname. "How long have you and Cy been friends?" Helen asked.

"A long time," Alana said. "So long I'd rather not remember. Makes me feel old."

I bet, Helen thought. I bet there's a lot you'd like to forget.

"I used to do odd jobs for him in the eighties," Alana said. "We weren't doing the deed back then. We didn't start screwing until he hired me to run his boutique and I had to work off my rent. The hard way."

She giggled, then saw Helen's face. "Oh, don't look at me like that," Alana said. "It's not like I'm breaking up his marriage. It's been dead a long time. He only stays married for the sake of his kid."

Right, Helen thought. Heard that one before.

Her face must have betrayed her.

"Hey," Alana said, "haven't you ever done anything you're not proud of?"

Bury my ex-husband in a basement, Helen thought.

Alana correctly read Helen's silence as guilt. "Thought so," she said.

But she couldn't read the rest of Helen's thoughts. She'd tolerated—even been mildly titillated by—Alana's carefree morals. Now Helen started putting together the bits she'd gleaned: Alana knew Cy, also known as Kef, from the bad old days when he ran drugs.

Cy gave her that coveted expensive outfit and Alana bragged, *I didn't even have to do anything disgusting.*

So what did Alana do? Did she make sure Joan would be at Riggs Pier the night of her death? How? Did she offer her a sales job at the boutique? A reference for a job at some other Riggs Beach restaurant or bar? Promise to take her to a beach restaurant for dinner?

That's my guess, Helen thought. But if I'm wrong, I'll cut off my access to Alana, and that will tick off Phil. Except he's already angry. Let's see how she reacts—or overreacts—when I press her about Joan. We're almost finished with lunch anyway.

"How does it feel to kill someone?" Helen asked.

Alana stopped eating her pie.

"What?" she said, putting down her fork.

"I said, 'How does it feel to kill someone?'" Helen repeated.

"I don't know what you mean," Alana said. But her eyes shifted uneasily. The wind grabbed her paper napkin and it fluttered away.

"You lured Joan to the pier so Cy could kill her," Helen said. "She would never get close enough to him. She couldn't stand him. That's how you got that outfit you wanted so bad. Maybe you didn't throw Joan off the pier, but you handed her over to the man who did."

Alana's easygoing attitude quickly flared into anger. "You're nuts!" she said, loud enough that people at the nearby tables stared at her again. "How can you even say that?"

"It's true, isn't it?" Helen said.

"I'm outta here," Alana said. "Pay for your own lunch."

She pulled a slim black wallet out of her purse, threw a twenty on the table and said, "Don't come into my store, ever again. If you set foot inside the door, I'll have you arrested for shoplifting."

She flounced off to Cerise, followed by the stares of the other diners.

Interesting, Helen thought as she walked back to her car. Alana never denied what I said. She just erupted into anger. She's guilty, but I can't prove it.

Something else about that scene bothered her. She thought she had it, but it escaped her mind.

I'm too hot and upset to think straight, Helen decided. It will come back.

Inside the Igloo, Helen turned on the air-conditioning and called Valerie.

"Helen," the TV reporter said, "I heard about that server who died. She was your source, wasn't she?"

"Yes," Helen said. "And she didn't commit suicide."

"I'm so sorry," she said, her voice soft with sympathy. "The station wouldn't let me cover the story because it involved Cy. But I still have my job. So far."

"Can you talk?"

"Not on a cell phone," Valerie said. "I'm finishing a story downtown. Meet me at Riverwalk by the gondola ride."

Riverwalk Linear Park was a pleasant paved walkway along the New River in downtown Lauderdale, lined with yachts and restaurants. Helen loved the slender black Venetian gondola moored there. It had been fitted with a motor and was driven by Captain Pierre in a straw hat and striped gondolier's costume.

Helen waited on a nearby bench and watched the yellow water taxi motor by. She heard Valerie clip-clopping in her high heels before she saw her.

The Valerie of the Crocs and cat T-shirt was once again dressed to kill. She wore elegant black-and-cranberry stilettos with a slim cranberry sleeveless dress.

"You look like your old self," Helen said.

"I'm still in disgrace," she said to Helen as she sat next to her on the bench.

"But putting on a brave face," Helen said.

"They won't let me say anything on camera, but I've been continuing the Riggs Beach investigation quietly on my own," Valerie said. "Commissioner Charles Wyman has an uncanny habit of getting gifts just before a decisive vote.

"He got a new pool from a contractor who wanted city business— and a deal on the price. You might say an impossible deal. He got a new car at an amazing price, just before the city bought its fleet. There are canceled checks and bills of sale, but Commissioner Wyman owns way too many expensive things for someone making his salary."

"Joan told me Wyman wanted Cy to give his daughter a wedding reception with steak and lobster dinners at the restaurant in January," Helen said. "Of course, Cy couldn't give that gift when his place burned down."

"There went Wyman's chance to sell his vote," Valerie said.

"Maybe he can get Commissioner Frank Gordon's vote at a discount," Helen said.

"Are you kidding? Gordon will charge him double now," Valerie said. "I don't think even Cy has that much money to burn. Gotta run, Helen," and Valerie was gone in a sophisticated streak of color.

Chic Valerie made Helen feel frumpy. She was already tired and discouraged. Helen hoped she could snag a glass of wine with Margery by the pool.

She was relieved that Phil's Jeep wasn't in the Coronado parking lot, and positively cheered that Margery was sitting by the pool.

"Come sit. Have some white wine and cashews," Margery said. The evening breeze lightly stirred her lilac caftan. Her necklace of deep purple abalone shimmered in the dying light.

Helen poured herself a generous glass of wine and grabbed a handful of cashews. She could hear Thumbs complaining all the way across the yard.

"That cat doesn't stop yowling all day," Margery said.

"He misses me," Helen said.

"More likely he misses food." Helen's landlady was no cat lover. "What are you going to do about that noise?"

"Nothing," Helen said. "I can't. Phil changed the locks."

"And didn't give me a key like he's supposed to," Margery said, "or I'd let you in to feed that fur bag. How's the murder case going?"

"Up in smoke, and I mean that for real," Helen said. She updated Margery on their latest failures.

"Do you think there's any chance Phil will forgive me?" Helen said. "I don't understand why he's behaving this way."

"Most women don't understand men," Margery said. "Women

are tough and practical. Men are romantics, especially guys like Phil. You didn't tell Phil about the blackmail when you got married, did you?"

"I meant to," Helen began.

"But you married him with a lie. And you've kept lying your entire marriage. Phil is hurt and disappointed. It will take him a while to get over it."

"What if he doesn't?" Helen said.

"You're a good private eye, Helen. You're practical. You'll find another PI job. You got over Rob and you'll get over Phil."

"But I don't want to," Helen said.

"You will. If you have to," Margery said.

CHAPTER 32

Helen was furious—almost as angry as Thumbs. She could hear her cat screeching and shrieking while she wrote her report about Daniel's pay-phone calling card. It was hard to believe that soft, furry body produced such harsh, intense sounds.

The big-pawed cat's cries were impatient, insistent and incessant. No wonder people thought felines were the devil's familiar, Helen thought. Thumbs was wicked loud.

She tried to concentrate on her report, but her head ached. So did her heart. Just stop, cat, she thought. Shut up, please. He answered with an otherworldly wail.

"Thumbs," she called through the wall. "Thumbs, it's me, Helen. It's okay."

He redoubled his efforts. Margery wouldn't put up with this noise much longer, Helen thought. And neither will I.

At 9:12 Helen searched her apartment for something heavy to break the glass slats in Phil's jalousie door and rescue her cat. The heavy pottery ashtray on the coffee table—a turquoise triangle. She grabbed it by one pointed end when she heard Phil's door rattle, then slam shut.

Thumbs stopped howling a few minutes later. Phil must have fed him.

The silence was a blessing.

Helen waited more than an hour for Phil to respond to her report. She gave him time to shower and eat. He usually checked his e-mail after dinner. She'd dug up first-rate information. Her facts contradicted his assumptions. Would Phil admit he was wrong about Daniel? Would he turn their investigation back in that direction?

She started checking her e-mail every five minutes, then every two. No *ding* announcing an incoming message. She kept her cell phone at her side. No ring. Her apartment grew chilly as the night deepened. Helen slipped on a sweater.

She gave him a full hour. Then fifteen more minutes, which stretched like taffy into half an hour.

Nothing. Not a peep. That man was pigheaded.

Phil won't admit I'm right, Helen thought. He sure as hell won't admit he's wrong. But I'm supposed to wear sackcloth and ashes because I made a mistake. Enough. I'm no martyr.

The silence grew so loud, it seemed worse than Thumbs' screeching. She couldn't stand the tension.

She flicked on her CD player—the Rolling Stones' "(I Can't Get No) Satisfaction." Mick's voice matched her mood. He sang with a sly, angry taunt. He insinuated. He sneered. And then he screamed.

Phil hated this rock classic. He liked Eric Clapton's overrated guitar sounds: CLAPTON IS GOD. Hah. That was Phil's favorite T-shirt. The Stones pledged their allegiance to drink and the devil, the way rock stars should. They didn't think they were God.

"Satisfaction" finished and she played it again.

And again.

That's when Phil erupted. "Hey, Helen," he yelled through the wall. "Can you keep it down?"

"Keep what down?" Helen shouted back.

"That shrieking you call music."

Helen opened her door. "It is music," she shouted. "The whole world says so."

"Not me," Phil said, slamming out of his apartment and glaring at her. "Keith Richards is nothing but a junkie. A brain-damaged junkie who fell out of a tree. He has holes in his head. For real."

"You have holes in your head if you think Clapton is better," Helen screamed. "He's a racist who wanted the wogs out of England. Nice guy, Phil. Real nice."

Her anger felt hot and reckless, as if she was skimming across a lake of fire, almost out of control. She was tired of being a humble mouse, through with repenting. She put her hands on her hips, threw her head back and glared at her husband.

Phil glared back, his shoulder-length silver hair loose, his lean face a dark red, hateful mask.

"Yeah, and how about Mick Jagger," he sneered. "The great Mick was shortchanged. His women didn't get any satisfaction. So much for sex, drugs and rock and roll. He—"

"Shut up!"

Margery stepped between the warring couple, hair flying, nostrils flaring, cords standing out in her neck. Her caftan surrounded her, an angry purple storm.

Now that she had their attention, her voice was soft, fast and furious. "I said quiet! Right now. Both of you.

"I had the misfortune to be the minister who tied the knot for you two. I should have strangled you both. What are you doing, disturbing the peace of my apartments at eleven o'clock? Arguing about rock stars like two half-wit teens. What is this? A stupid contest?

"You, Phil, shouting that Mick Jagger has small equipment. You think that's news? He calls it the 'tiny todger.'

"You, Helen, insulting Eric Clapton. Like he cares.

"I've tried to stay neutral, but no longer.

"Helen Hawthorne, you're a fool. You should have told the police about Rob. You should have told us you were being blackmailed. But you said nothing. You've paid dearly for that lesson.

"Phil, you're an idiot. You've acted like a jerk ever since Helen confessed. Yes, she was wrong. But you were, too. You should have waved your arms, shouted, pouted and then forgiven her. She would have been grateful and you two could have lived happily ever after. Instead, you've been a two-bit drama queen."

Margery pointed an angry, red-tipped nail first at Phil and then Helen. Helen suddenly realized that for the first time ever, Margery didn't have a cigarette in her hand.

"I've had enough of both of you," their landlady said. "You're squabbling when you should be solving a major case. A nice woman died and a good man may lose his business. And that poor server was murdered helping you ingrates. Have you found her killer yet?"

She glared at them both.

"Well? I didn't think so.

"Listen and listen good, both of you. You will work out your difficulties, or you will leave the Coronado. You have forty-eight hours or you're both evicted. Got that?"

A tiny mew came from Phil's apartment.

"If I hear another sound from that bellowing fleabag, he goes to the pound."

Phil shrugged and ducked into his apartment to quiet the cat.

Helen couldn't stop the electric rush of adrenaline through her body. She was too angry to sleep or even sit still. She headed for her car. She needed a walk along the water to cool down.

Helen meant to stop at Fort Lauderdale Beach, but the Igloo had been to Riggs Beach so often lately, the Cruiser headed there automatically.

Cy's parking lot was nearly empty. The wind carried the dead campfire scent of the burned restaurant. She could see Sunny Jim's yellow trailer locked up for the night. Why were his security lights so dim? And why were there no lights on the beach? Riggs Beach was a tourist town. That meant bright lights and noise.

Of course, she thought. It's turtle season. Turtles outrank even tourists in South Florida.

From March to October, two-hundred-pound loggerhead turtles crawled ashore to lay their eggs on the South Florida beaches. Lights were banned to save the two-inch long hatchlings. The baby turtles followed the moonlight to the sea but were distracted by bright lights. Before the light ban, newly hatched turtles were killed trying to cross the highway, led astray by the glittering hotels. Some even turned up at a hotel tiki bar.

Tonight, no artificial lights outshone the bright white moon.

In the moon glow, Helen saw couples strolling on the sand. They made her feel safe walking alone. She locked her purse in the car, stuck her keys in her pocket, and gave Cy's parking lot the second ten-spot of the day.

She walked into the wind, hoping to tire herself out. The ocean breeze helped cool her fury. The sand stung her face and made her cry.

These tears are caused by sand, she thought. Not because of my lost love and ruined marriage.

And I'm a liar as well as a fool. Helen stared out at the moon-silvered sea. The long day had caught up with her. She wanted to sleep.

She turned around and hiked back toward the pier. The moon softened the dark ruins of Cy's restaurant. Helen stopped dead. She saw a shadow moving around Sunny Jim's trailer. The wind was playing tricks with her eyes.

But she moved closer to the trailer, the damp sand silencing her steps. Now she could see the trailer's door was open. And that was no shadow. A husky man in black was hauling a heavy white plastic bucket, liquid splashing over its rim.

Water?

The wind carried a familiar scent—gasoline.

The man in black slipped inside and tossed gasoline on the walls, wooden floor and plywood pull-down desk.

No! she thought. He's going to burn down Jim's trailer. She reached for her cell phone to call 911, then realized it was in her purse, locked in her car.

Where were those couples strolling on the sand? She scanned the shore for someone, anyone, but the beach was as deserted as if a lifeguard had ordered everyone to leave.

The moon slipped behind a cloud. The whoosh of the waves and the soft sand covered Helen's approach. Now she could reach the rack of paddleboards with the paddles stored on top. She slid a plastic paddle off the rack and hid in the shadows alongside the trailer. The man in black emptied a trash can in front of the trailer, then added a stack of free newspapers and poured the last of the gasoline onto the pile. Helen nearly choked on the fumes.

She was close enough to see he was wearing a black sweat suit with a hoodie. His body, face and hair were hidden, but the dark clothes didn't disguise his powerful shoulders and muscular arms. He took out a disposable lighter and held the flame to the gasoline-soaked trash.

Helen heard the *whump!* as the fire ignited.

"Hey!" she cried.

He looked up, surprised, then launched himself at her as Helen swung the paddle. She whacked him on the shoulder. Hard. He stumbled and fell but scrambled back up. He charged Helen a second time.

I have to stop him, she thought. He's strong, but so am I.

This time, she put all her muscle—and her anger—into that swing.

She walloped the side of his head with a resounding *thwack!*

Stunned, he stumbled toward the fire. Flames ran up his back and jumped onto the hood. Now his back, arms and hair were on fire. He started to run toward the ocean.

"Drop down!" Helen shouted. "Running feeds the flames."

He kept going and she tripped him with the paddle. He fell face-first into the shallow water, writhing and screaming.

"Turn over, turn over!" she shouted, but he was too panicked to pay attention. She pushed at his shoulders and her sweater caught fire. She felt the flames sting her arms. Helen ripped off the sweater, then soaked it and her arms in the cool seawater. The pain was bearable.

The man in black was lying in the water, eyes closed. He seemed to be unconscious, possibly from the pain. He was quiet at last.

So quiet, she could hear the screaming sirens.

CHAPTER 33

· · · · · · · · · · · · · · ·

"It hurts!" he moaned. "It hurts. Arggghhhh!"

Helen was back in the emergency room again, this time at Riggs Beach General Hospital. This ER's walls were as flimsy as the ones in St. Louis. Helen listened to another medical drama in the room next door.

Her arms were wrapped in cool, damp gauze that did little to relieve her own pain. It was two in the morning, and she expected a long wait.

She knew the man moaning and shrieking: Randy, the diver who'd probably killed Ceci Odell. The man she'd saved after he set fire to Sunny Jim's trailer. Every time he screamed, she winced.

I don't like you, Randy, she thought. I hate what you did. But I couldn't bear to watch you burn.

Helen tried to harden her heart. He'd killed Ceci Odell, an innocent tourist. He didn't deserve pity.

Randy's ER doctor sounded sympathetic. "I know it hurts, Randy," she said, "but we have to remove the burned cloth and tissue on your back. We can't let these burns get infected."

"Can't you give me something for the pain? Please!" Randy begged.

"We have," the doctor soothed. "I can't give you more pain meds for a while. Just a little more."

"Ahhh!" Randy wailed. Helen jumped. The diver sounded like he was in the room with her. He was crying from the pain. Coward. He didn't care how much Ceci had suffered.

Helen shut her eyes and wished she could shut her ears. She didn't enjoy Randy's torment, however much he deserved it. Even the minor burns on her arms stung like an everlasting sunburn.

She heard her exam room door open and looked up, hoping the doctor had arrived at last. But her visitor was Phil. Not the angry, arrogant, argumentative Phil of a few hours ago. This was her Phil, with the soft silver hair and the slightly crooked nose, wearing her favorite blue shirt. This time, she was sure he wore it for her.

He smiled tentatively and asked quietly, "How are you?"

"Where's Margery?" Helen asked. Her heart was pounding so hard she could hardly talk. "I called her. I didn't call you."

"She's at home," he said. "She came over and told me what happened. I wanted to see you alone. She was right, Helen. I am an idiot. Forgive me."

He looked at her bandages and said, "Can I kiss you?"

"Carefully," she said.

His cool lips touched hers, but he brushed against her arms and she flinched in pain.

"I've hurt you," he said, his voice soft with concern.

More than you can imagine, she thought. But I'm feeling much better.

"My arms sting a little," she said. "My sleeves caught on fire when I tried to put out the fire. That's why I'm wearing this lovely hospital gown."

"I love you," he said. "I was wrong. I have so much to tell you, but this isn't the place. I'll make it up to you, I promise. Please tell me you weren't burned trying to save Sunny Jim's trailer."

"No, I went after the guy who set it on fire. I hit him and he stumbled and his clothes caught on fire. He's screaming in the next room, with second- and third-degree burns. He was wearing cotton sweats."

"Cotton?" Phil said. "That goes up like a torch."

"I think he's in bad shape," Helen said. "Do you have your note-book with you?" She put a finger to her lips.

Phil nodded and produced the small spiral notebook and pen from his shirt pocket.

She wrote, "Randy the diver is in the next room. RB cop outside door."

He wrote back, "Saw cop. Can U text me?"

"Purse in car at RB," she wrote.

"I'll go for some water and be right back," Phil said out loud, in a failed faked attempt to sound natural. "Would you like something?"

"No, thanks," Helen said.

Randy's doctor must have left. The diver was quiet at last.

Phil returned shortly with a white coat over his arm. He slipped it on, then wrote, "Found in the doc lounge. Going to see Randy."

Helen watched through the glass door as Phil handed the Riggs Beach officer a folded bill and said, "Why don't you take a half-hour break, Officer? No need for you to stand here. He won't be going anywhere."

"Thanks," the cop said, pocketing the bill.

How much did Phil give him? Helen wondered. Twenty? Fifty? Was anyone honest in Riggs Beach? She heard the door open to Randy's exam room.

"Can I have that pain shot now?" Randy asked, his voice low and weak.

"I don't know," Phil said. "You'll have to ask a doctor. I'm here to give you bad news. You're going to die."

"What do you mean?" Randy sound more alert and very frightened. "That's not what the doctor said. The real doctor. Who are you?"

"A private eye. You were a busy boy tonight, Randy. You bought two gallons of gas at the Riggs Beach BP station near your home at ten twenty-one," Phil said. "It's on the station's security tape. Put your purchase on a credit card. Not smart."

"So?" Randy said. The fear was gone. "I wanted to mow my lawn."

"You don't have a lawn—or a lawn mower," Phil said. "You live in a rat hole near the beach. You set fire to Sunny Jim's trailer tonight. Arson is a felony. That fire was started with gasoline."

"They haven't arrested me," Randy said. "That cop is out there to protect me."

"Protect you?" Phil said and laughed. "From what? Or should I say who?

"Here's what you don't know, Randy. When you're arrested and go to the hospital, the cost of your medical treatment is billed to the arresting agency."

"That's cool," Randy said. "I don't have health insurance."

"Not cool," Phil said. "Riggs Beach hasn't arrested you. Now, generally, the cops wait to make the arrest until after you leave the hospital."

"I'm gonna be in at least a month, maybe longer," Randy said. "I might need skin grafts." He sounded cheerful at the awful prospect.

"I'm no doctor, but that back looks pretty crispy," Phil said. "Are you going to be transferred to a burn center?"

"They're going to admit me to the hospital," Randy said. "They'll send me to the burn center in Miami tomorrow afternoon. Get my own private ambulance. Think I'll have a siren?"

Helen wondered if the pain medication made him sound like this, or if Randy was a ditz.

"Probably not," Phil said.

"Either way, all I have to do is stay in bed," Randy said. "It's a drag lying on my stomach. Can't watch TV. Maybe they got special ones at the burn center. I'll know by tomorrow afternoon."

"If you live that long," Phil said.

"The doc says I will," Randy said.

"And I say you won't," Phil said. "Who hired you to burn down Sunny Jim's? Bill Bantry? You used to work at Bill's Boards."

"I quit," Randy said.

"Right after you got a big payoff," Phil said.

"Not from Bill," Randy said. "He don't pay nothin'."

"Commissioner Frank Gordon?" Phil said.

Randy snorted contemptuously.

"Then it's Cy Horton, Riggs Beach bigwig and restaurant owner," Phil said. "Cy hired you, didn't he? He paid you to kill Ceci Odell and Joan Right."

"I never killed Joan," Randy said.

"I believe you," Phil said. "I also believe you're a dead man unless you tell me who hired you to kill Ceci Odell."

"Like I said, I ain't talking."

"Think about it," Phil said. "I've got enough to tie you to Ceci's murder. You rented an underwater scooter the day of her death. The dive shop identified your photo. A cell phone video shows you in the water near Riggs Pier when Ceci was murdered and you didn't go to her rescue. In fact, you went in the opposite direction."

"A video?" Randy sounded wary.

"You can't move anymore without nosy people and their camera phones," Phil said. "There's a witness, too. He wondered why you didn't help a drowning woman. He saw you drag her under."

"No!" Randy made a noise between a yelp and a shriek.

Was he denying what the witness had seen or what he had done? Helen wondered.

"Yes," Phil said. "You're going down, Randy. You committed two felonies: murder and arson. Both are death penalties, especially killing that nice tourist lady, Ceci Odell. Florida doesn't like it when tourists get murdered. It's bad for business."

"Leave me alone," he whined. "I hurt."

"I bet you do," Phil said. "When you get more pain medication, you're going to fall asleep. But are you going to wake up? What will keep that Riggs Beach cop outside your door from putting a pillow over your face? Or injecting your IV line with a lethal dose of pain-killer?"

"Why would he kill me?" Randy asked. "I haven't said anything."

"People babble when they're on drugs, Randy," Phil said. "I've got contacts in Riggs Beach. Remember when I met you in that bar? I tracked you down because some of your friends talked to me. Sold you out for a beer.

"Detecting is thirsty work. I could go back to those same bars and say you wanted to cut a deal. Word would get back to the wrong people, and guess what? One less beach bum. Nobody would care, Randy."

Helen heard a long silence. Was Randy thinking about his hopeless situation? she wondered. Phil had done a masterful job of bluffing. Randy didn't know that Joan's video was worthless and Kevin's testimony could be demolished by a good defense attorney.

"I can help you, Randy," Phil said. He sounded like a kindly older brother. "I know a special agent at FDLE."

"What's that?" Randy asked.

"Florida Department of Law Enforcement. State police agency," he said. "Investigates corruption. I'll call him in the morning. If he's interested, he can arrange for protection. I can't make any promises, but he might put in a good word for you if you cooperate."

Silence.

"Tell me quick, Randy," Phil said. "You wanna live or die? That cop's coming back in five minutes. I bribed him, Randy. Fifty bucks. If I can get to him, so can someone else. Now, who hired you?"

"It was Bill. Bill Bantry," Randy said. He was crying. "He hired me and my buddy to steal some boards and ruin Sunny Jim's business at spring break. He thought Jim would close. But Jim had insurance. Bill was pissed. There isn't enough business for two paddleboard rentals on the beach. He wanted me to kill a tourist and ruin Sunny Jim's business for good."

"Why did you pick Ceci Odell?"

"It didn't matter who died," Randy said. "Just so it looked like an accident."

Helen thought that was the worst part of his confession. Ceci was killed because someone had to die. Her murder wasn't even personal. "Bill said morning was the best time because of the high tide, and it would look like an accident," Randy said. "The day before, I called Jim and pretended I wanted to make a reservation for eight, because that's how many boards he has. He said he couldn't do it. Two boards were rented for ten o'clock. I only saw one woman get into the water and she was kinda wobbly. It was easy."

Helen shivered, and not from the hospital air-conditioning. Randy seemed to be bragging.

"And you hated women tourists after your famous manatee ride," Phil said.

"Killing that lady tourist was like a bonus," Randy said. "I got paid for revenge. Stupid YouTube video ruined my life. I wudda killed her if I could have, but she lived in Canada."

"How much did Bill pay you?" Phil asked.

"Five thousand cash. He bitched about it. He had to cash in one of the CDs he got from his mom and pay a penalty. I left town afterward. Bill put me up at a cabin he owns in Stuart. Had me a nice little vacation. Then Cy called. He tried to get me to kill Joan Right, the waitress, but I wouldn't."

"So your buddy Bill talked after he used you," Phil said.

"No!" Randy said.

"Somebody talked," Phil said. "Word got out that you're a killer for hire. Why didn't you kill Joan?"

"I knew her. I couldn't do that to somebody I knew."

"Did you warn Joan?" Phil asked.

"No," Randy said. "I was too scared. I heard stories that Cy made people who crossed him disappear. I had my own self to think about.

"I didn't trust Cy and didn't want to work for him. I was scared of Bill, too. Word is he offed his old lady and they never found her. That's why I had some insurance. I learned something from that viral video. Recordings are powerful. When Bill asked me to kill a tourist, I recorded the conversation with my cell phone and then bought me a new phone."

"Where's the phone with the recording, Randy?" Phil asked.

"Hidden in my car trunk. Under the spare tire. It's parked at Riggs Pier. Rusted orange Ford Fiesta, dented right fender. I used to drive a real car, not that junker."

"Good boy," Phil said. "You better hope the Riggs Beach cops didn't search your car. I'll call the FDLE agent and see if he's interested in saving your sorry hide. Meanwhile, I'll see if your grandmother can come here and watch you until you're moved to the burn center."

"I don't have a grandmother," Randy said.

"You do now," Phil said.

CHAPTER 34

"Where is my grandson? I wish to see him immediately." Helen recognized that voice. Margery. She stormed into the emergency room at four in the morning, magnificent in her chaos.

Helen watched from her ER cubicle as their landlady swept through in a lavender Chanel suit. The suit had an ethereal shine in the sad late-night fluorescent light. Margery's elegant ropes of pearls and gold clinked delicately, the soft sound of money. A large-brimmed hat dipped over one eye.

Margery puffed on a cigarette in an ebony holder. Helen thought that was overdoing it.

A sturdy short-haired nurse in puke green scrubs planted herself in front of Margery. "You can't smoke in here," she said, a brave bull-dog barking at a goddess. "And you can't park your Rolls in front of the emergency room entrance. That's for ambulances."

Rolls? Helen wondered. Where the heck did Margery get a Rolls at this hour?

"I didn't park the car there," Margery said. "My driver did. You may tell him to move it."

"Not till you put out that cigarette." The nurse had the white skin and nearly colorless eyes of a cave creature. "It's a fire hazard."

Helen admired the nurse for standing her ground. Margery was formidable. The nurse waited, hands on hips, until Margery stubbed out her cigarette and stowed her cigarette holder in her Chanel handbag.

"There," Margery said. "You may talk to my driver now." Dismissed.

Helen was surprised that the tough little nurse left. Margery stalked straight to the ER cubicle with the Riggs Beach cop posted in front of it. He started to say something, but Margery glared him into silence.

She threw open the door and said, "Randy, darling, what have these awful people done to you?"

"I—" Randy said.

"Sh!" Margery said. "Don't say a word, sweetheart. You let Grandmama handle everything." Accent on the "grand."

Phil raised an eyebrow and Helen smiled at him. He wrote a quick note: "Margery watching R till I call FDLE. Told her to be rich bitch."

"Doing good job," Helen wrote.

I should be dead tired, she thought, but I'm too happy. Phil came to see me. He still loves me. I still love him. It will be rocky for a while, but we'll work it out. Phil can take me back home as soon as I'm discharged.

The ER doctor had examined her half an hour ago and confirmed that her burns were minor. He covered them with a soothing ointment, wrapped them lightly in gauze, and told her to take Tylenol for the pain. Now Helen was waiting for her discharge paperwork.

A young coffee-skinned man in maroon scrubs knocked on the door of Randy's cubicle and said, "Randall Henshall?"

No response.

"Randall is sleeping," Margery said. "He needs his rest."

"I'm Curtis," the young man said. "I'm here to take Mr. Henshall to his room. He's being admitted until he can be transferred to the burn center in Miami."

"Very sensible," Margery said, as if the hospital needed her approval.

Helen watched Curtis wheel Randy expertly through the ER, threading his way around wheelchairs, carts, and an old woman with a walker.

Randy was lying on his stomach, draped with a sheet from the waist down. His back was covered with white gauze and stained with patches of red and yellow. Helen hoped the yellow was ointment. An IV line snaked out of his left hand.

Helen thought his young face looked collapsed. His eyes were sunken in dark pools and his mouth was open. He was either asleep or passed out.

The Riggs Beach cop and Margery followed in the stretcher's wake. Margery flirted outrageously with the young cop. "Tell me," she said. "Is a big, strong man like you bored standing outside a door?"

Helen rolled her eyes. Phil grinned. The cop seemed charmed.

"Grandmama Margery will stay with Randy until Cousin Phil arrives at nine in the morning," Phil said. "That's when visiting hours start."

"How's she going to stay in his room?" Helen said. "Visiting hours are over."

"She'll wait until Randy's settled, then slip into his room."

"And the staff won't see her?" Helen asked.

"The nurses and aides are run off their feet," Phil said, "when they're not putting data in the computer or taping sign-out reports for the next shift. I doubt they'll notice she's there. If they give her trouble, Margery will make a fuss about calling her lawyer and demand to see the hospital administrator. That's why she has the Rolls parked outside."

"What about the cop?" Helen said.

"She's already made a cash contribution to his retirement fund," Phil said. "You saw how Margery sweet-talked him. She'll keep talking to him until it's safe for her to go back into Randy's room. The cop thinks she's a harmless old lady."

"He's not the first man to make that mistake," Helen said.

An aide arrived with Helen's paperwork and a T-shirt she could wear home. She listened to the instructions, then signed the papers. At last, she was free.

Helen and Phil walked out of the ER together into the cool, dark morning. The light breeze stung her arms.

The hospital parking lot was nearly empty, except for the ghostly silhouette of the Rolls-Royce under a bright light near the staff lot. A uniformed chauffeur in a peaked cap sat in the front seat.

"Look how straight that poor chauffeur is sitting," Helen said. "There's nobody out here, but he's not relaxing. His deportment is perfect."

"For what he's paid, it should be," Phil said. "Besides, we're out here. And you don't know who's looking out a window. Hospitals are hotbeds of gossip. He's paid to be seen."

"Where did Margery get a Rolls in the middle of the night?" Helen asked.

"She rented it," Phil said. "That's a 1960 Rolls-Royce Silver Cloud. Luxurious but understated."

"It shouts old money," Helen said.

"That's the idea," Phil said. "It's good advertising. The hospital staff—and the administrators—know someone who can cause a lot of trouble is here."

Phil's Jeep was parked crookedly in the visitors' lot, as if he'd abandoned it and run inside. Helen smiled when she saw that. Another love token.

He opened the door for Helen. She carefully leaned her head on his shoulder as Phil drove toward the Coronado, and inhaled his familiar smell of coffee and sandalwood. It was good to be with him again.

"I'll start calling Calder at six," Phil said.

"Who's that?" Helen said.

"Calder Honeycutt, the FDLE special agent. I want to tell him about Randy. I hope I can reach him before nine. That's when I go back to the hospital so Margery can go home."

"When are you going to get some sleep?" Helen asked.

"When I know that Randy is safe with FDLE," Phil said. They were stopped at a red light on Federal Highway, the only car on the road.

"It was sheer luck that Randy decided to burn down Sunny Jim's as I was walking along the beach," Helen said.

"You were so brave," Phil said. "And so foolish. When I think I could have lost you for good." He carefully kissed the top of her head. "You still smell like smoke and gasoline. You risked your life to save that worthless punk."

"I didn't care about him. I wanted to save the case," Helen said. "We know Bill of Bill's Boards hired Randy to kill Ceci. Randy recorded that conversation. FDLE can also prove Bill cashed in a five-thousand-dollar CD and trace the money to Randy. Plus he stashed Randy at his place in Stuart. His fingerprints will be all over it.

"We know Cy wanted Randy to kill Joan Right, but Randy refused. Cy must have found another way to murder her. How do we prove it?"

"None of the pier surveillance cameras were working the night Joan was murdered," Phil said. "They were damaged by the fire. I checked Sunny Jim's cameras, but they only cover the area around his trailer. I've got photos of Cy leaving Alana's apartment and pictures of her coming home the night Joan was killed."

"Do you know the autopsy results yet?" Helen asked.

"Not yet," Phil said. "They aren't usually released during an ongoing investigation. Joan didn't die at the hospital, so I don't think Jim's nurse friend can get them for us. Cy's never going to confess."

"Alana's the key," Helen said. "She's an accessory to Joan's murder. She won't confess, either. She's tough as nails. But I know she somehow persuaded Joan to go down to the pier. Joan was too afraid of Cy to be alone with him.

"Cy paid Alana for that service. I saw the expensive outfit he gave her the day after Joan died—a sixteen-hundred-dollar dress. Alana worked for that gift, and she told me she didn't have to do anything disgusting."

"What'd she mean by that?" Phil asked.

"She didn't have to have sex with Cy," Helen said. "She did something to earn that gift. He doesn't throw money around."

That triggered a thought. Throwing. Money. Where was someone throwing money? Helen's brain was too tired to hold on to it.

"The weak link is Alana," Phil said.

"But how do we get her to say she's an accessory to murder?" Helen asked. "She won't talk to me anymore."

Helen saw the furious Alana pulling a twenty out of her wallet and throwing it down. A slim black wallet. Why did that scene nag at her?

"Want to get something to eat?" Phil asked. "Maybe downtown?"

"That's it!" Helen said. "The wallet. The black wallet."

"What's a wallet got to do with eating downtown?" Phil said. "You lost me."

"When Joan and I ate downtown, she took out her wallet to pay the tip. She had a beautiful black Gucci wallet. It cost about five hundred dollars, way more than Joan could afford."

"There are lots of fake Guccis," Phil said.

"No, I've worked in retail long enough to know the real thing," Helen said. "She said a boyfriend gave it to her. The day after Joan died, I confronted Alana at lunch. She pulled out a slim black wallet.

Phil, it was the same wallet—and Alana can't buy expensive wallets, either. Cy gave her Joan's expensive wallet as a gift."

"How do you prove that?" Phil asked.

"Women's wallets have all sorts of little compartments and zippered sections," Helen said. "We tuck things away in them. I have my cell phone number and a coded version of my ATM password hidden in mine. Somehow, we have to get our hands on that wallet. No, you have to get your hands on that wallet. She'll call the cops if she sees me in her store."

"How do we get her to take out her wallet?" Phil asked. "Would she give money to a charity?"

"Not a chance," Helen said. "Only person she cares about is herself."

"Suppose she got a small refund check—say, fifty or sixty dollars? Would she take it?"

"In a heartbeat," Helen said.

"Then I think I know how to get her to open that wallet," Phil said. "We'll work on it after Randy is safely in FDLE custody."

They were back at the Coronado Tropic Apartments. The old art moderne building glowed white in the darkness, and the palm trees rustled softly. All the lights were out.

"We're home," Phil said. "Helen, will you come back to my place? Come back to me?"

"Oh, yes," she said.

"I love you," he said. "I always have. I always will."

"And I love you." Helen tried to put her arms around him, but they hurt too much. "I wish I could hold you."

"We'll have lots of time for that when you're well."

"Let's go home," Helen said. "To your place."

"Our place," he said.

CHAPTER 35

Helen awoke to the smell of hot coffee, the sound of Phil singing off-key—and an empty bed. He greeted her with a careful kiss and a cup of coffee.

"You didn't sleep last night," she said.

"I didn't want to hurt you," Phil said. "Besides, a two-hour nap would have made me feel worse. I've got some amazing news. I tracked down Cal Honeycutt at seven this morning. Our timing couldn't be better. FDLE has been investigating corruption in Riggs Beach for more than a year. They're convening a grand jury next week. They've got lots of information about bribery, but no homicide.

"Randy could wind up being a star witness. Cal got a search warrant for Randy's car. If that cell phone recording is as good as Randy says, and he's willing to testify, Cal will take over by two o'clock this afternoon."

"You thought the transfer would take a day or two," Helen said.

"Cal's moving with lightning speed. This Riggs Beach investigation is the case of a lifetime. Cousin Phil has promised to babysit Randy at the hospital and relieve Margery this morning."

"What time is it?" Helen asked.

"Eight fifteen," Phil said. "Margery should be home in about an hour and a half. You can watch her arrive in style. Don't forget, once I'm home from the hospital, we'll go get Alana."

"And my car," Helen said. "It's still at Riggs Beach. Along with my purse."

Phil kissed her again, left her a twenty-dollar bill and a credit card "in case you need anything" and was out the door. Helen stretched luxuriantly and felt the sharp sting. Her burned arms still hurt, but they were better. Everything was better this morning.

Thumbs came up to Helen for his morning scratch. When she came home earlier, he'd tried to sleep with his head on her arms, but the pain was too much. Helen cried out, and Thumbs spent the rest of the night sleeping at her feet.

She took a careful sponge bath in the sink, washed her smoky hair, put on fresh clothes and spread a light coat of ointment on her burns, then stuffed the credit card and money in her pocket.

Helen poured herself another cup of coffee and stepped out into the brilliant sunshine, where she saw an even more dazzling sight. A uniformed chauffeur with dark wavy hair opened the door of a Rolls-Royce Silver Cloud. Out stepped Margery, a vision in lavender Chanel, ropes of pearls—and that cigarette holder.

"Thank you, William," she said.

"My pleasure, Mrs. Flax," he said, and bowed. He climbed into the driver's seat and the Rolls purred away.

Helen waved to her landlady. "Lady Flax," she said. "Would you care to join me for a cup of coffee?"

"Soon as I ditch these clothes," she said.

By the time Helen was back with a mug of coffee and a plate of cookies, Margery was settled in a chair by the pool, wearing a purple cotton caftan.

"Nice outfit," Helen said. "But quite a comedown from the Chanel suit."

"More comfortable, though," Margery said. She wiggled her tangerine-painted toes in her purple sandals and took a long drag on her Marlboro.

"You got rid of the cigarette holder," Helen said.

"Too much trouble toting it around," Margery said. "But it was fun last night. Don't get a chance to use a theater-length holder much anymore."

"You sure looked theatrical," Helen said. "I didn't realize cigarette holders have different lengths."

"Four," Margery said. "They kept the nicotine stains off your gloves, back when ladies wore gloves everywhere. Both went out of style about the same time. The short cigarette holders were called cocktail length. Dinner-length holders were about six inches long. The one you saw, my theater-length holder, was a foot long. If you really wanted to put on the dog, you got out the opera length. I think mine's about twenty inches long and made out of Bakelite. The theater length was the best I could do in a hurry."

"You looked amazing last night," Helen said. "Like a movie queen."

"Thanks. It was fun playing grandam," Margery said.

"How's Randy?"

"In a lot of pain and scared spitless," Margery said. "As he should be. He's starting to realize how much trouble he's in. I'm glad that Riggs Beach cop was stationed outside his door all night. He was a living reminder that Randy's a dead man unless he talks. I think by the time FDLE gets him, he'll be very cooperative. How are your burns?"

"Not so bad," Helen said. "Kind of like a bad sunburn. No blisters."

"Did you and Phil make up?"

"Mostly," Helen said. "We still have a little way to go. What did you say to him to change his mind?"

"Me? Nothing," Margery said. "But if I can give you a piece of advice, your trip to the hospital gave him a chance to get off his high horse without losing his pride. Don't ruin this opportunity with your own stubbornness.

"Oh, I signed for a FedEx package for you. Stop by and pick it up."

Margery had sixty thousand dollars sitting on top of her fridge and didn't know it, Helen thought.

In St. Louis, she'd picked the bag of blackmail money out of the Dumpster on the way to the airport and sent it to herself. She'd planned to use it to start her new life if Phil didn't forgive her. Now she didn't need to. It was nice to have an emergency stash.

"Thanks for the coffee," Margery said. "I want to take a nap."

It was only eleven o'clock. Phil wouldn't return for at least three hours. Helen was too nervous to sleep. She walked off her jittery feelings along the shady streets. The Coronado was in a part of old Lauderdale that was quickly disappearing. Soon the small, candy-colored Caribbean cottages and the sleek midcentury duplexes would be torn down for hulking mansions and charmless condos. Winding streets like these would be widened, straightened and improved.

She stopped to scratch the ears of a brown spaniel waddling along with its owner and tried not to smile. Dog and man both had brown eyes, brown hair and portly bodies. She admired a garden where a surreal staghorn fern clung to a tree like a many-clawed monster. White moth orchids fluttered in pots on the turquoise-painted porch.

A fit young mother pushing a jogging stroller raced by. Helen didn't see an ounce of baby fat on the ponytailed mom's muscular body, but she moved with determination. She watched an old couple with faded eyes and cottony white hair helping each other along a section of broken sidewalk.

Will Phil and I help each other like that in forty years? she wondered. Will we still be in love?

The quiet street ended at busy Federal Highway. Helen avoided the roaring traffic by strolling through a small palm-lined shopping center. She stopped at a closet-sized bookstore with a red awning. There, in the window, she saw the perfect present for Phil.

She saw Phil's Jeep when she got back to the Coronado and stashed her present in her apartment. Then she knocked on Phil's door.

He answered, wearing a short-sleeved khaki shirt and pants, his silver hair pulled back into a ponytail.

"You look very workmanlike," Helen said.

"I hope this gear works," Phil said. "I'm trying to pass myself off as a Riggs Beach city worker so we can get Alana's wallet."

"How's Randy?" Helen asked.

"In an ambulance on his way to the Miami burn center," he said. "He's now FDLE's problem. Cal has Randy's cell phone. Let's go see if we can convince Alana to talk. Cal said he thinks he can work a deal for her, but only if she'll testify against Cy."

"I can't go inside Alana's shop with you," Helen said. "What do you want me to do?"

"Wear black and lurk by the door until I have her wallet," he said. "Then come in."

"Do you know what the wallet looks like?" Helen asked. "I can show you one like it on the Internet."

She called up a Gucci leather goods site and pointed to one photo. "See? Long wallet with room for a checkbook. Black on black leather with nine gold studs along the flap."

"Got it," he said. "Now you have to change clothes."

Helen ran back to her apartment, changed into a black T-shirt and pants, and added her black straw hat. Phil was waiting outside her door with a clipboard.

"You look like a glamorous gunfighter," he said.

"What's on the clipboard?" Helen said.

"A list of names and addresses of other people signing for the refund for the overcharge," he said.

Helen noticed about half of the names had signatures beside them. "Very authentic," she said.

"The hard part was trying to create different signatures," he said. He tapped the board. "Under this, I also have envelopes that supposedly contain checks, including one for Alana. Shall we?"

Phil and Helen were silent on the short ride to Riggs Beach. This was a different kind of quiet, not a tension-packed silence. Now they were united in their silence, gathering their strength for the coming ordeal.

Phil parked his car in the Riggs Beach lot as tired, sunburned beachgoers were packing up their gear to go home.

"I think we got here at the right time," Helen said. "People are leaving the beach. There's a better chance that Cerise will be empty."

They walked quickly to the boutique. Phil peeked in the window. "One customer," he said. "Is Alana a blonde?"

"Tall, slender, long blond hair, dangly earrings?" Helen said.

"That's her," Phil said. "As soon as she rings up this customer, I'm going in."

The customer seemed to take forever. She and Alana chatted about the weather, the sunshine, a sale coming up next week. At last, Alana handed the woman her hot pink shopping bag and she was out the turquoise door.

"I'm going in," Phil said, as if he was storming an armed stronghold. Helen pulled down her hat and studied the clothes in the display window.

"Hey, there," Alana said.

"Are you Alana Roselli Romano?" Phil asked.

"I am, but why so formal?" Alana said. Her voice was an invitation. Helen's hackles went up.

"I need your full name if I'm going to give you some money," Phil said, flirting right back.

"You're a lot younger and better looking than Ed McMahon," Alana said.

"I don't have nearly as much money to give away," Phil said. "But I am prepared to give you a check. You live in the apartment upstairs, 10792 A1A, Suite 2?"

"I do, but why are you asking?" Alana sounded wary.

"You've overpaid your city water bill by five dollars and twelve cents for the last ten months," he said. "I have a refund check for fifty-one dollars and twenty cents." He tapped the clipboard. "It's not a lot." Phil sounded apologetic.

"I'll take it!" Alana said. "I love free money."

"Hardly free," Phil said. "You've already given it to the city. I'm just giving it back. I'll need to see your driver's license or some other photo ID. Then you sign here and I'll give you the check."

Helen could see Alana duck down behind the counter, pop up with her purse and plop it next to the register. She rummaged inside and pulled out a slim black wallet with gold studs along the edge of the flap.

Phil grabbed it out of her hand. "I'll take that," he said.

"Hey, I'm calling the police." Alana picked up the phone.

"Please do," Phil said. "Then you can tell them what you're doing with a dead woman's wallet. Helen!"

Helen slapped the CLOSED sign on the turquoise door and locked it.

"You!" Alana hissed. "I told you to stay away from here."

Helen ignored her. Phil tossed her the wallet and Helen began emptying the compartments on a display table. The driver's license, credit cards and library card all belonged to Alana. So did the ATM card and checkbook. Helen ignored the money and explored the other compartments.

Now she was frantic. There was nothing in this wallet to show it had belonged to Joan. Nothing.

Helen opened a long zippered section, then felt under the leather flap with her finger. Jammed into the corner was a pink raffle ticket, number 176591. Joan Right's raffle ticket for the Mercedes.

"Found this," Helen said. "It's a chance to win a Mercedes."

"That's mine," Alana said.

"Really?" Helen said. "Then why does it have Joan Right's name, address and phone number? Were you going to give the Mercedes to a server?"

"Where did you get the wallet, Alana?" Phil said.

"Cy," she said. "Cy gave it to me. As a gift."

"And we know where Cy got it," Phil said. "He gave you another present to convince Joan to come down to the pier alone so he could kill her."

"You wanted that peach dress in the worst way," Helen said. "That's how you got it. You talked Joan Right into meeting you at the pier so Cy could kill her."

"You can't prove that," Alana said, but her voice trembled.

"Don't have to," Phil said. "I'll also call Channel Seventy-seven, and their investigative reporter can video the wallet and raffle ticket. Helen will swear it belonged to the late Joan Right, who mysteriously committed suicide.

"After that story runs, I'll call the Riggs Beach police and tell them that you have the dead woman's wallet—and Cy gave it to you. Where did he get it, Alana? Nobody will believe he found it on the beach. Not after his weepy speech on TV about how much he wanted to help poor, worried Joan. Even a force as crooked as Riggs Beach won't cover up that.

"Are you going to tell them you're only an accessory, that you didn't kill Joan?" he asked. "Are you going to say Cy did?

"How long do you think you'll last in a Riggs Beach jail, Alana? You know what Cy did to Joan. He can hire some beach bum to get rid of you. Heck, he could probably hire a cop. Next, we'll hear how you hung yourself in your cell out of remorse. That's an ugly way to die, Alana."

"No! No! Let me go. I have some money. I can pay you," she said.

"Not interested," Phil said. "But you may want to talk to a special agent with the state. He's investigating corruption in Riggs Beach. He might—and I say *might*—cut you a deal in return for your testimony."

"Then get him," Alana said. "Call him right now."

The sexy, lighthearted Alana was gone. Now she seemed haggard and badly used.

"Not yet," Phil said. "Answer one question first: Why did Cy kill Joan Right?"

The color had drained from Alana's face. She put her hands on the counter to stop them from shaking, took a deep breath and said, "He knew Joan was meeting with a woman PI who drove a white PT Cruiser. She was hanging around the restaurant the night it burned. So was that investigative reporter for Channel Seventy-seven. He couldn't have Joan talking to the press or a private eye."

Alana doesn't know I'm the woman private eye, Helen thought. I was careless and let Joan get killed.

"Hurry," Alana said. "What if Cy stops by for the day's receipts?"

"Then you're in a heap of trouble," Phil said. "So answer quick. Why didn't Cy bribe Commissioner Wyman for his vote?"

"Once the restaurant burned down," Alana said, "Cy couldn't hold a reception for Wyman's daughter, so he lost the chance to influence his vote. Wyman's too careful to take cash. Cy would have paid for the reception and given Wyman a phony bill."

"Which Wyman wouldn't pay?" Phil asked.

"Oh, no, he'd write a check for it," Alana said. "But Cy would never cash it. Wyman makes sure he has bills of sale and receipts for everything."

"Thanks," Phil said. "I'll make that call now."

He speed-dialed a number on his cell phone and said, "Agent Honeycutt? I have someone who wants to talk to you. The person I told you about. How soon can you get here? Twenty minutes? Good."

He clicked off his phone and said, "He's on his way."

A woman wearing a T-shirt with a tabby cat curled under a palm tree rattled the door handle.

Helen went to the door. "We're closed," she said.

It was after dark when Helen and Phil left Cerise and walked back to the parking lot along the beach. The sea was smooth silver, stretching to infinity. Helen and Phil walked along the water's edge, holding hands.

"Things turned out better than I dreamed," Helen said. "We can close Sunny Jim's case, and Randy and Alana are safe, thanks to FDLE."

"We also know who killed Joan and Ceci," Phil said.

"Valerie's career is saved," Helen said. "I called and she'll be there when Bill is arrested for murder for hire. I also told her she wants to be at the Riggs County Courthouse tomorrow morning when the grand jury is convened."

"FDLE can't say what's going on—not yet—but Valerie will be first with the story," Phil said.

"Her courthouse sources are good," Helen said. "Cal may not be able to talk, but she'll find a leak somewhere."

"Joan's autopsy report showed she fought her killer," Phil said. "The medical examiner got DNA from the skin under her fingernails. Cal says Cy has healing scratches on his hands and arms. If the DNA matches, they'll have Cy for murder one."

"Alana's and Randy's testimony should help the case," Helen said.

"When Cy is charged with murder, Valerie will report that story, too," Phil said.

"Best of all, Rob is gone for good," Helen said. "And we're back together. Why did you forgive me?"

Phil gathered her into his arms. "Because I was wrong," he said.

"I was wrong, too," Helen said.

"But I was worse," Phil said. "The night Rob was killed, I lied to the police about his death and covered up what I knew. I was guilty of the same thing you were. I just couldn't admit it. It was too easy to fall into that trap."

Helen silently agreed but said nothing.

Phil reached into his pocket and handed her a key. "It's the new key to my apartment," he said. "You already have the one to my heart. I don't know what else to say, except I love you."

"And I love you," Helen said.

This time, when he took her into his arms, the pain was gone.

EPILOGUE

Helen and Phil paddled out on the silk-smooth ocean, admiring the sunrise. Helen heard a small splash and saw a red snapper leap up in the water near her board. The ocean was that clear. She had a fanciful notion that it was the fish she'd saved on the beach.

"This morning is so beautiful," Helen said.

"And so are you," Phil said.

She smiled at her husband and nearly lost her balance.

"Whoa!" he said.

She righted herself just in time.

The early morning paddleboard session was a thank-you gift from Sunny Jim, along with a substantial bonus. He even paid Margery's limo rental bill.

"You saved my business and my reputation," he said.

The newly elected Riggs Beach City Commission voted to renew Sunny Jim's beach location lease for five more years.

The firefighters had managed to save all eight of Sunny Jim's paddleboards and eleven paddles. Insurance covered the rest of the damage. Jim was glad he'd backed up his data in his Riggs Lake computers. Now that there's only one paddleboard concession on Riggs Beach, Jim's business is booming. He bought Bill's paddleboard equipment at fire-sale prices.

Bill Bantry did not get away with murder this time. He was convicted of the murder for hire in the death of Cecilia Odell and sentenced to thirty years in prison. He served only five. Bill was killed in a prison-yard fight.

Daniel Odell collected the million dollars from Ceci's life insurance policy, then lost it in bad investments within a year.

Maureen Carsten, Ceci's best friend, discovered that she was pregnant three months after Ceci died. Her husband had had a vasectomy. He divorced his unfaithful wife. Daniel told Maureen to "get rid of it." He didn't want a child.

Maureen, pregnant and newly divorced, wept to Daniel's parents that their son wanted her to abort their only grandchild. Daniel reluctantly married his lover, after his parents threatened to disinherit him.

He looks very tired these days. Daniel Odell Junior still doesn't sleep through the night.

Maureen Carsten Odell gained forty pounds after the birth of the baby. She can't seem to lose the weight. Daniel padlocks the fridge door after dinner.

Valerie Cannata broke the story of the arrest of Bill Bantry of Bill's Boards, and the FDLE investigation into bribery, corruption and murder in Riggs Beach. She won two more Emmy Awards for her exclusive coverage of the murders of Ceci Odell and Joan Right.

Valerie's contract with Channel Seventy-seven was renewed with a substantial raise. She bought another bookcase to hold her new Emmys.

Alana Roselli Romano was charged with being an accessory after the fact to the murder of Joan Right. In return for her cooperation with the authorities, she served six months in prison and two years' probation.

Cy's frequent text messages helped establish that he used Alana to meet Joan Right at the pier. Alana currently works at a Riggs Beach T-shirt shop and lives in an apartment with a view of the alley.

The chief of the Riggs Beach police resigned and was charged with six counts of grand theft and eleven counts of official misconduct. Five officers and Detective Emmet Ebmeier were also convicted of taking bribes and multiple ethics violations.

Ebmeier forfeited his house, thirty-foot sailboat, Harley, Mercedes and BMW. The other officers were also forced to forfeit any possessions related to the bribery.

Randall Travis Henshall pleaded guilty to murder for hire and arson. In addition to his incriminating recording of the conversation with Bill Bantry, his cell phone had several text messages that backed his claim. Randy had three operations for skin grafts on his back. Because he cooperated with the long investigation, he was sentenced to twenty-five years in prison.

Cyrus Reed Horton was charged with multiple offenses, including the first-degree murder of Joan Right. Facing the death penalty, he ratted out Commissioner Frank "the Fixer" Gordon. For his testimony against Gordon, he received life without the possibility of parole. Cy works in the prison kitchen.

Joan Right was buried next to her parents in a private ceremony in Riggs Beach. Helen, Phil, Kevin and the rest of the staff of Cy's on the Pier held a sunset memorial service for their friend on the beach.

"You were kind, brave and hardworking, Joan," Kevin said. "You were loved by your friends and colleagues. You will be missed."

Helen floated a wreath of purple orchids into the water and said, "I will remember you, Joan, and your courage. May you have eternal rest." Afterward, Kevin told Helen and Phil, "You gave my friend justice. Thank you. Fat, lazy Cy is sweating in the prison kitchen, working harder than we ever had to. And he's paid even less than we were."

Commissioner Frank Gordon was convicted of multiple counts of bribery and sentenced to thirty years in prison and a fine of five hundred thousand dollars. He was unable to sell his home to pay the fine and the lawyer's fees. His house, pool and a half acre of waterfront property were washed away when his seawall crumbled during a tropical storm.

His wife divorced him and married an orthodontist. His stepson has straight teeth.

Commissioner Charles Wyman was convicted of bribery in return for gifts, including a thirty-foot cabin cruiser, a new shingled roof, pressure washing and painting of the exterior of his home, five thousand square feet of wall-to-wall broadloom, two Mercedes and a low-flush toilet. He was sentenced to ten years in prison and five years of supervised release, fined one hundred thousand dollars and forfeited all the proceeds from his offenses.

Wilma Jane Wyman's wedding was canceled when her father was arrested. Her car salesman fiancé said her father's reputation was bad for his business image. Wilma Jane works as an exotic dancer at a joint that features "burgers and babes."

Riggs Beach mayor Eustice Timmons and the other members of the Riggs Beach City Commission resigned and were charged with multiple counts of bribery and ethics violations. They were sentenced to a total of more than two hundred years in prison.

Helen suffered from recurring nightmares after Rob's death. She received a call that no one had claimed Rob's body in the St. Louis County morgue. Helen arranged for a quiet funeral for her ex-husband. Phil insisted on flying to St. Louis with her.

No one attended Rob's burial except Helen and Phil. The funeral and other expenses cost fifteen thousand dollars, the amount Rob had demanded the night he staggered into Kathy's backyard. Helen thought it was worth the price to finally bury her ex and her guilt.

The night they returned, Helen gave Phil the gift she'd bought him at the little store: a classic edition of *Crossroads: Eric Clapton*.

Phil gave her a new special edition of the best of the Rolling Stones. He is learning to appreciate the Stones, particularly "Let's Spend the Night Together."